"What's wrong, Danovan?" She sounded as confused as he felt. "Is it me?"

"It's not you. Us working together and...being together messes with my head sometimes." He ran a hand through his hair.

Mixing business and pleasure had destroyed his last life.

"Look, I want you," he said. "But I've also asked you to put a lot of faith in me with the winery. I don't ever want you to think that I used this—" he waved a hand, indicating them both "—used *us*, to influence your decision."

She tilted her head. "I can't decide if you're sweet or the most egotistical man I've ever met."

Yeah, join the club. He had never felt so conflicted and unsure of himself. "You are in my blood, Indigo Blue."

He ran a finger down her throat, to where the first button of her blouse halted his progress.

Dear Reader,

Since Widow's Grove is surrounded by wineries, one of the books in the series just *had* to take place on one, right? Except the only thing I know for sure about wine is how to consume it! I enjoyed the research for Indigo's story and hope you enjoy visiting The Tippling Widow.

If you're ever in the area, stop by and sample the cabernet—it's fabulous.

Oh, and watch for the cameo appearances of the characters from the first two books in the series!

The next book? I had readers ask what happened to Bear, the big scary guy from *The Reasons to Stay*, so the next in the series will be his story.

Stay tuned, ideas are still growing...

Laura Drake

PS I enjoy hearing from readers. You can contact me and sign up for my newsletter through my website, lauradrakebooks.com.

LAURA DRAKE

Twice in a
Blue Moon

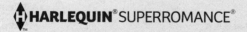
HARLEQUIN® SUPERROMANCE®

Recycling programs
for this product may
not exist in your area.

ISBN-13: 978-0-373-60918-5

Twice in a Blue Moon

HARLEQUIN®
www.Harlequin.com

Printed in U.S.A.

Laura Drake is a RITA® Award-winning author of romance and women's fiction. She's a city girl who never grew out of her tomboy ways, or a serious cowboy crush. Laura's realized her dream of becoming a Texan and is working on her accent. In the remaining waking hours, she's a wife, grandmother and motorcycle chick. She currently writes for Harlequin Superromance. Find her online at lauradrakebooks.com and on Twitter, @PBRWriter.

Books by Laura Drake

HARLEQUIN SUPERROMANCE

Her Road Home
The Reasons to Stay

Visit the Author Profile page
at Harlequin.com for more titles.

To my Alpha Dog, who, no matter how fast I pedal,
is waving from the top of the next hill,
cheering me on.

And telling me to hurry up.

Thanks for always waiting, Babe.

Acknowledgments

I'm not much different than Indigo; I may know a
cab from a zin, but not much more.

A huge thanks to Jeff Wiens of Wiens Family
Cellars, who offered to answer this author's every
ignorant question...and even helped on plot points!
His family winery in Temecula, California, was my
template for The Tippling Widow.

If you're ever in the area, check out their
wonderful wines! Tell Jeff I said, "Hey."

www.WiensCellars.com

The Hollywood Informer

Hollywood was rocked last week by the death of our beloved Harry Stone. Undoubtedly one of the most influential personalities in the history of film, Harry was Hollywood's best-known director and one of the wealthiest filmmakers in the world. We'll miss him not only for his sparkling genre-bending movies, but for his iconic bigger-than-life personality.

But apparently Harry's not done rocking the town.

In our *EXCLUSIVE* interview inside, Harry's daughter and reality show superstar, Brenda Stone, reveals the juicy details of Harry's will! And guess who's *not* in it? Harry's four-decades-junior wife, Indigo Blue. Apparently the opportunistic 'masseuse to the stars' will have to hit the road with her massage table, because she got nada.

The Informer is gratified to see that sometimes, even in this town, Karma works. Blue dug for gold and came up with rocks. We sincerely hope this is the last time we have to mention her name within these pages. Like Townshend wrote, "Let's forget you, better still."

Goodbye, sweet Harry. This town will miss you.

CHAPTER ONE

"COME ON, BABY BLUE. I may not have Harry's bucks, but I've got a place in Malibu overlooking—"

"You booked a massage, Carlo. I am not on the menu of services." Indigo Blue grasped the man's muscular forearm, removed it from around her neck and lowered it to her massage table. Soft light from the matching Tiffany lamps caressed the burnished skin and smooth muscles of Hollywood's latest action hero, Carlo Bandera. Soothing new-age rainforest sounds flowed from the spa's hidden speakers.

"I get that you don't want to commit, babe. That's cool."

Pouring coconut oil into her palm, she rubbed her hands to warm it, attempting to ignore the massive boner tenting the towel draped across Carlo's crotch. Starting at the bottom of his rib cage, she slid the heels of her hands up and across his considerable pecs. She leaned in, adding her weight to release the tension in the huge muscles.

His arms snaked around her and pulled her onto his chest, trapping her hands underneath her. "I've got five hundred bucks for a BJ."

She pushed against him, but his arms were steel

bands. He didn't even flinch. Panic pumped into her bloodstream, impelled by her racing heart.

"Harry Stone could've had any broad in town, and he chose you." He gave her the look she'd seen him use in his last movie. The heavy-lidded, smoky one that liquefied female costars. "You must be incredible—it'd be worth five hundred."

"Back off, Bandera. *Right now*." Adrenaline raced through her, demanding flight or fight. But the caveman Casanova's balls were out of her knee's reach.

"Aw, honey, you'll change your mind once you see the goods…"

When he used one arm to whip off the towel, she twisted away, sliding easily thanks to his oily chest.

"This appointment is over." She stepped to the door, but her hands were slick. She couldn't turn the knob.

Bandera sat up, a slow smile spreading across his face, his member throbbing. "From what I hear, you gotta need the money, Blue." He slid his legs off the table.

She shot a glance around the dim room, looking for a towel to wipe her hands. They lay stacked on the other side of the table. *Figures*.

He stood. "If you're *that* good, I'll refer my friends."

Using two hands, tendons in her forearms straining, she twisted the greasy knob. It slipped, but then finally turned. She flung the door open. It hit the wall with a hollow *boom*. She stalked through the crowd from a just-released rumba class, leaving the door gaping behind her.

Her client's indignant yell didn't douse the burn in her gut.

I can't do this anymore.

Only a week into her old job and this was the third and scariest pass so far. She'd told herself that she'd been spoiled with the cushy life—but it was more than that. Before Harry, the upscale clientele of Las Brisas had at least shown respect for her skills and service. Now she was accosted on a daily basis. She snatched an Egyptian cotton towel from a stack, wiping her hands as she walked through the gym, hyperaware of the curious eyes that followed her.

This was not going to work. She needed a new plan.

As with everything he touched, Harry had changed her. She was no longer the free-spirited, starstruck newbie, grateful for a dream job teaching yoga to starlets and massaging famous muscle. But without Harry's love and unswerving loyalty, who was she now? She didn't know.

But she wasn't this.

A crushing blanket of loss had descended the morning she woke to find the lifeless body of her mentor, her love, her best friend, cooling on the mattress beside her. After that Harry had belonged to everyone: the press, his fans, his daughter. In their hands, the funeral morphed from the quiet family ceremony Harry had wanted into a nightmare of Hollywood proportions complete with limos, television cameras and paparazzi.

Indigo pushed open the door to the women's locker room, hollow to the marrow of her bones. She put her hands on her knees and leaned over, waiting for a wave of dizziness to pass. When had she last eaten?

But a decent meal wouldn't touch this emptiness. The problem was much deeper.

The commune where she'd grown up had been a large sheltering womb that, after high school, had shrunk to the point of claustrophobia. She'd fought her way out, choosing to be born instead between the glamorous thighs of Hollywood.

It was only later she learned her surrogate mother was a narcissistic whore.

That was the last time she'd trusted her gut. Lost, and one bad choice from disaster, she'd met Harry.

"Indigo Blue. It sounds like a streetwalker's name." A chalkboard-squeal voice drifted from the first row of teak lockers.

"The only reason anyone invited her to parties at all was because she had Harry wrapped around her ring finger. How do you suppose she did that?"

"See? We're back to the streetwalker thing."

Blood pounded up Indigo's neck, flooding her face with heat. She eyed the exit, but her car keys were in her locker. Tightening her stomach muscles, she walked on. Coming abreast of the lockers, she glanced to the two underwear-clad plastic surgery billboards. "Monica, you may want to stick with those voice lessons." She covered the bitchy words in fake-sincerity syrup. "You're still strident, dear."

That shut them up. She grabbed her stuff and got the hell out.

TWO DAYS LATER, her Louis Vuitton luggage open on the bed, Indigo stood before her walk-in closet, which was bigger than her childhood bedroom. She surveyed the yards of satin, spandex and sequins, seeing her Hollywood life recede like the view in the long end of a telescope.

That's how it felt—as if, at twenty-seven, she'd already led three separate lifetimes: the tomboy who'd grown up wild on the Humboldt County commune, the star-struck yoga instructor and the celebrity wife of an aging Hollywood icon.

Thanks to her mom and Harry, two of those lives had turned out well. The one in between, the one she'd been in charge of? Epic fail. She turned away from the closet. Whatever lifetime came next, she sure wouldn't need *this* wardrobe.

Mom wanted her to come home to People's Farm, but her experience at the spa had taught her that going backward didn't work. Thanks to the skills she'd learned there, she could put her portable massage table under her arm and start her next lifetime almost anywhere.

And in the ass-end hours of last night, she'd decided to begin that life at the winery—the one remnant of this life that was truly hers. Maybe she'd find Harry's spirit where they'd been happiest.

Closing the luggage, she glanced around the bedroom, listening one last time for a whisper of Harry. All she heard was the whine of the pool pump through the open French doors. She now understood the phantom pain that amputees felt for a missing limb, because of the gaping hole in her that Harry had left. What would happen to her now, without his steady guiding hand on her shoulder?

Everyone believed she'd married Harry Stone for his money. Still, she'd thought she'd made a *few* friends in the four years they'd been married. But the past two months proved that all the naïveté hadn't yet rubbed off of Indigo Blue. She shook her head, picked up what was left of this life and walked downstairs.

Claws on marble echoed in the two-story vestibule, getting closer. She dropped the load and knelt as Harry's basset hound, Barnabas, careened around the corner, huge feet pistoning until he gained traction and barreled into her.

"Oof. Well, hello to you too, big guy." Avoiding drool, she knelt to pet him from soft ears to whipping tail. "The Wicked Witch of the West will be here soon. Let's spare ourselves that drama, eh?"

"Well, I may be a witch, but that's not Toto." Brenda Stone swept in on stilettos instead of a broom. "And *you* are no Dorothy." She flipped her salon-perfect blond tresses over her shoulder and strutted over on shapely, tanning-bed-brown legs. "Give me your house key, and open the suitcases."

Indigo stood, fists clenched at her sides. "You think I'd steal something?"

"Listen up, bitch." The diva waved a carmine talon in front of Indigo's nose. "Daddy's gone. I don't have to put up with your shit for one more second." She planted a fist on her hip. "Now, are you going to open up? Or do I call the cops?"

They were once "friends." That was before Indigo understood the Hollywood definition. She would have accepted Brenda's aversion to having a stepmother her own age, but Brenda had made it clear that the competition wasn't for Harry's love—but for his money.

Indigo spread her arms. "If I'd wanted any of this, I wouldn't have insisted on a prenup leaving all of it to you." The only things she wanted from this house were Barney, her wedding rings and a few of Harry's T-shirts to sleep in.

"Yeah, like anybody believed *that* story." Brenda

sniffed, her eyes crawling over the luggage. "Open them. Now."

Indigo bent and popped the locks on the first suitcase, tasting bitterness in the back of her throat. Sure, Brenda was all about money. But Indigo knew that deeper in her hate-shriveled heart lived an insecure, jealous little girl, and that was Indigo's unforgivable sin. Not that Brenda *was* that little girl—but that Indigo knew it.

A few minutes more, and you're done with all this forever.

She flipped open the suitcase. Slapping the drama queen silly would sure feel good but would only supply more fodder for the gossip rags. Harry deserved better. Guts churning, she gritted her teeth and opened the next.

Ten minutes later the inspection was over, leaving Indigo feeling as violated as a cavity search.

"Just because I'm a nice person, and since you didn't try to steal anything else, I'll let you keep the Vuitton." Brenda raked a proprietary gaze over the marbled entryway and the Tara-style staircase, then back. "You were less than nothing before you met my dad. You're now free to go back to that." She flicked a hand in Barney's direction. "You're taking that filthy animal, right?"

Indigo snapped the last lock shut and looked into Barney's droopy eyes. "Are you ready?" Taking his tail wag as assent, she stood, grabbed the handles of the suitcases, and left this lifetime behind.

"I WAS SORRY to hear about your baby girl, Danovan." Reese Winters sat across the executive desk at Winter Wines. His wrinkles were set in nervous lines, as if waiting to get a root canal. With no Novocain.

Danovan DiCarlo felt the same but knew if it showed, this interview would be over. He shut his mind to the words that delivered the brass-knuckle punch to his chest. "You're aware that I have a degree in agribusiness from UC Davis, and that I worked my way up at Bacchanal Winery to become one of their trusted vintners. But what you may not know is that I single-handedly took their sauvignon line from ten percent of—"

"Danovan." Reece's fingers drummed the edge of the desk.

"Yes, sir." He leaned forward, anxious to make his next point. He was just getting to the good stuff.

"Spare me the résumé. You know I can't hire you."

"But, sir, I'm an excellent manager."

"My respect for your abilities is what got you this meeting. I'd wager you haven't gotten many others. Am I right?"

"Well, I'm just now starting to—"

"Son, I don't believe the rumors the family is putting out about you." He leaned back in his burgundy leather chair. "But that doesn't matter. They buy my grapes."

"You're going to let the Boldens dictate—"

"I am. And so is every other winery in the area. What's more, you knew that when you set up this appointment." He pushed his chair back and stood. "I don't mean to stand in as your daddy, but it seems somebody needs to." He put his knuckles on the desk and leaned in. "You got a bad deal. But you have to admit, you had some…input into your situation."

Danovan shot to his feet. "I didn't come here to—"

"So, I have to ask you." He squinted across the desk. "Did you learn anything?"

Heat pounded up Danovan's neck until his face throbbed, engorged with it.

"No one ever choked to death swallowing his pride, son."

Sanctimonious sonofabitch. If Winters hadn't been old enough to sell wine to King Tut, Danovan would have pulled him across the table by the collar of that polo shirt and vent his frustration. Instead, he snatched the file folder of documentation from his chair, retrieved his résumé and dropped it in the folder. Even if all Danovan had left was a string of dynamite-rigged bridges, he couldn't afford to burn any. Anger drained out of the hole that opened in his guts.

He looked across the desk and saw the truth in those mournful blue eyes. In his own twisted way, the old man was trying to help.

"I appreciate your time, Mr. Winters." He squared his shoulders, did an about-face and marched out of the office, through the huge tasting room and out the front door of the winery. Finally, standing beside his car, he let out the breath he'd been holding.

I'm firmly and durably screwed.

He slammed his hands on the hood. When Winters agreed to see him, he'd had a glimmer of hope that one grower in the valley had a big enough set of balls to stand against the Boldens. But apparently they'd stopped making them that size.

He unlocked his Land Rover with a click. He pulled the door open, and the smell of almost-new car washed over him as he settled into the seat. If he didn't find a job soon, he'd be forced to sell this last sweet perk of his old life. He inserted the key and fired the engine.

Sure, he could widen his search. He probably should. Napa Valley had more prestige, anyway. But there still would be the issue of a recommendation from his last employer. Who would an owner believe—the largest winemaker in central California, or a prospective hire? He pounded his fist on the burled wood dash, startling a passing tourist.

Besides, dammit, he liked it here. He may have chosen the Central Valley right out of school because it was a small pond he could make a big splash in, but sometime over the past five years, he'd become attached. He liked the quaint small-town feel of downtown Widow's Grove. He liked the prissy Victorians that lined the King's Highway into town. But mostly, he loved the land. The rolling, golden hills dotted with live oaks quieted his edgy restlessness.

But not his drive.

Throwing the car into Reverse, he backed out. Goddammit, he wasn't leaving until he'd interviewed at every winery he could get through the door of. The colossal screwup with Lissette might have trashed his ego, and his daughter's death, his heart, but the Boldens were not taking his career, too.

It was all he had left.

INDIGO WANTED TO go out the way she came in, so she chose Pacific Coast Highway. It took longer, but she and Barney weren't in a hurry.

The heavy mantle of Hollywood lightened with each mile of road that passed under her tires. This town wasn't just a geographical location, but a state of mind—and she was delighted to change states. She played Harry's favorite CDs, singing along with Van Morrison as the sun tipped over its summit to begin its descent to the sea.

"What do you think, Barney? Are you ready for an adventure?" His woof was hopeful, but his doleful eyes gave her guts a wrench. They were leaving Harry behind.

But the moment of doubt didn't stay. They were only leaving the Harry that belonged to Tinseltown. *Her* Harry was still with her—in his wisdom that lingered in her mind, and in his love that would always be in her heart.

At the Topatopa Bluffs of Ojai, she began looking ahead instead of back. Maybe she'd return to her roots and become a "gentlewoman farmer," helping with the vines. She pictured herself in a floppy hat and canvas gloves, bending to snip fat bunches of grapes and putting them in a basket.

Or maybe she'd use the grand hostess skills Harry had taught her, welcoming customers and pouring wine. After she learned more about wine, of course.

She'd loved Harry's Uncle Bob. His winery outside Widow's Grove had been their favorite getaway between Harry's projects. They'd sit sipping wine on the porch of Bob's cozy log cabin, watching the sun sink into the vines. It was timeless and peaceful—the only place Harry was able to really relax.

Bob was a spare raisin of a man, as if he'd been left too long on the vine in the late summer sun. She supposed she felt so instantly at home around him because he reminded her of her mother in the way he seemed inseparable from the land.

It was Bob who had finally resolved the stalemate that delayed her and Harry's marriage for two years. Ever aware of their age difference,

Harry had wanted to be sure she was cared for after his death. But she'd refused to marry until Harry signed a contract leaving her nothing.

It had been easy to stand resolute through all of Harry's rants, because it didn't matter to her if they ever married. All she ever wanted was Harry. Uncle Bob informed his nephew that if he remained stubborn, he'd lose everything. Bob's respect and acceptance was balm to her singed soul following the tabloid firestorm that erupted over news of her and Harry's courtship.

Uncle Bob's death two years ago had come as a shock to them both, but Indigo had one more—he'd left the winery solely to her. Apparently Harry wasn't the only one who worried about her future.

She and Harry had traveled together to the winery once after Bob's death, but the magic had vanished with its owner. Harry hired a manager, and the winery became just another line on their tax form.

Now she was going to see if it could be more.

She watched the surf racing to keep pace with her car, realizing her future was in an odd sort of balance. Her first lifetime in northern California as a free-spirited earth child had been the polar opposite of her lifetime in the other end of the state. Like Goldilocks, she could only hope that this one, in the middle, would be just right.

With Santa Barbara in the rearview mirror,

champagne bubbles of excitement rose in her chest. As the car blew out of the Gaviota Tunnel, the sun and land exploded in a blaze that burned onto her retinas. The hills flowed away in golden waves and the road wound between them, lazy as a snake in the sun. Old red barns nestled at the bottom of the valleys, and cattle wandered along paths that their forebears had etched into the hillsides.

Peace blew in on the wind, brushing her face, settling on her skin. She smiled.

Almost there.

A little while later she was rolling into Widow's Grove—and it was like visiting an old friend.

There's a new antiques shop where the hardware used to be. Oh, Harry, look, there's Hollister Drug where we got those great strawberry shakes. Remember that waitress with the crystal in her tooth and the '50s waitress uniform and hot pink hair?

She turned onto Foxen Canyon Road, the precision straight rows of winter-barren grapevines undulating over the hills that she and Barney passed. The basset's long ears flapped out the open window as he sniffed the air. Indigo tried it, too, pulling in the scent of dirt and growing things. "You remember this, don't you?"

"Woof."

"Well, this time we're here to stay." She drank

in every hill, every landmark and every mailbox on what was, as of today, her road home.

They turned in at the sun-faded sign that read, "Tippling Widow Winery. Home of distinctive wines since 1978."

"We'll have to get that sign repainted," she said. "It doesn't make a very good impression from the road." Dead leaves blew across the asphalt as they drove up the wide drive, unpruned denuded vines keeping pace on either side. "I wonder how the harvest was this year."

The drive opened to a small, deserted parking lot that ended at the tasting room. The steel-roofed wooden building, painted in buff and redwood, was shaded by a wraparound porch. Square wooden tables and chairs rested in its shade. She pulled up and parked.

The place was so empty it seemed abandoned. Weeds grew among the rosebushes at the base of the porch, complete with wind-blown trash accents. What was the manager thinking? This would look awful to potential customers.

Where *were* the customers? The place should be bustling with tourists this time of year. Warning bells jangled in her head.

When Barney whined, she got out, gathered him in her arms and lifted him down. He wandered off the sidewalk, sniffed, then watered some weeds. As she closed the car door, the fecund scent of fermentation—a sure sign that the crop was being processed—calmed her unease a bit.

Until she walked closer and spied the cobwebs gracing the tables and chairs of the porch. And they were not fake Halloween leftovers.

She pulled the handle of the glass door—it was locked. She cupped her hands and looked in, though she couldn't see much of the shadowed interior.

What the hell is going on? "Barnabas, come."

He stopped sniffing and, collar jingling, trotted after her around the building, along the nine-foot-tall solid wood fence, to the working side of the winery. She pulled the metal door at the back of the pole-barn building. At least it was unlocked, and the lights were on. Barney followed her in, and she let the door close. No genteel trappings here—just concrete floors, stainless steel wine fermentation tanks, skylights and industrial lighting overhead.

"Hello?" Her voice echoed off the high steel ceiling. "Anyone here?" She held out her hand, palm down. "Barney. Stay."

He sat, plump feet splayed.

She walked farther in, peering around raised fermentation vats and stepping over hoses.

In the last row, a pair of jeans-clad legs stuck out from under a vat, several wrenches spread on the floor beside them. "Hello?"

The legs didn't move. Had he hit his head?

Had something collapsed? Alarm skittered up her spine and scurried along her nerves. Jogging over, she knelt beside the legs and bent to peer under the vat. An old man lay, eyes closed, a tonsure of curly gray hair wild around his head. No blood. She reached out and touched his leg. Then shook it. "Hey, you okay?"

His lips parted, belching a snore.

"What the hell?" She snatched a wrench from the floor and banged it against the metal tank.

With a snort the man woke, jerked and smacked his head on the tank. "Jaysus!" He put a hand to his forehead and glared at her through one blood-shot eye. "Why'd you go and do tha'?"

A miasma of stale wine breath unfurled. She recoiled and stood, then backed up a step.

"Cantcha' see I'm workin' here?" The man rolled out from under the vat. "Who the hell're you?"

"Indigo Blue. The owner." The remnants of adrenaline in her system congealed to a sticky wad of anger. "You're not working. You're shit-faced."

It took some precarious butt balancing and grunting, but the man eventually sat up. "I'm not. I was resting my eyes. This work isn't easy, you kn—" He scratched his scalp. "Who'd you say you were, again?"

She didn't want to ask her next question— didn't want to know. She put her thumb and forefinger to the ticking bomb behind her eyebrows. "Please. Tell me you're not the manager."

He smiled, revealing a missing incisor and delivering another lethal dose of boozy halitosis. "I am." He stuck out a hand. Then, realizing it held a wrench, he dropped the tool, and winced when it clanged on the cement. "I'm Cyrus Delaney. Proud to meetcha." He held out his square, dirty hand again.

She shook only the ends of his fingers. The pretty dreams she'd imagined on the drive here detonated, gone in an instant. "Why isn't the tasting room open?"

"The bitches up and quit, that's why."

When he turned to get to his knees, she didn't slam her eyes closed fast enough. A close-up of his butt crack seared into her brain.

"How long ago?" She moaned.

"Oh, I think it was…uhnn." He gained his feet. "Around about a couple weeks ago, reckon."

Questions hit her brain with the heavy thud of bullets hitting raw meat. Then the hollow-pointed one hit. "Why isn't it cold in here?"

She didn't know much about making wine, but Uncle Bob always kept this room at a steady sixty degrees. Fermentation might be a natural event, but uncontrolled, it resulted in vinegar, not wine.

He looked around. "Yeah, why in't it? That's a good question." He tottered away, swaying right and left, as if his knees didn't bend.

God help me. She pulled her phone from the back pocket of her jeans and hit speed dial. Then, catching herself, she pushed End.

There was no cell tower where Harry was.

What now? Dread zinged along nerves made brittle by the adrenaline dump.

Who am I to decide?

Oh, sure, she'd made lots of decisions as a married woman in regards to running the household, party planning—the mundane white noise of everyday life. But Harry, or his staff, had taught her all that. And though he was gone now the thought of him, no more than a phone call away if she needed help, still resided in the back of her mind. His presence had always been a comfort. And a safety rope.

She swallowed a burr-edged nugget of fear. This fiasco was hers to fix. There was no one else. The winery had been Uncle Bob's baby. Harry's haven. Failure meant she'd always carry the guilt and shame of losing that. It would be like losing them all over again.

She looked up at the metal roof. "Harry, you know I suck at this."

The only original idea she'd ever had was moving to Hollywood. And if Harry hadn't stooped to lift her up, dust her off and take her in, no telling where she'd be now. Giving BJs to up-and-coming stars? Worse?

A shudder rattled through her so hard her bones

shook. She took a breath, then headed in the direction she'd seen her "manager" take.

She found him fiddling with the thermostat on the wall beside the tasting-room door.

"It's not coming on." He frowned at the dial as if maybe he'd merely forgotten how it worked.

Thank God she'd gotten the business checkbook from the accountant before she left LA. "Who do you call when this happens?"

"Never happened before." He smacked his lips. "I'll be right back. I need…" He pulled the metal door open, and dim lights came on in the barrel room—a glass-walled display room of oaken barrels of product. He went deeper, into the darkened tasting room, turned the corner and disappeared.

Indigo followed. She could see the sun through the windows out front, but the shaded porch left the tasting room in shadows. What wasn't hard to see was the gray-on-black form lifting a bottle to his lips. Anger fired in her chest and shot through her so fast that white sparks drifted across her vision. She put her hands on her hips. "We have an emergency here. The entire year's stock could be destroyed, and you're drinking? You've got to be kidding me!"

The shadow lowered his arm. "Well, I was just gettin' some fortification, then I was going to—"

"You're fired." She might not have the experience to make good decisions, but at least they wouldn't be clouded by alcohol. She'd seen enough red-veined noses and yellowed eyes to recognize chronic alcoholism when she saw it. "Get your stuff and clear off." She strode past what she knew to be the long burled-wood bar, with racks of wine behind, to the counter with a cash register next to the door.

"You can't do that, missy. I been here for a long time." She heard the slosh of a bottle being lifted.

"Bullshit. I just did." Where was the phone book? She dug around under the counter. At least the light was better up here. Her intestines gurgled a warning, but she didn't have time to worry about that now. "Get your stuff and get off this property. Aha." She pulled out the thin Widow's Grove phone book. "On second thought, wait right there for a minute. I'm following you out. I want to be sure some of the product is left when you're gone."

Once she'd looked up an air-conditioning company, called and extracted a promise that someone would be out right away, she walked to where Delaney stood, grumbling under his breath. "Let's go." She led the way into the warehouse and to the back door.

Barney stood when they walked up.

"What kinda dog is that?" Delaney slurred.

Barney sniffed the man's pants leg then, lip curling, backed up.

"One with good taste." She held the door and her breath when Delaney brushed by her.

"You won't get away with this, lady. I'm going to the EDD."

"You do that. Please. And I'm only guessing here, but I'll bet when I contact the tasting room staff, they'll have plenty they'll want to say to the labor board themselves." When Barney scooted out behind her, she let the door fall closed.

Delaney walked to the loading zone and turned to go up the hill.

"Hey, where are you going?" She and Barney jogged to catch up.

"To get my stuff. I moved into the cabin." He huffed, trudging up the hill.

"Bob's place?" Outrage fisted her hands as she imagined the cozy little log cabin defiled by this drunken slob. "Oh, no, you didn't."

"It was sitting empty." He jerked a thumb over his shoulder. "And the bed down there was lumpy." The cabin came into view as they crested the hill. The grapevines marched right up to the edge of the dusty yard, and the setting sun washed the old log walls golden.

She half expected to see Bob and Harry sitting in the wooden chairs, feet up on the railing, sipping merlot.

But they weren't. Indigo's chest squeezed her heart in a painful spasm of nostalgia.

Delaney went on grumbling about the slights he'd borne in his life as they stepped inside.

"Oh, no." The air went out of her in a whoosh.

The bear-tapestry-upholstered couch was sagging and stained. The Navajo rug was pocked with cinder-blackened holes, some possibly as recent as the foot-high ashes that spilled out of the huge fireplace.

Bottles, cups and filthy dishes occupied the low coffee table and graced every flat surface. The air was close and stale, smelling of garbage. Barney snapped at a buzzing fly.

All the pain she'd held inside since Harry's death gathered, filling every space in her body, pushing, pushing. Every slight, every abuse, every loss started to boil. Her skin tightened in an attempt to contain it, but the pressure built in her soft parts—in her gut, behind her eyes.

She clapped her hands over her ears as the pressure exploded from her in a howl of pain. "Getoutgetout-getout. Get out before I kill you!"

Delaney flinched, his mouth open.

Barnabas threw his head back and howled, raising the hair on her arms.

Delaney scrambled, snatching clothes from the furniture, stumbling between the bathroom and the bedroom.

She couldn't watch. Couldn't bear seeing the rest of the house just yet. Sinking to her knees, she gathered Barney in her arms, but the dog wouldn't be consoled. His howls echoed through the large two-story room as if he, too, were pouring out his grief. She rocked him in shaking arms, whispering to him in an attempt to calm them both.

Delaney shuffled back and forth, loaded down with boxes, clothes hanging out of them. She wasn't letting go of Barney to look through them. Knowing firsthand how demeaning that was, she couldn't do it to another human being, even someone as useless as this manager.

Besides, everything precious had already been taken.

CHAPTER TWO

FROM THE PORCH, Indigo watched the ex-manager's rattletrap truck pull out onto the road below. "Well, it's up to you and me now, Barn."

The dog lifted his mournful face.

"Cheer up, bud. We may suck at making decisions, but we can't do worse than *that* guy."

A lead blanket of responsibility dropped onto her shoulders, making it hard to draw a full breath. No one to look to. No one to call. The success or failure of Harry's last lifeline was in her hands. Her incompetent hands.

Oh, come on. You're not totally clueless. After all, you've run your own yoga business.

A tattered remnant of a memory floated through her mind, of a carmine-red scrap of a dress that had cost her more than a good chunk of her bank account.

Yes, and that worked out so well. She slammed her mind shut on it.

She should start shoveling out the cabin. Turning, she stepped to the open door, then hesitated. The sun dipped below the edge of the world. The breeze blew colder than it had a moment ago. The dark played in the straggling vines, and she thought she heard the scurrying of rat-like claws in the dirt.

Ghosts whispered from the open doorway.

Blue? She's a little chit, but I'm just glad to see Harry's still got the interest.

He'll tire of her. Smart men always do, once they start thinking with their bigger head.

You were less than nothing before you met my dad. You're now free to go back to that.

The ghosts chuckled, breathing the smell of boozy sweat-stained sheets and failure into her face. Turning her back on the past, she blindly reached for the knob and shut the door.

She'd deal with the cabin when she felt stronger. "Let's go, Barn."

As they walked down the hill to the winery, a white panel van pulled into the parking lot, the name of the air-conditioning company she'd called on its side.

The dog woofed.

"It's okay, Barn. The cavalry drives panel trucks nowadays." She unlocked the front doors for the repairman, but that was about all the help she could render, having no idea what a compressor looked like, much less where it was located. She told him where she'd be and left him to it, imagining dollars ticking by on a taxi's meter.

She and Barn walked through the tasting room and took the door on the left that led the way to the manager's quarters. She shot a glance to the ceiling. "Oh please, God, I can't take any more today." Bracing herself for the worst, she opened the door.

Encouraged by a faint whiff of stale Lysol, she walked down the long hall, opening doors as she went. The first on the left revealed an abandoned office with windows that looked onto the parking lot. The next door was to a long room. Empty barrels and equipment littered the floor. Behind the door on the right stood the industrial washer and dryer, the deep working-man's sink between them.

The next room on the right was the manager's living quarters, and their home until the cabin was shoveled out.

She opened the door and sniffed. "It's safe, Barney. Come on in." Set up like a room in one of those extended-stay hotels, the apartment had a small kitchen area on the right, a two-person dining table to the left, and a neatly made double bed before her. Crossing the room, she turned left to check out the bathroom. The shower/tub combo, sink and toilet all gleamed.

Thank God the cleaning crew didn't quit too.

Problems lay tangled in her mind like huge piles of string. She had no idea where to begin unknotting them.

First things first.

A short while later, on her last trip to the car unloading what she and Barney would need for the night, the repairman found her in the hall.

"I've cobbled together a temporary fix, ma'am, but frankly, your whole system is held together with bubble gum and cat hair." He squatted to pat Barney. "It'll need to be replaced."

"The whole thing?" The taxi meter in her head whirred.

"Well, some of the duct work could probably be salvaged." Head down, he studiously petted an adoring Barney, whose tail whopped the metal doorjamb with a hollow bong.

She didn't want to know. "How much?"

He named a figure that stole her breath, and a considerable chunk of the business savings account. But you couldn't make wine without a consistent temperature. Even she knew that. Should she call another company for a second quote? She bit her lip. Businesses would be closed by now. Tomorrow might be too late.

Bong. Bong. Bong.

"Jeez, Barney." She grabbed his collar and pulled the little traitor away from the door. He'd always liked men better.

What to do? Nothing had gone right since she'd stepped foot on the property. She'd known when she took this path that she'd have to trust in her intuition, but she hadn't known that the weight of responsibility would be so heavy. It smothered her last flicker of energy. She looked up at the repairman's young, guileless face. Surely she could trust a face like that. "How long will it take?"

"We don't have a unit that large in stock. I'll need to order one. Should take a week to ten days to get here."

"Will the cat hair hold out?"

He smiled. "If it doesn't, you call me. I'll keep it running until then, no charge."

He should. The price he quoted for labor alone would send his kid to college for a year. What would Harry do? A chill wind filled the place in her chest where Harry used to be, howling around the cracks in her cobbled-together life. She crossed her arms to cover the void and chose the easier option. "Yeah, okay, order the parts."

She followed him out, locked up behind them, then returned to the manager's quarters. The bed beckoned. She longed to fall onto it, curl into a fetal ball and welcome sleep's respite. Instead, after a long, lingering look, she set up her laptop on the kitchen table and fired it up, then wandered into the kitchen area to find a bowl for Barney's food. Her stomach growled, but the shelves and drawers revealed only dime-store dishes, bent-tined silverware and a few pots and pans. The fridge was empty save a box of baking soda that sure hadn't been put there by the manager.

She poured Barney's food into a chipped cereal bowl with Mickey Mouse tap dancing around the rim. She knew she should eat something. The stress of the past month had her jeans gapping, hanging off her hip bones. A bevy of women in

Hollywood would kill for a size zero, but they sure wouldn't want the grief and worry that had gotten her there.

You've got to start taking care of yourself. There was no one else to do it.

Tomorrow.

Barney finished his dinner and slopped half the water out of the other dish. Ears dripping, he meandered to the side of the bed and collapsed on the worn braided rug.

They were both out of shape. She'd go to town and stock up on healthy food and restart her yoga routine tomorrow. Plopping into the chair, she jiggled the mouse to refresh her laptop. It would take a lot more than discipline to deal with the rest of the mess that was the winery.

She knew little more about wine than to order white with fish and red with beef. Her education would have to come first. She searched the internet for books on wine making but found most either were for home hobbyists or were way-over-her-head technical. Then she hit pay dirt. *The Complete Idiot's Guide to Starting and Running a Winery.* "That sounds about right." With a click, she downloaded it to her e-reader.

The next knot in the pile of tangled string would be trickier. She'd need to find a winery manager who could do it all: vintner, cellar manager and vine steward. Her experience with the "manager" today had been a lesson in what happened when you left precious things in the hands of others. So, he or she would also have to be willing to teach her.

She needed someone she could trust.

She signed on to her simple business accounting software program and subtracted the cost of the new air-conditioning from the checking balance. She swallowed the knot of dread-laced acid at the back of her throat and added one more to the list of job requirements.

The future manager must be willing to work for next to nothing.

"Yeah, that should be an easy ad to write." She did a search for a central California winery job board, trying to conjure the words to put lipstick on that pig.

DANOVAN SQUINTED AT his computer screen and read the post again, hoping to glean more information.

Wanted: Winery Manager
A great opportunity to get in on the
Grand Reopening of a boutique winery with a
solid reputation for outstanding wines.
Great working environment!
Please apply in person to
The Tippling Widow Winery,
Widow's Grove, California

He'd never heard of The Tippling Widow, but that wasn't surprising. Mom-and-pop operations lay scattered in the hills all over the valley.

Reading between the lines of the sunny ad, it was clear that this would be a lot of work for little acclaim. He squared his shoulders. This job was far beneath him. He'd been a lead vintner at one of the largest winemakers in all of California.

Had being the key point.

He flipped to the Bacchanal website. His own smile met him. A flashy photo of the favorite son raising a glass of Pan's Reserve Cab, his father-in-law's arm around his shoulder.

His breath whooshed out. The family hadn't changed the website yet. No surprise there. He was still stunned to blasted stillness inside…the family must be too. His daughter's cherubic smile drifted across his vision, softening the edges, blurring it. He pulled his mind from the darkness. He had to keep moving forward. There was nothing left behind.

Who was he kidding? If the owner of Tippling Widow hadn't heard of his epic ousting at Bacchanal two weeks ago, a simple phone call to check references would remedy that. Failure bubbled up, turning his skull into a witch's cauldron of funk. Should he even bother applying?

He glanced at the walls of the crappy apartment he wouldn't be able to afford next month. What choice did he have? Gathering the scattered chunks of his career, his ego and his regrets, he wrote down the address of The Tippling Widow. He had to try.

When he first pulled into the parking lot, he thought the place abandoned. But a basset hound lumbered around the corner of the covered porch to the front steps and sat down, staring at his car. He shut off the engine.

What are you going to say when they ask about your last job?

"Hell if I know." His voice bounced off the windows and back at him. He'd just have to dance around the truth. A little. He checked his hair in the rearview mirror, then, résumé in hand, stepped out.

Unpruned vines in untidy rows straggled up and down the hills like drunken soldiers.

Well, at least here you'll be needed. Retucking his custom-tailored dress shirt into his favorite slacks, he smothered the *last chance* whisper in his mind, slapped on a salesman's smile and strode toward the porch.

Taking the drooling dog's thumping tail as a gesture of goodwill, he stepped around it on the way to the door. At the sound of sweeping coming from the right, he turned. A broom appeared from around the corner, followed by a small, thin woman in a faded T-shirt and spandex pants that ended below the knee. Golden-highlighted brown hair escaped a red bandana to fall around her sweaty face.

He might have to give up the Land Rover, but if this was an example of the help around here, at least there'd be some perks to the job. "Excuse me."

She squeaked and jumped, her Keds actually leaving the porch. She raised a French-manicured hand to her chest, her deep brown eyes huge.

"Could you tell me where I could find the owner?"

She tucked a hank of hair behind her ear and shot a look at the roof of the porch, her lips moving silently. The broom fell with a clatter, and she scrubbed her hands on her slim thighs and extended a hand. "I'm Indigo Blue, the owner. The working owner," she said with a blush and an apologetic smile.

He knew that name. His mind sorted data, trying to remember from where. Her hand was soft, warm and fine-boned. She might be a working owner, but with hands like that, she hadn't been for long. "I'm Danovan DiCarlo. I've come to apply for the manager position."

"I only posted that opening last night. I never dreamed anyone would be by so soon." Her hand slipped from his. "I'm sorry to be a mess. Please, come in."

She led him to the front door, stopping to

pet the hound. "This is Barnabas. The Tippling Widow mascot."

He followed her, wishing he could shake the hand of whoever invented spandex. He'd always been a leg man. The muscles in her calves were fluid in flexion. Her thighs were long and firm, and her ass…legendary. Suddenly, the name clicked. That body had graced the cover of the Hollywood rags Lissette consumed like trendy cocktails. This was Harry Stone's arm-candy wife. What the heck was she doing here?

She led the way through a high-ceilinged, timber-framed tasting room, through a door and into an office. At least, at some point in the past, this space must have been an office. Large arched windows looked out onto the front lawn, and the wood modesty panel told him there was likely a desk under the piles of paper.

She lifted a stack of wine trade magazines from the guest chair. "Have a seat." She looked around for a place to put the magazines. Not finding room on the desk, she dropped them into a corner. They hit the dirty carpet with a muffled *whump*. She walked around the desk and lowered herself into a scarred high-backed leather chair as if it were a throne. "I'd apologize for the mess, but I'm afraid once I start, I'd never stop."

"If everything was shipshape, you wouldn't need me." He gave her a salesman's smile and handed his résumé to her over the paper piles.

Given Harry Stone's money, Danovan figured that finances shouldn't be a problem. And once he took over, she could go back to Hollywood. This job was looking up.

The light from the dirty window fell on her heart-shaped face as she read. Flawless pale milk skin, her mouth a bit too wide and big, sad eyes. Not just the sad within them, but in their shape, tilting down a bit at the outside edge. She turned the page with long, elegant fingers.

She looked up, and their gazes locked. He recognized the pain in those big eyes from what he saw in the mirror every morning.

Why so sad? He froze for a heartbeat, afraid he'd said it out loud.

ARROGANT AND FULL of himself. Indigo studied her potential employee, not caring that he stared back. She had nothing to hide. Profiles like his graced Italian coins. He had a spade-shaped face: broad forehead, arresting wide-spaced brown eyes. There was a diagonal line through one of his heavy brows. At first she thought it was a razored fashion statement, but looking closer, she saw it was a scar. It, along with a slightly crooked nose, just made him look rugged. And a strong jaw narrowing to a squared-off chin only added to the effect.

Oh, Harry, your cameras would love this one. And he *knew* how good-looking he was. He wore handsomeness as casually as he did his expensive clothes. Hollywood was full of men like this, bursting with charm and hubris. He had no way of knowing she'd been inoculated against that type years ago. "Why would you want this position?" She read from the résumé. "Cum laude in agribusiness from UC Davis, you worked your way up to lead vintner at one of the largest growers in the area within three years." She dropped the paper and studied the man it supposedly explained. "You are obviously overqualified."

"Actually, I'm looking to this job as a way of completing my education." He leaned back, resting his hands on the chair arms. "I need to know how to start up a winery if I hope to own my own someday." His eyes traveled around the dingy room. "No offense meant."

"None taken." She kept the wince on the inside. "I'm hoping our grand reopening will be *like* a startup."

"'Our.' Do you have a partner?"

The corner of her mouth lifted. "Not unless you count Barnabas." Might as well scare him off before they wasted too much time; she had a lot to do today. "I can't afford to pay much."

"What is the salary?"

She told him.

He wasn't as good at hiding winces as she was. "I have an idea." His thumbs beat a cadence on the chair arms as he considered. "What if I accept your salary and we work out a percentage split of the profit?"

Her eyes widened. "What do you mean?"

"If I can't increase the profitability of your winery, I only receive the salary you're proposing. But if I succeed, I get, say, fifteen percent of the profit I generate." He stopped tapping and raised his hands, palms up. "This way you're assured that I'll do my best, because I have skin in the game. And you wouldn't lose anything that you didn't have to begin with."

She searched for holes in his logic. "I'd have to think about that."

He gave her a Hollywood smile. "Fair enough. Why don't you give me a tour and tell me your plans?"

"Follow me." She stood and led him to the hallway. "Our wines have enjoyed a solid reputation for years. I hope to continue that." When she stopped in front of a door, he opened it. "Since I have a background in yoga and massage, I plan to reopen as a boutique winery *and* spa. I think it would give us a unique twist."

The room was long and narrow. "This would be great for my yoga classes." She stepped in and flipped on the lights. "I'll install mirrors all along this wall and put reflective tinting on the windows for privacy. I'll wall off a small room at the end for massage and aromatherapy."

"Really." He didn't actually put his nose in the

air, but his tone was the auditory equivalent. "I'm not big on all that new-age woo-woo, but you may be right. Rich women love it."

Great. Arrogant and opinionated. Well, he didn't need to approve of her—just respect her, as the owner. "Not only rich women. I'm going to encourage the local women to participate as well." She pulled the door closed and led the way down the hall.

He's only the first applicant. Hopefully the next will be better.

"These are the manager's quarters. Barney and I are camping out here until I can get moved into the cabin at the top of the hill." Glad she'd thought to make the bed this morning, she unlocked the door and stepped in.

He looked around, his gaze lingering on her open suitcase. "Nice."

Of course her fuchsia underwear lay on top like a Frederick's of Hollywood advertisement.

Wondering if he referred to the apartment or her underthings, she stepped around him, walked across the room and kicked the suitcase lid closed, sure her face was the same shade as the lingerie.

"Why did you leave your last position?" She leaned against the wall and crossed her arms.

His assurance faltered as something flashed across his face—shock maybe. But it was gone before she could be sure.

"I'm the lead vintner at Bacchanal." He slipped

his hands into his pockets. "They don't know I'm looking to take my career in another direction, so I'd appreciate it if you wouldn't contact them. My other references should tell you what you need to know."

CHAPTER THREE

"I SEE YOU'VE worked as an assistant vineyard manager…" She consulted the résumé before her. "…Craig. But I need more than that. I need a generalist."

The earnest-faced young man leaned forward in the guest chair. "I know. But I learn fast. I thought I could start in the vineyard then advance."

"I appreciate your aspirations and your attitude. But as you can see—" she spread her arms "—it's just me. I need someone who knows it all." *And who can teach me.* "I'll hold on to your résumé for when I can affo—expand enough to require a vineyard manager." She stood. "But thank you for coming by."

The kid stood and extended a hand. "I hope you do keep me in mind. I'm looking for an opportunity to move up."

From the office window a few moments later, Indigo watched his car peel out of the parking lot, leaving a haze of dust and desperation.

That was the last interview. The posting had run for a week, and she hadn't had a call in three days. As Harry would have said, "It's time to kill the engineer and start production." But there had only been six applicants, and two had ended the interview when they heard the salary. One had the nerve to chuckle on the way out.

She lifted the three remaining résumés from the desk. The old man would be a great teacher, but with his huge-knuckled, arthritic hands, she had doubts that he could withstand the physical work required. She dropped his résumé in the overflowing trash can. The next looked great on paper, but two of his references had sung the same song about complaints from the serving staff. Sexual harassment complaints. Since the manager would live on the premises and Indigo's closest neighbor was a half mile away... She shivered, imagining a knock at the cabin door late at night. Or maybe not even a knock. His résumé followed the rest into the trash.

That left one. She studied the heavy ivory paper. *The arrogant Italian.*

Yes, his attitude bugged her, but she was used to that. After all, if arrogance was a crime, all of Hollywood would be incarcerated. She'd checked his references. No one had a bad word to say about Danovan DiCarlo, from his expertise to his knowledge to his work ethic.

But something still nagged about him. Like the shredded remnants of a dream upon waking, something lingered, leaving her with an uneasy feeling and the memory of his sad smile. Her hands swept the papers on the desk into stacks, almost without her being aware that she'd done so.

Whenever she was upset, her body craved movement, as if action could help sort the knots in her mind.

What was it about him?

For one thing, he's overqualified. He'll walk as soon as he gets a better opportunity.

But he already had a better job than she was offering.

How very convenient for him.

Are you looking for reasons not to hire him?

"Yeah, I am, kinda."

Barney looked up from the blanket that she'd put in the corner for him.

On what grounds? A feeling? *What a joke.* She was batting O-fer when it came to being able to trust her feelings.

Maybe she should broaden her search to include the entire country. But that would take time, and meanwhile, money was flowing out of the checkbook with damned little coming in.

The chair squealed when she collapsed against the back. In spite of her vow to make her own decisions, and regardless of how it felt to cave this early, she lifted her phone from the desk to call in a lifeline.

Uncle Bob's baby was just too important to risk on *feelings.* Especially hers.

"The People's Farm. This is Sky."

"Hi, Mom."

"Indigo! How good to hear your voice. Tell me what the winery's like. Have you settled in?"

Indigo could hear the bustle of the market in the background. The commune had barely been feeding itself when her mother took over and expanded the operation until they had surplus to sell. Her mother was half late-blooming flower child and half drill sergeant. The combination worked, for now the organic farmer's market she'd begun drew people from three counties.

"Not settled yet, but I'm working on it. First, tell me what's happening there." She smiled at her mother's happy chirping about business and growing things. Wistful thoughts drifted in with her mother's voice, but Indigo knew that as much as her childhood had been peaceful and pastoral, she'd no longer be happy living that simple existence. Hollywood had stripped her of the innocence required for membership, and like a hymen, once broken, innocence wouldn't grow back. She shivered.

"Indigo? Are you there?"

"I'm here, Mom, sorry."

"What's wrong?" Metal pellets of worry clicked in her voice.

"Not a big deal, I'm just calling for some advice." She needed a lifeline, not a life preserver—her mother couldn't save her, only she could do that. "I'm about to hire my first employee. How can I know he's the right person?"

Her mother chuckled. "Lord knows, I made enough mistakes in the beginning to sink this place."

"That's what scares me." She wriggled in the chair to shake off her body's craving for movement. "How do you decide?"

"First, do your research. Then you take a leap of faith."

"I was afraid you'd say that. I always sucked at the broad jump."

"Indigo Blue. What's going on?"

She'd never discussed the dirty details of her life in Hollywood with her mother. In the beginning, she'd been too proud and embarrassed to admit that her pretty teenage dream had become a nightmare. After Harry, it had been easier to tell her a version closer to the truth. "Let's just say I've learned some things the hard way, okay?"

"Of course you did. That's the only way we learn." Suddenly her voice barked, "No, Moon, not there. Put the radishes beside the arugula. It's more visually appealing."

"You're busy. I'll let you go." She didn't want her mother digging further into her past. Indigo's stories wouldn't stand up to more than casual interest.

"Honey, you know how to do this. Go to a quiet place, put on some soothing music and open some lavender oil. Just trust. The answer is inside you."

"I will, Mom, thanks. I'll talk to you soon." She

clicked End. Her mother meant well, but meditation wouldn't fix the winery's problems—knowledge would.

She'd read through the *The Complete Idiot's Guide to Starting and Running a Winery* three times and had learned enough to know that she didn't know enough. Running a winery from a book was like a blind man attempting brain surgery.

Which led her back to the résumé that lay, front and center, on the newly tidied desk.

"Shit. Why am I putting myself through a mental rat maze? I don't have a choice." And that rankled.

AT THE SOUND of a car engine, Danovan came back to himself and took a quick glance around the grassy hill dotted with marble rectangles. No visitors marred the perfect green lawn. Thank God. The family might have reclaimed his wife, but damned if they'd keep him from his daughter. He scanned the drive coming up the hill. He wasn't prepared for another confrontation. The cuts to his soul might have healed, but the scars were red and shiny, too tight.

He bent and placed the nosegay of baby's breath and tiny white roses on the headstone below the name Esperanza DiCarlo. He'd named her for the hope she'd brought, but the few months between the two dates below her name reminded him that hope was fragile.

"Sleep, *cara*. I will visit again soon." He wiped a drop of regret from his eye and turned away.

He opened the door of his Range Rover and dropped onto the seat. The phone rang. "DiCarlo," he answered.

"Mr. DiCarlo, this is Indigo Blue, of The Tippling Widow Winery. You applied for my generalist position earlier in the week?"

As if he could forget either the job or the husky quality of the owner's voice. "Yes, Ms. Blue."

Her laugh was as smoky as her voice. "I think we'd better be on a first-name basis if we're to work together."

Thank God. He let out a breath it seemed he'd been holding forever. He'd sweated out the past four days, waiting for both the splash page on the Bacchanal site to be changed, wiped clean, as if he'd never existed. And for a call from Indigo, telling him she'd chosen someone else.

"That is, if you still want the job, based on the terms we discussed."

"Oh, yes, I want it." It might not be good form to smile in a cemetery, but his daughter wouldn't be offended; wine was in her blood on both sides. "I can start tomorrow, if you'd like."

"Don't you have to give notice at your current position?"

Crap. He'd been so sure he wouldn't land the

job that he hadn't planned this far ahead. Thoughts ran through his mind in a blur, like a manic news feed. He snatched at one. "I put in notice after my interview with you."

"A bit sure of yourself, aren't you?"

Her voice might be smoky, but he now remembered that smoke sometime came from ice. Dry ice.

"Oh, no, not at all." His panicked brain snatched at another speeding excuse. "I'm committed to my new course. If you hadn't hired me, I'd have looked in Napa." That was the truth—he'd planned to start looking on Monday.

"I see."

His gut clenched at the silence on the line. He wanted to jump in, to convince her. But his father had always told him, "When you're in a hole, stop digging." So he stopped.

After a lifetime of agonizing moments, she spoke. "How about tomorrow, say, ten?"

"Yes, of course. See you then. Thank you." He hung up and started the car. If she thought that a vintner's hours ran on Hollywood time, she had a lot to learn. And for as long as she stayed, he'd teach her.

But he didn't expect that to be long at all.

He drove down the hill to the exit. *Oh, that's nice. She's put her trust in you, and you lie to her.* When a wasp's sting of guilt hit, he soothed it with the vow that he'd fulfill his side of the bargain.

He'd run the place to the best of his ability after she scurried back to the Cush Life. He owed her that, for giving him a second chance. Even if she didn't know she had.

He drove to the apartment that would no longer be his home, whistling a Paganini concerto.

This job would be a great do-over. He had every intention of doing it right this time.

INDIGO SCRABBLED THROUGH the office desk's lap drawer, searching for the scrap of paper she'd seen among the ancient business cards, crumpled receipts and leaky pens. "You should have started on the cabin yesterday." *Or the day before.* Odious as it would be, setting Uncle Bob's home to rights should be her job alone. But with Danovan reporting for work in the morning, she'd have to vacate the manager's quarters, and the only other bed on the property was in the cabin. She was out of time and needed help.

"Ah, here it is." Squinting at the smeared numbers, she dialed.

"*Hola,*" a lilting feminine voice said.

"Hello. Is this Rosalina?"

"*Sí,* señora. Can I help you?"

"You own the service that cleans The Tippling Widow, right?"

"Yes."

Indigo blew out a breath. "We need to talk."

"We did not do a good job?"

"Oh, no. You've done a great job. That's why I'm calling. I need help cleaning the cabin on the premises. You know, the one at the top of the hill?"

"*Sí*. Señor Bob's."

At the tenderness in the woman's voice, a bubble of sadness rose into Indigo's throat. "Yes, that one." Her voice squeezed around the blockage, coming out skinny.

"But the manager, he no let us in there."

"He doesn't work here anymore. I'm Indigo Blue, the owner. I'll be living in the cabin, but…" She searched for words that wouldn't scare the woman off. "It needs a good going over before I move in. Could you send someone today?"

Papers rustled. "No one free today. We can come next week. That's our normal schedule."

"No one? Are you sure? Could you check again? I really could use some help."

"I am so sorry, missus. No one today."

Her heart shriveled to a small ball. She should have known it would come to this. It was her job to do, really. "You mean you don't come every week?"

"The manager, he tells us no."

She couldn't afford it, but they were making and selling a food product; a clean facility was a must. And her time would be better spent learning than cleaning. She forced the words past the banker side of her brain. "Can I get on a once-a-week schedule, including the cabin?"

When they'd worked out the timing, Indigo thanked her and hung up.

One more call to go. "Cross your toes, Barney."

The carefree mutt looked up from his blanket and yawned.

"Okay, a good-luck yawn. I can live with that." But just in case, she threw a prayer to any god listening before dialing the next number.

"Yes?"

"Is this Sandra Vanderbilt?"

"This is Sondra." She drew out the name, as if chastising the mispronunciation.

"Yes, sorry, Sondra." She didn't stretch it. "I'm Indigo Blue, the owner of The Tippling Widow. I'm calling to—"

"I wondered when someone would call. Do not ask. I will not work with that vinous degenerate."

Note to self—search Google for vinous. "If you mean the former manager, that's no problem. He's gone. I understand from the records that you are the serving staff manager."

"I *was*." Delicate sniff. "I enjoyed working for Robert, but since his death the place has gone downhill to the point where I was embarrassed to admit I worked there."

Robert? Uncle Bob was salt of the earth. He was no more a Robert than Indigo was a Bambi. "Well,

I intend to change that. I have already hired a new manager, and I was hoping you would agree—"

"Whom?"

"What?"

"*Whom* did you hire as manager?"

Indigo had heard that I'm-dealing-with-an-idiot tone before, but never from an employee. She might live in the country now, but the taint of Hollywood uppity was still fresh in her nostrils. And it burned. Dammit, she'd come here looking for some respect. Why rehire a snotty employee? Indignation filled her chest, squaring her shoulders. She took a breath to tell Sooondra to pound sand.

Then a shotgun blast of reality hit her inflated chest, and all the indignation bled out. *You need this woman.* A complete staff turnover was more than The Widow could survive right now. After all, Indigo didn't know enough about wine to interview, much less hire, competent serving staff, and Danovan wouldn't have the time to interview *or* train them. "Danovan DiCarlo is the new manager."

"Oh, reeeally?"

She would have given quite a bit to know what caused Sondra's surprise, but damned if she'd ask this woman for gossip. Loosening her jaw muscles, she bit her tongue.

Sondra sniffed. "I suppose I could consider that, though I am contemplating several other opportunities."

"I plan to honor Bob's dream to make The Tippling Widow wines the pride of the region. Surely, given your years of loyal service, you'd want to be a part of that?"

"I would. For a ten percent increase in salary."

You can't afford it. Besides, she's bluffing. Indigo's gut told her she was right. She put a hand to that notoriously unreliable part of her anatomy. *But what if she's not? You sure don't have the knowledge to do the job.* Not yet, anyway.

Sondra broke into her thoughts. "I'm waiting to hear about another position. Why don't I just call you back next week?"

One big mistake at this point could be the weight that sank The Widow. Figures streamed through Indigo's mind. "I'll give you five percent more, but only if you can convince the rest of the serving staff to return."

Another haughty sniff. "They will follow wherever I lead."

Without choke collars? "Good. Contact them and all of you report for work at…" Blood pounded to her cheeks. "What time do you usually start?"

"Nine-thirty. The doors open promptly at ten."

"I'll see you then, Sand—Sondra."

"You will." *Click.*

Indigo stared at the dead phone, then dropped it onto the desk. Bob had made running the winery seem effortless, yet she'd not encountered one easy task since she'd set foot on the property. Well, hopefully that would change tomorrow when the new manager showed up. She imagined Danovan DiCarlo galloping up the drive on a white steed, skidding to a stop at the porch steps.

She snorted. *Like I'm some damsel in distress.* She glanced out at the empty porch. The cobwebs swayed in the breeze, and trash fluttered in the weeds. The tasks she was capable of doing could fill several pages of lists, but the ones she was incapable of could fill a book the size of Webster's dictionary. *Okay, so I am in distress. But it's not going to be a chronic condition.*

She'd only need all of them—Danovan, Sondra and her crew—until she got her feet under her and some experience. Then, if any of them weren't working out, she'd fire them and start over.

The vow soothed her chapped ego. "Hey, Barn. Wake up."

The dog opened droopy eyes.

"How'd you like a hamburger? We have to shovel out the cabin yet, but we need a break."

Fifteen minutes later, she pulled into the gravel parking lot of the barn-red, low-slung building that the wooden sign declared The Farmhouse Café. She parked, turned off the engine, then sat frozen, watching two ghosts walk to the glass entrance door. The painfully young woman smiled up at the much older man as if he held the secret to life and was about to bestow it upon her.

Her savior. Her love. Her Harry.

In the suddenly too-hot car, the older but not much wiser woman sat mesmerized, swamped by yearning.

Harry's long gray hair was held in his signature ponytail, and his face was saddle-brown with white lines from squinting into location suns. The couple was too far away for Indigo to see his eyes, but she didn't need to. She remembered the sky-blue sparkle that had always been there just for her.

Harry had never seen her as the tainted mess he'd stumbled upon that horrific morning. He'd just picked her up, washed her clean and treated her like she was something special—like a diamond that someone had dropped in mud. And because he'd believed it, over time, Indigo was able to believe. Because of that look in his eyes.

The python of grief in her chest writhed, constricting her heart, squeezing a sob from her throat. She closed her eyes, wrapped her arms around herself and rocked, trying to charm the snake back to sleep.

A cold nose nudged her elbow, burrowing until Barney's head lay in her lap. He let out a long sigh that ended in a whine.

She ran her hand over the velvet head. "We are truly a mess, Barn." She leaned back in the seat. "This place has great cheeseburgers. What do you say we drown our sorrows in some grease?"

When she looked up, the ghosts were gone. She

snapped a leash on Barney's collar, gathered him in her arms and clambered out. Not a graceful exit, but Barney's legs were too short to jump out on his own. Together they crossed the almost deserted parking lot to the door the ghost couple had entered.

She slipped the leash over a metal post at the entrance. "Sit, Barn. I'll be back with your burger in a few."

A bell clanked against the glass door when she pulled it open and stepped into chilled air laden with the smell of bacon. Looking around, she noted the silvered wooden floor, the old pot-bellied stove in the corner—and the fact that she was the lone diner. Except for the ghosts, who sat in the booth by the window.

She turned away and walked to the long Formica bar with chrome and red vinyl stools. The cook's window framed a happy picture—a large man, white T-shirt riding up his ripped biceps, bent a blonde woman over his arm, kissing her. No, not kissing—consuming her.

Indigo's heart stuttered, then pounded heat through her: the base of her throat, beneath her breasts, at the back of her knees. A wicked whip-lash of jealousy bit deep, and yearning spread, burning like alcohol on the cut.

She must have made a noise, because the couple turned their heads. They separated, and the woman put a hand to her poofed-up French twist.

"Oh, hello." She trailed long nails down the man's throat, and Indigo saw his shiver. With a last private smile that said she knew exactly what that did to him, the blonde walked away, entering the restaurant through a swinging door. She smoothed her hands over the too-tight-to-wrinkle white pantsuit, her cheeks only slightly pink. "Hon, before you go getting the wrong idea, we're married." She flashed a Hollywood-worthy smile.

Indigo slipped onto a stool. "Hey, don't mind me."

"Welcome to the Farmhouse. I'm Jesse, and that sexy hunk back there is Carl."

The giant waved a hand in her general direction, but ducked his head, suddenly busy, a bit pink in the cheeks himself.

"You're not from around here, are you, hon?"

"I am now." Indigo snatched a menu from behind the napkin dispenser.

"Well, Widow's Grove is a great town. I'll bet you'll like it here." She tilted her head and tapped a long carmine nail on her cheek. "You look familiar."

"My husband and I used to eat here." She resisted the urge to glance to the booth behind her. "Years ago."

"Well then, welcome back…" Jesse raised a blond eyebrow.

"Indigo. Blue." Seeing the cogs turning in Jesse's

eyes, she ducked her head to scan the menu. "Could I have a veggie omelet?" The smell of bacon taunted her. "No, wait. Make that a bacon cheddar omelet." She closed the menu, vowing to eat better—tomorrow. "And could I also get a hamburger patty without the bun for my best guy out there?" She glanced to the door, where Barney sat patiently waiting, watching her every move.

"Oh, what a cutie! Of course you can, hon."

"Coming up," the giant in the kitchen window said.

"Let me guess. You're settling in Widow's Grove because you missed our great cooking, right?" Jesse smiled, leaned a hip on the counter and waited.

Oh, she's good.

Indigo should know—she'd been grilled by the best reporters in Hollywood. Jesse's down-home style was much easier to take. She couldn't help but return the smile. "Only partially. I'm the owner of The Tippling Widow Winery."

"You are?" Jesse's full lips pursed. "We were so sorry to lose Bob. He was a good man. One of the old guard around here. Did you know him well, hon?"

"Yes." Indigo knew a small-town gossip when she saw one. She wasn't discussing her relations with a stranger. Especially since it would lead back to Harry. The snake in her chest shifted, and she rubbed her breastbone to settle it back to sleep. She took a breath and focused forward instead of back. "I'm going to make The Tippling Widow a winery Bob could be proud of again." Local rumors spread fastest. The Widow's troubles wouldn't be news here.

She looked up just in time to see the tumblers fall into place in Jesse's eyes. "Oh." Sympathy replaced curiosity. "Harry Stone is—was—"

"Hamburger's up, Jess." The Nordic hunk slid a small plate through the window.

Jesse retrieved the dish and set it on the counter.

"Excuse me." Indigo grabbed the hamburger patty and hustled out the door to deliver it to Barney.

Dammit, she'd hoped to make a new start here, where no one knew her. She should have known better. Her name was so distinctive and Harry so famous... Squatting, she set the plate in front of Barney. He wolfed the burger, tail whipping.

Funny how it was easier to deal with Hollywood's ire than to endure sympathy from a well-meaning stranger. *On the flipside, if this woman is the gossip you think she is, she'll pass the word, and at least you won't have to explain to everyone you meet.* She stood and forced herself to grasp the door, wishing she could snatch Barney's leash and trot to the car.

CHAPTER FOUR

WHEN THE ANTIQUE clock over the mantel gonged twice, Indigo dropped the floor brush into the bucket and pulled off her rubber gloves. *Two in the morning and I still have to make the bed.* She sat back on her heels at the edge of the bathroom floor, then pushed to her feet. At least she had a fresh bed to fall into. She dug a knuckle into the cramping muscle in the small of her back. She'd earned it hauling the mattress in from its airing on the porch.

Her hard work had paid off. She walked into the great room of Uncle Bob's cabin, proud of the warm glow of lamplight on clean paneling. Someone would have to be hired to haul away the mountain of crap she'd tossed out the back door, but she'd worry about that tomorrow.

Burnished copper-bottom pots once again hung where they belonged over the stove. The starched gingham curtains were pulled back from a window that worked as a mirror, reflecting the room. After a rocky start, losing her breakfast after touring the bathroom this afternoon, her mood had lightened with every room she restored. Her body ached, and she might have to burn these clothes, but she'd been right—this was her job to do.

She ran a hand over the wooden grapes in the hand-carved mantel. "Welcome home, Uncle Bob."

AT EXACTLY NINE-THIRTY that morning, a woman strode through the door of the tasting room, two women in her wake.

Sooondra. She was willowy as a Lladró porcelain. Her perfectly straight ash-blond hair fell to the middle of a butt sculpted, no doubt, by hundreds of Pilates sessions. Her tasteful pencil skirt and crisp white tailored blouse were all business, and the high heels that tapped a staccato beat across the wood floor made the elegant line of her leg even longer. Her face was a juxtaposition of soft and hard that made it difficult to look away. Wide-spaced elongated eyes over sleek, soft cheeks ended in a chin that could slice paper. Stopping in front of Indigo, she flipped a sheaf of hair over her shoulder with a smooth, precise move. She looked like an Afghan Hound at a Westminster show: aloof, entitled, untouchable.

She sniffed and glanced around. "Well, it's still standing."

Well, la-de-da. Ms. Perky Ass has arrived. Indigo gritted her teeth in what she hoped looked like a smile. "It's a bit rough, but the cleaning crew won't be here until next week, so our first job will be getting this place ready for business."

Sondra looked down her long nose. "You do not expect serving staff to do manual labor."

Indigo shrugged, holding her hands out to the empty room. "I don't see any customers to serve, do you?" She dusted her hands, then offered one to shake. "I'm Indigo Blue. You're Sondra, obviously. Will you introduce me to your coworkers?"

Sondra shook the ends of Indigo's fingers, then turned, displaying the women behind her with a game show model's flourish. "This is Natalie Baddorf." A petite brunette in soft camel slacks and a white blouse just like Sondra's, tipped her head. "She's a wine professional and server. Her expertise is eclipsed only by my own." She turned to her other minion. "And this is Becky Stiles, the salesperson for the gift shop, and my cashier."

My cashier?

Becky looked like a copper penny among diamonds, a fresh-faced redhead with a dusting of freckles across her nose. She smiled then burst forward to give Indigo's hand a firm shake. "I'm glad to be back, Ms. Blue."

This could be a strong team. Sondra and Natalie's expertise and high class would impress the wine aficionados, and Becky's charm and girl-next-door looks would keep newbies from being intimidated. "I'm glad to meet you all. We're going to have to roll up our sleeves because it's up to us, along with our new manager, to turn The Tippling Widow into a winery Uncle Bob would be proud of." She lifted from the bar three dark green aprons with the winery's logo across the breast: the name in script, with the *I*'s in *Tippling* and *Widow* the stem of a wineglass. "And we're starting today." She handed out the aprons, then slipped the last one over her own head, crossed the strings behind her and tied them in front.

Sondra's chin lifted, and she eyed the apron in her fingers with an arched brow.

This was the moment Indigo had worried over. And over. If Sondra wouldn't follow orders, this wasn't going to work. What would happen then, Indigo didn't want to contemplate. Uncle Bob had trusted these women, and Indigo didn't have the knowledge to even interview for these positions. She stilled herself, though she could almost hear the stress humming through her like electricity in a high line.

Natalie and Becky stood holding the aprons, watching their boss's cue for what to do next.

Sondra gave a theatrical sigh. "We can't work in this filth, regardless." She dropped the apron on the bar. "I won't need this to supervise." She glanced at her charges and clapped her hands. "Well, ladies, what are you waiting for? We don't have a minute to spare if this tasting room is going to be fit for customers."

Barney's collar jingled when he trotted into the room.

"Is that a *dog*?" Sondra made it sound like *cockroach*.

Barney skidded to a stop at Indigo's feet, and she leaned over to play with his ears. "This is our mascot, Barnabas. Barney to his friends."

"Oh, how cute!" Becky bent to pet him.

"Do not touch that. You cannot have an animal in the serving room. It's a clear health-code violation."

"It's an FDA recommendation, not a hard rule. It's up to the owner's discretion." She straightened and leveled a stare at Sondra. "And I'm the owner."

The area at the base of Sondra's nostrils went white. Her gray eyes went dark. She stared back.

No one moved, even at the sound of boots clumping across the wooden porch.

"Hey, look who's here! My old pal Sandy." Danovan strode up and enveloped Sondra in a huge hug. "I knew there was a beautiful woman missing from my life."

Sondra air-kissed both his cheeks and smiled up at him. "Danovan DiCarlo, you big flirt. I should have known that if a woman inherited a winery, you'd be working there."

He released Sondra as if she'd just scalded him. When he turned to Indigo, his cheeks were pink. "Reporting for duty, Ms. Blue. Er—Indigo."

He wore nothing special: suede boots, chinos and an ivory cotton button-down shirt with the sleeves rolled on his tanned forearms. But he still managed to look like a cover model with his sexy eyes, a crooked smile and the testosterone that he wore like cologne.

Indigo pulled herself from the shock of seeing Sondra tease. "Morning, Danovan. Let's go to my office to talk." She turned to Sondra and her entourage. "Nice meeting you, ladies. We'll catch up later." She led the way across the floor to the wooden door marked Employees Only. He was there to open it before she could reach for the handle.

She felt back in control once she sat behind her desk. Danovan took the office chair. "You're a friend of Sondra's?"

The incredulity must have bled into her tone, because he smiled. "She and I worked together at another winery. Sandy's a pussycat."

She blew back her bangs. "So is a panther, but I wouldn't want to try to pet one."

He laughed.

With his charm, he probably *could* tame a wildcat. "Let's get started." She gathered her bullet list of questions from the desk. "Since I'm not even sure where to begin, I think it best if I just shadow you for now, don't you?"

"That's a good idea." He leaned forward, elbows on knees. "I'd like to inspect the vines first, then move on to the production facility. Before anything else happens, I need to assess where we are so we can put together a plan to get The Widow back on her feet. All right?"

"I'm right behind you." She stood. "Oh, by the way, the manager's quarters are clean and ready for you to move in."

"Thank you. I'll do that after work today." He stood and gestured to the door. "Shall we?"

HE NOTED A fine tremor in her hand when she reached for her notes. *She hides it well, but she's nervous. At least I'm not the only one.* Hopefully the last-chance jitters he put on with his clothes this morning would wear off as the day went on.

He led the way to the vines, noting the drainage, exposure and sheltering along the tree-lined border. It was obvious that Bob Stone understood grapes. Nurturing delicate vines was a labor of love that required a scientist's knowledge, a shaman's intuition and strong parenting skills. He squatted to inspect a vine, gratified to see strong bud nodes and new shoots while his boss rattled off facts she must've looked up since he last saw her.

"The vines are a hybrid with the European *Vitis vinifera*, which I understand to be a good thing."

"The best. What else do you know?" He dug his fingers into the too-hard soil.

"Our grapes are Cabernet Sauvignon and merlot on the red side, and a Chardonnay on the white. Those are European. Uncle Bob was experimenting with a few American zinfandel varietals before he passed away."

He grunted a reply and brushed dead leaves from the base of a vine to inspect for bugs.

"I think it looks pretty good out here, no? A little tidying maybe..." Her voice trailed off to a wish.

He brushed the dirt from his hands and straightened. His boss stood pen in hand, ready to make more lists. He hoped she'd brought enough paper. "It looks like nothing has been done since pruning last winter." He gazed over the messy rows that sprawled down the slope of the hill. "The debris from last year's crop needs to be removed, and the soil tilled. We're already late putting up this year's trellis and tying the tendrils to it. All the support posts need to be tested and loose ones pounded back in. We need to put together a spray schedule for fungus and determine what fertilizer the soil needs. Do you know when the last soil analysis was done?"

She scribbled fast, her tongue caught between her teeth. "Um...soil samples?"

"Never mind. I'll find them. Let's go."

She finished writing then jogged to catch up. He led the way to the covered outdoor grape crush pad and press, noting that they were at least clean. They wouldn't be used until the crop was harvested in the fall, but all looked in order.

When they reached the production facility, he held the door for her.

She ducked under his arm. "When I arrived ten days ago, the AC was out. Luckily, it had just happened." She pointed to the ceiling. "The repairman finished replacing the whole thing earlier this week."

Shiny aluminum ductwork snaked across the ceiling. "What'd it cost?"

She named a figure that was a third higher than it should have been.

He cleared his throat. "That is…"

She scanned his face with a look of innocent hopefulness, like a young girl who just asked for verification that there *was* a Santa.

"Fine." He cleared the gruff from his throat. She would have enough to worry about by the time he was done. No need to make her feel bad about a decision that it was too late to rectify.

She led the way through the shipping area. Cardboard boxes stacked on pallets filled the floor.

"Where are your—our warehouse employees?"

She glanced to the empty shipping tables and the abandoned forklift beside them. "We'll have to hire some."

"No shippers? Don't we have orders waiting to be filled?"

"Not so much." She put her lists and her pen down on a case and turned to him. "Look. I'll be upfront with you. The last manager was a lazy drunk. The employees quit. I haven't asked around about our reputation, but the trickle of orders tells me what I don't want to know."

She jammed her hands into the back pockets of her jeans, which squared her shoulders. And pulled the green apron tight across her chest. "Getting The Widow in shape is going to take a lot of work. I know it. Now you know it." Her chin came up. "But it'll be so worth it. I can tell you exactly what it's going to be like." She looked off into the warehouse, but he was sure she wasn't seeing metal walls or new ductwork. "We'll have a pond in front with those fancy goldfish. Customers sipping wine on the front porch will be able to hear the ornamental waterfall. We'll have wedding receptions on the lawn. I'll teach yoga classes and aromatherapy and do massage." Thick brown hair curtained her face when she ducked her head, but not before he saw her pink-stained cheeks. "I have ideas. I know looking at it now makes all this sound crazy. But this could be so much more than just a place to sell wine."

"Well, with you and me working together, we'll make that dream happen."

She had her aspirations. He had his. He imagined a dark bottle with a black label that read: Di-Carlo Select Merlot.

He shook his head. This dreaming thing was contagious. "We'd better get started if we're going to get all that done." He smiled at her and got a tentative one in return. She was a naïve dreamer, but damned if she wasn't a good-looking one.

Rein it in, DiCarlo. That's what got you in trouble last time. He'd learned the hard way that work and women didn't mix.

He stopped at the glass wall of his office, overlooking the bottling line. He'd love to begin work in the adjoining lab, but first things first. "I'm going to find those soil sample reports and see what other information was left by the last manager."

"All right. I'll be in my office, trying to scare up a couple of warehouse employees."

"Could we go over the financials later? I need to know where we stand so we can determine how many more employees we can afford to hire."

"Sounds like a plan." Hope mingled with the dreams in her brown eyes before she walked away.

Lucky thing she didn't know what an unlikely hero she'd hired. But Indigo's enthusiasm was catching. Jitters gone, he walked into his office, his step light.

And for the first time in months, his spirits lifted from the floor of hopeless.

SEVEN HOURS LATER, Danovan returned the test tube of wine to the wire rack and jotted one last note. He'd found the testing equipment dusty and outdated. Apparently the last manager believed that tasting wine in large quantities was superior to using chemistry. And the wine quality showed it.

His stomach growled, protesting his decision to turn down his boss's lunch offer. But he'd been trying to get his arms around the production end of the business. He closed the spiral notebook. Time to fill her in on his armload of problems.

His steps echoed in the dim production building. No reason to burn lights in a deserted warehouse. The bottling line disappeared into gloom, and the fermenting tanks looked like boulders in a dark canyon. He passed through the barrel room into the lit-up tasting room. The long wood bar gleamed, the slate floor had been washed and there was not a cobweb or speck of dust to be seen. Looked like the retail employees had been busy. He flipped off the lights on his way out.

Pushing open the door to the private wing, he was surprised to find Indigo's office dark. Had she forgotten they were going to meet? Damn, he'd wanted to review those financials tonight.

As he walked to the door of his quarters, he figured he shouldn't have expected otherwise from a Hollywood A-lister.

Clang! "Dammit!"

The sound came from across the hall. He pushed open the door to the long storage room.

All he could see of his boss was her jeans-clad

legs. The rest was obscured by a stainless cylinder she lugged blindly across the floor.

He stepped forward. "Here, let me have that."

She squeaked and dropped the fixture.

Luckily he made it there in time to catch it. "What are you doing?" He set the drum on the floor between them.

She put a hand to her chest. "God, you scared me." With her other hand, she swiped hair out of her eyes. "Spring cleaning. This is going to be my yoga studio."

An imprint of dirt streaked her reddened face and continued down her sweatshirt. Her smell bridged the gap between them—not sweaty, exactly, but more an intensification of her normal scent—earthy, natural. She must have been at this awhile, because the room was empty save this drum. Maybe he should rethink his A-lister assumptions. "Why didn't you ask for help?"

"Because what you were doing was more important than manual labor, which is about all I'm qualified to do."

"Well, next time, come get me. This is heavy." He lifted the drum. "Where do you want it?"

"Just out in the hall for now." She held the door for him.

He set it to the side of the exit door and dusted his hands. "Have you eaten?"

She shook her head.

"I'm starving. But it's too late for a run to town."

He tipped his head to the apartment door. "You leave anything to eat in there?"

"Yes, but—"

"Good. I'll make us something. Come on." He unlocked the door with the key she'd given him earlier.

She hovered on the doorsill a few seconds. Then, as if making up her mind, she stepped in, brushing by him. "Danovan, why don't you get your things from your car? By the time you're done, I'll have food ready."

Good as her word, once he'd brought in the last armload of books, Indigo had soup and sandwiches on the small table.

"Looks great. Thank you." He held out a chair for her then sat opposite.

"It's just grilled cheese, and soup from a can."

"Sounds good to me." He took a bite of the sandwich. The bread was tangy and crunchy, the cheese rich and hot. "Hmm. This doesn't taste like any grilled cheese I've ever had."

"It's rye, with sharp cheddar and Swiss cheese. I used to make it all the time for..." Her lips twisted in a spasm. Then it was gone. "I used to make it all the time."

"Well, it's damned good."

"Thanks." She sipped a spoonful of soup. "I called the unemployment office today, and I'll have a couple of warehouse workers interviewing tomorrow. I'm hoping one man can handle both stock and shipping. We can't afford specialists at the moment."

"Good thinking."

"How are we doing from your viewpoint?"

He took a bite to avoid answering. He didn't want to ruin her dinner. Besides, he didn't have the whole picture yet. He swallowed.

He saw that look of hopeful watching.

She's your boss. You owe her the facts.

But that look made him hold back.

He couldn't help it. He loved women. Not necessarily in a lustful way, though there would be many who would dispute that. He just appreciated the gender. From toddlers to little old ladies, he was endlessly fascinated by the way their minds worked, so differently from his. He loved their organizational and multitasking abilities. He loved their delicate bones and envied their mental strength. He loved their softness, their chattiness, their smell.

He loved their smell.

"Well?"

"Do you mind if we discuss that tomorrow after I've reviewed the financials? I'd like to have the complete picture before I make suggestions for expenditures."

Her brows pulled together, a sure sign of the worry he was trying to save her from.

He shifted in the chair.

"Okay. But first thing tomorrow, right?"

With his finger, he traced an X over his heart. "If you'd like, I can make out a list of things to be done." He knew that would appeal to her book-keeper soul. "I'll prioritize it."

She picked up her spoon. "Good."

They ate in silence for a minute.

"Why wine?"

He looked up. "You mean, as a career?"

She nodded. "Is your family in the industry?" Her tone was casual, but she didn't fool him.

She's digging. She doesn't trust you.

"Hardly." He wiped his lips with the napkin. "My father is a federal appeals-court judge, and my mother is the headmistress of a girls' prep school in Georgetown. My brother is a Wall Street trader, and my sister is a partner in a big CPA firm in Seattle."

"Wow."

"Yeah, no pressure being the youngest swimming in that gene pool." Seeing she was done, he lifted both their plates.

She started to rise.

"I'll get the dishes and cleanup. It's my apartment now, after all." He carried the dishes to the sink. "I didn't like school much as a kid. Didn't get why I had to know about ancient Greece and quadratic equations." He located the dish soap under the sink. "But I always loved growing things. My mom says I drove the gardeners nuts, digging up the daffodils as a toddler." He ran the water until it was hot, then plugged the sink, squirted in some detergent. "The wine bug hit in high school. My parents appreciated a nice red and it turned out I was lucky to be born with a sensitive palate." He started with their dinner plates. "I was subscribed to *Wine Enthusiast* by tenth grade and couldn't wait until I could legally attend wine tastings."

"I'll dry." Indigo walked up, a kitchen towel in her hand. "I've heard high school drinking stories, but they didn't sound like that."

He rinsed a plate and handed it to her. "You 'heard.' Does that mean you didn't drink in high school?"

"I mean I didn't attend high school. I grew up on a commune in northern California. I was homeschooled. Nothing but natural, healthy living."

He started on the soup pot. "Somehow that doesn't surprise me. You have a natural look about you. Sounds like an idyllic childhood."

"It was." Her smile was happy and sad all at the same time. "But, trust me, I made up for it later."

"In Hollywood?" He wondered what was behind that bittersweet smile, but it winked out.

"Oh, I almost forgot the financials." Her words came out snipped off at the ends. She wiped her hands on the towel and dropped it on the counter. "I'll go get them."

Then she was gone, the door swinging shut behind her.

Well, there's a no-fly zone if I ever saw one. He finished the dishes and rummaged in the cabinets until he found where they all belonged.

She rapped on the door, pushed it open, but didn't step in. She reached across the small space to hand him a slim file folder. "Here you go. I've got to get back to the cabin and feed Barney. I'll see you in the morning." She turned away.

"Hang on. It's pitch black out there. I'll walk you home." He reached for his jacket.

"No, I've got it covered." She waved a flashlight.

"It's no bother. I don't feel good about—"

"Look." She put a hand on her hip. "I'm not helpless, or incompetent. I'm capable of walking a hundred yards in the dark by myself."

He raised his hands. "Yes, ma'am."

She turned and marched down the hall.

He closed the door. *Better this way.* He didn't need to know what shaped the soft and hard edges of Indigo Blue in order to work for her.

But he wondered, just the same.

CHAPTER FIVE

"UNHHH." INDIGO COLLAPSED in a heap on her yoga mat, paying for neglecting her morning routine. The Firefly Pose, one of her favorites, was now beyond her.

Barney just watched, head on his thick paws.

She untangled her arms and legs to lay with her head on her hands, two inches from his nose. "That's it, Barn. Starting today, we're back on our workouts."

He licked her face.

She swiped her cheek then sat up. "Yeah, I know you like them." Why shouldn't he? She'd logged a ton of miles jogging the Hollywood hills, hauling him behind her in a wagon. "Lucky for you, I found a wheelbarrow in the junk from what will be my yoga room. I actually think it'll work better than our wagon. We'll try it out tomorrow." She pushed herself to her feet. "We'll get weird looks, but we're used to that, right?" That was saying something. She'd been considered odd in Hollywood, where eccentricity was an art form.

She padded to the kitchen to make a latte. Luckily, her espresso maker had been a Christmas gift from Harry, so the Wicked Witch couldn't claim it. Starting today, it would be the only indulgence she allowed herself. She closed her eyes as the milk began to steam, the sound propelling her back to the mornings when she'd make two. She and Harry would drink them while they traded sections of the paper in bed. Her dream ended with a last hiss and sputter.

The coming sun was only an aura on the horizon. As she stepped barefoot onto the wood boards of the porch, the crisp air hit her exposed skin and damp leotard. Shivering, she set the cup on a small wood table and scooted back inside to grab a sweater. Barney trotted ahead on the return trip, then down the stairs to examine the vines that began ten feet from the porch. She settled in the Adirondack chair, pulled her legs up, wrapped the bulky sweater around her knees and took a deep breath of dirt and early morning air.

It doesn't get any better than this.

She sipped her coffee, and hope rose with the progress of the sun. Doubtless the day would bring more worries to pile on the old. But right now—in this moment—her jumble of emotions bowed before the perfect day. The home that Bob built at her back, Harry's sweater wrapped around her and the view of the grapevines they'd all loved sent tendrils of peace spreading through her core, unfurling in her dark, empty places. She savored it, trying to trap the feeling inside for later, when she'd need it.

Maybe it would all work out; she just needed to give it time to—

"Holy shitballs!" Danovan popped from behind a grapevine four rows in to her left.

"Jesus, dog!"

When she recovered from surprise, she called, "Barney, come!" The thump of big feet came closer and, ears flapping, her laughing dog barreled around the last row, vaulted the steps and skidded behind her chair. "What happened?"

Danovan strode to the end of the row, annoyance plain on his face. "Damned dog stuck his cold nose in my crack!"

She couldn't help it. Hiding her face in a fistful of sweater, she giggled. "Shitballs? Really?"

His face turned a shell pink that matched the last tint of sunrise at the horizon. "Sorry."

After a final indelicate snort, she forced herself to stop. "Thanks for the laugh. Feels like I haven't done that in forever."

Today he wore a blue jacket and his jeans were dark below the knee, stained with dew. He stopped at the rail of the porch and leaned on it. "Can't you keep that mutt on a leash?"

"Aw, Barney was just being friendly."

"Well, he and I don't know each other well enough to be on butt-sniffing terms." And from his tone, they never would be.

"You don't like dogs?"

"Not particularly."

How could you trust a man who didn't like dogs? "Whyever not?"

"They're always jumping on you, wanting attention. They're just so...easy."

"You have a problem with easy?" *Not from the way I've seen women react to you.*

Though she had to admit, she could understand the attraction. Something about the hardness of the planes of his face and the softness of the look in his eyes as he surveyed the rows tugged at her. That and the sadness clinging to him...

He turned toward her and stared straight at her. There were gold flecks in his eyes. And interest.

She snatched her gaze away. It wasn't as easy to do as it should have been. "Never mind." She put her feet down. "You want coffee?"

"No, thanks. I've got to get—"

"I'm talking fresh brewed latte." She waved her cup. Barney walked from behind the chair, tail waving. She put a hand on his silky head. "Besides, Barney insists. He's sorry."

The corner of Danovan's mouth lifted. "Well, maybe one."

"Come on up and have a seat while I get it."

Holding the sweater closed, she opened the screen door and stepped in. She kind of owed him after cutting him off at the knees last night. But when he'd pushed...she'd balked. The cabin was so isolated and it had been dark. She didn't really know Danovan DiCarlo.

She cleaned out the press, refilled it and snapped it back into the machine. While the coffee brewed, she ran to the bedroom and threw on sweat pants, a sweatshirt and fluffy slippers. She refused a look in the mirror on her way out of the bedroom. After all, he wasn't a guest. He was an employee.

From his glance when she returned, he noticed the quick change. She handed the latte over the porch rail. "Don't you want to sit?"

The cup almost disappeared in his long-fingered hand. "I'm good here, thanks."

Had he picked up her fear last night? Or was he worried about keeping a professional relationship? "Any time. Nothing better than enjoying this view with a latte."

"You're right about that." He sipped, studying the vines like a king surveying his kingdom. "I love the peace I get from checking my vines as the sun comes up."

The willpower she'd discovered this morning gathered in her upper chest, hardening, pushing back her shoulders to make room. His proprietary gaze on her vines flash-froze that willpower into crystals of resolve. *His kingdom, only for now.* "Can I get those textbooks from you today?"

He turned to her, the tiny tilt of his head conveying surprise. "Sure thing."

She was eager to discuss the state of the business, but wouldn't do it in slippers. "I'm going to catch a shower. I'll meet you in your office in, say, twenty minutes?"

TWO HOURS LATER, Danovan looked from his list to his boss. The downward tilt of her eyes gave her a perpetually sad look, but as he recited the winery's long list of problems, her face changed to an expression as mournful as her dog's.

She dropped her head onto the desk. "It's hopeless, isn't it? You can tell me. I can take it."

He snorted. "Yeah, you look like you can take it. But luckily, you won't have to. This is all fixable."

She lifted her head, disbelief narrowing her eyes. "Really?"

"With a lot of work."

Her shoulders lost some roundness. "I'm not afraid of work." She leaned back in the chair.

Those smooth, manicured hands were testament to what she considered work. Most likely her former "work" was planning Hollywood parties and supervising housekeeping staff. But that opinion he'd keep to himself. "Good. That'll help."

He stood and stepped to the white marker board behind him. He uncapped the black marker and made three columns. "Let's categorize and prioritize the most time-critical items, so we can make a plan." He wrote WINE at the top of the first column. "Last year's product has faults." He pointed the marker at Indigo. "Not flaws. You'll learn in the wine chemistry book I loaned you that faults are repairable. Flaws go down the sewer." He wrote the first bullet point. "Our merlot is not acidic enough, the Chardonnay is too acidic. Thankfully it's in the final racking stage and not yet bottled. I can fix this in a day. We'll add more items to this list, but this is the most time-critical."

He moved to the second column and wrote VINES at the top. "We need to aerate the soil and fertilize. Like, yesterday." He wrote the bullet point. "I haven't found any fungus, but we have to keep a close eye on the humidity and the water content of the soil. But first, there's the cleanup we talked about the other day." She scribbled more notes. "This should already have been done, and we have no vineyard rats."

"At least there's *some* good news." She shuddered. "I hate rodents."

He covered a smile with his strict teacher's glare. "Those are employees. We call the vineyard workers rats."

"Oh." She frowned. "And I suppose we have to pay that species?"

He turned back to label his third column, RETAIL. "Sales are down. We'll need a marketing plan and an advertising budget."

She leaned forward in the chair and propped

her forearms on the paper-strewn desk. "That's something I *can* do."

He lifted an eyebrow. "Marketing or a budget?"

"Both." She didn't buff her fingernails on her shirt, but the pride in her voice was the equivalent.

A Hollywood showcase wife/marketing exec/ accountant? Either she was delusional, or there was more to Indigo Blue than could be found in a Tinseltown gossip rag.

"I'll rough out a budget, Danovan, but I'll need your requirements for the first two columns." She closed her notebook. "That'll determine my budget for the last column."

"What do you say we circle back this afternoon? I'll do some research and have the numbers for you then."

"Sounds like a plan." She stood, eyes on the marker board. "I'll see you later."

INDIGO KEPT HER head up walking out, but once out of view of Danovan's glass-fronted office, her feet slowed, dragging cement blocks of hopelessness. She remembered driving here, going north along the coast, envisioning walking amid the sun-kissed vines, wearing gardening gloves, a floppy hat and a swingy skirt, a wicker basket over her arm.

How naïve she'd been.

Well, I'll just have to learn faster. She forced

her spine straight. *It's important for the owner to project confidence.*

She traversed the barrel room. At least here there were signs of progress. Through the window-wall she could see the tasting room; clean, light and airy, the high wood-beamed ceiling and slate floor gave a welcoming look.

We have customers! Her step lightened. She pushed open the door. An older couple stood at the bar, heads bent, listening to Natalie while sampling wines. A bright flash of color on the porch caught her eye. A group of spandex-clad bicyclists sprawled in the chairs on the porch, laughing and talking. *There must be fifteen of them!* Her smile started in her chest and rose to her mouth.

Sondra slipped from behind the bar and glided over.

Indigo even smiled at her. "Well, it's a start, no?"

Sondra gave her a condescending look. "Two customers hardly constitute a start."

"But…" Indigo pointed to the porch.

"They're not customers. They're resting from their ride. Bicyclists drink Gatorade, not wine." Sondra had turned releasing a long-suffering sigh into an art form. She put a hand on her waist. "What do you plan to do about this? It's hardly worth our time, waiting on two customers every four hours."

Cables cut, the elevator of joy in Indigo's chest

plunged. But an identical one full of indignation rocketed. "I'm working on that. Any suggestions you or your staff have would be appreciated. It would also help if you'd begin spreading the word in town that The Widow is open for business again."

Sondra's lips tightened.

"And in the meantime, I am paying you, even if it is to wait on only two customers every four hours." Indigo slammed her mouth shut before she could vent more frustration; she turned and strode for her office.

She couldn't work on a budget until she spoke with Danovan again. So she picked up the first tome on the large stack that he'd left on the edge of her desk.

The Chemistry of Wine. She rifled through pages filled with atomic diagrams and twenty-letter words. "Not titillating, but if this is what it takes…"

When she settled in her chair, Barney whined from his bed in the corner.

"I don't know what you're complaining about. I'm not making you read it."

Three hours later, the grinding of her stomach pulled her attention from the book. She finished a note, laid down her pen and stretched. She was pretty proud of herself. Skirting her way through the hard-core chemistry and dry-as-dust prose, she'd managed to glean a basic understanding of flaws, faults and fermentation. She put her notes in her stopping place and closed the book. "Barney, did you realize that 2,4,6-trichloroanisole is responsible for cork taint? Who knew?"

Barney yawned.

"Don't you dare go back to sleep." She lifted her purse from the drawer and the flyers she'd created from the desk. "We're going to town. We have things to do."

She felt like a coward, but that didn't stop her from leaving by the side door to avoid the ninja throwing stars in Sondra's gaze. Those damned things cut deep, shredding her confidence, her dignity and her carefully constructed owner facade. Barney led the way around the back, and they jogged up the hill to the car like kids playing hooky.

Such a pretty day. The sun-dappled road wound under the trees, and when they broke out of the shade, the light almost blinded her. She grabbed her sunglasses and hit the button to lower the windows.

As he always did, when the window on the world opened, Barney stuck out his head. She smiled at his look of bliss, sniffing the air, wind puffing out his lips and pulling back his ears. As they wheeled through town, people turned to stare.

Thanks to the internet, she knew the only place for what she wanted was Coast Hardware, on the way to the town of Solvang. She snagged a parking place in front and helped Barney out.

Tied to a bike rack in front of the store was the ugliest bulldog she'd ever seen. Mostly white, but with the pink of his skin showing through. A pink scar zigzagged down his back. He sat, tongue lolling, drooling on the sidewalk. Though the dog looked as though he were smiling, she approached with caution. Barney's tail moved in a slow, "hello, I think" wave.

The dog stood on stumpy muscular legs, his butt wiggling in glee.

Barney walked up and gave him a sniff. The bulldog licked his face and flopped on his side, exposing his belly. Barney sat looking like an old man trying to figure out what to make of this damp, happy thing.

"You two play nice. I'll be back in a bit, Barn." She tied the leash around the bike rack and, with a last look over her shoulder, walked through the door.

She hadn't seen a store like this since she'd left Humboldt County. A small-town operation, they carried a variety of products, catering to tourists up front, selling postcards, beach balls and souvenirs. She wandered the aisles, just in case...

Pay dirt. Tucked between the pool blow-up toys and the beach towels was a stack of yoga mats. She gathered each and every one in her arms. They weren't heavy, but they were awkward.

Deciding not to backtrack for a cart, she waddled to the home section.

She turned a corner while looking at the signage overhead and ran into a body. "Oof."

A strong hand gripped her elbow. "Hang on there, Miss. You all right?"

She looked around the mats to a man in jeans, a T-shirt and a black carpenter's apron. The plastic pin on his shirt read, "I'm Tim. How can I help you today?"

"Here, give me those. I'll get you a cart." He took the mats from her and laid them on the cement floor. Then he was gone, jogging down the aisle before she could protest, returning a few seconds later with a shopping cart. "Here you go, Miss." He lifted and dropped the ungainly mats in.

"Thanks. I should have done that from the beginning."

Blue eyes in a tanned face sparkled as he looked her over. "I'm here to help in any way I can."

Somehow, she didn't think he was referring to her hardware needs. She dropped her smile. "Could you just tell me where I'd find mirror tiles?"

"I can do better than that. I'll take you there." She followed him to the end of the tile aisle.

"We have the gold-veined variety, or plain, in several sizes. Which were you looking for?"

"Plain."

"You didn't look like a seventies kind of lady to me."

She scanned the boxes, avoiding his smile and his invitation to flirt. "What are the largest squares you have?"

"Twelve-by-twelve."

She sighed. It would take forever to mirror the entire wall in her new yoga room that way.

"What are you using them for?" He must have caught her hint, because his voice was all business.

"I'm mirroring a long wall."

"In that case, I suggest mirror sheets. Much easier to install, and they look more modern, too."

He took her around the corner to show her a display bathroom with the sheets installed. They looked like a silver mosaic up close, but if she backed up, she could see herself in them. If you weren't happy with what you saw in the mirror, with a shift of focus, you'd disappear. These would be wonderful. "But they're expensive, aren't they?"

He pointed to a roll on the pallet rack below the display. "Actually, they're cheaper than the tiles. It's easier to manufacture and transport these."

"Great! I'll need to work out how many I need."

"And I'll need to check stock. Come with me." He led her to a desk with a computer and held out a chair for her. "How large is the wall?"

He sat in the other chair, grabbed a calculator and did the math. The total he came up with was less than she'd feared—and they had them in stock. She handed over her credit card. The expense for the spa side of the business would come out of her meager personal account. It seemed important that she be able to track the profit that her knowledge brought to the winery.

"Do you want them delivered?"

She bit her lip. No way seven rolls would fit in her Audi. "I'm afraid you'll have to." She recited the address of the winery for his records.

He pulled a business card from his carpenter apron and wrote on the back. "I'm Tim Benton, manager of the store. That's my cell number." He handed it over. "We'll get this out to you by noon tomorrow. But you let me know if there's anything else I can do for you." He had laugh lines at the corner of his eyes when he smiled.

She took the card and stood. "Thank you. You've been very helpful."

Wheeling the cart to the front of the store, she realized she was no longer a normal woman. Yes, she was still mourning Harry, but it was more than that. It wasn't only that she had no interest in sex; she had no interest in the opposite sex. She couldn't imagine ever dating, much less... As if Harry had taken all that with him when he left her.

But that was okay. She'd had *everything* for four years. More love, intimacy and companionship than many women had in an entire lifetime.

She returned the cart from where Tim had gotten it and gathered the yoga mats.

It was only selfishness that made her want it back—want Harry back. A lonely wind whipped through her chest, sucking it hollow.

She wrestled her way through the door to find Barney alone and forlorn on the sidewalk. She stashed the mats in the trunk of the car and strode back to liberate her dog. "Come on, Barn, we have no time for the lonelies. We're on a mission."

CHAPTER SIX

DANOVAN PUSHED HIS cart past the iceberg lettuce to the fresh portobello mushrooms. The only so-called food in his cupboards came in cans, and the fridge was worse: a box of baking soda, a tub of margarine and a lone egg. He'd been on his way to talk to Indigo when he noticed her car gone, so he'd decided to get this chore out of the way. He'd be up late working, and he couldn't survive much longer without real food.

He unrolled a plastic bag and put two perfect mushrooms in. *Maybe some fresh basil—*

"Well, look what crawled into the light. I'll just grab some of that roach spray in aisle five."

The familiar voice made its usual nails-on-a-blackboard screech across his brain. His neck burned. "Go away, Roxy."

He didn't turn. He didn't need to see the roof-of-the-mouth *tsk* of irritation or the hair flip that always followed.

"I'm not surprised you can't face me. Frankly, I'm amazed you have the balls to show your face in public. Hasn't anyone stoned you yet?"

The heat climbed to his ears. He froze his shoulders to keep them from doing the same. "I believe being stoned is *your* specialty." He pushed the cart to the broccoli, hoping she'd totter off.

"I mean, decent society usually shuns men who murder babies, don't they?"

Fury shot from the chained box in his chest. It surged through him, a red-hot fountain of lava. He spun and spit out his next words. "Don't. You. Dare."

Startled, she shrank back a step, whipping her head of black witch's hair right and left to make sure they weren't alone. Seeing other shoppers, the fear fled her foxy face, replaced by a twist of malice. She leaned in. "Lissette never loved you, you know. She used you for sex. And I'll bet you're not even good at—"

She stopped with a squeak when he leaned in, only a breath away from the skin of her face. The words came out hot, squeezing past the molten fury in his throat. "You are a spider, sucking the goodness out of people. When you're done feeding, you cut the husk out of your web and move on to the next victim." He forced his fingers to release her arm. "Get away from me. You're not worth it."

He wrapped his fists around the basket handle to give them something to squeeze besides her neck. Walking away, he thanked God she had enough self-preservation instinct not to follow.

He'd never liked Lissette's party-girl BFF. The feeling became mutual when he'd turned down Roxy's under-the-table advances. In the beginning, Roxy was an infrequent visitor—only around when Lissette wanted a dance on the wild side. But like a wasting disease, she soon took larger and larger chunks of Lissette's naïveté until, at the end, his ex-wife had more in common with Roxy than with Danovan. And things went downhill from there.

The fury had burned through his thick layer of insulation, baring his own truth.

He'd taken Lissette's innocence first.

"COME ON, BARNEY, almost done. Next stop is lunch, I promise."

With a sigh, Barney stood and plodded out of the shade.

She'd asked almost every business on Hollister to put her flyer in their window. The drugstore ahead was the last. Hopefully the eye-snagging lime-green advertisements would get the word out that Widow's Grove would soon have a yoga spa because her personal checking account was evaporating like a puddle on desert sand.

When they reached the blond brick of Hollister Drugs, she tied Barney's leash to the trunk of a small tree sheltering the sidewalk and walked to the door. The buildings downtown blocked the spring breeze and the blazing sun had raised the temperature to summertime levels. She stepped in, grateful for the air-conditioning that bathed her warm face. The smell of grilling meat from the old-fashioned soda fountain to her left pulled her feet that way. Her mouth watered, and her stomach ground out an SOS.

The lunchtime crowd was long gone. Only one couple shared a milkshake at a tiny wrought iron table in the sea of black-and-white checkerboard tile. Her heart swelled, ponderous with sadness. She turned away from the familiar ghosts, stepped to the bar and perched on the red vinyl stool.

The soda jerk stood polishing a glass, snapping her gum like machine-gun fire. She wore a pink '60s throwback A-line dress, a white frilled apron and a pink pillbox cap perched on flamingo-pink shoulder-length hair. The rims of both ears were encrusted with stud earrings, and her lipstick and short nails were both painted black. She looked like the love child of Joanie from *Happy Days* and Marilyn Manson.

"Hi. Do you have a menu I could look at?"

Snap, snap. The girl rolled her eyes to a menu board on the wall and kept polishing.

"Okay, great. But first, could I have some water for my dog?" She pointed out the window, where Barney watched her, looking worried she'd forget his burger.

The girl put down the glass. "I think that dog needs a few Xanax. He's got serious depression issues."

Indigo smiled at him and held up a finger. *Hang on, Barn.* "It's nothing that a hamburger patty won't fix."

The girl reached under the counter and pulled out a Styrofoam to-go box, filled it with water and handed it over. *Snap, snap, snap.*

"Thank you." Indigo glanced at the board. "Could I also have a plain hamburger patty for Barney, and I'll take…" She scanned the menu board. *Salad. Or maybe a BLT.* "A strawberry milkshake." She slid off the stool to take the water outside.

How often did you get a milkshake made the old fashioned way, with whole milk, full-leaded ice cream and fresh strawberries? *Tomorrow. I'll start eating better tomorrow.*

When she returned, she sat, mouth watering, relishing the sound of the mixer whirling in the metal cup. When it stopped, she asked, "Could I have it to go?"

Snap, snap, snap, snap. "Sure."

"Is it okay if I leave a flyer in your window?"

"Depends. What of?" She poured the lumpy pink heaven into a huge cup. "I wanted to put up a poster once, for a battle of the bands between Bullets and The Mangy Sherpas for Valentine's Day. Boss didn't like it." *Snap, snap.* She flipped Barney's burger.

"Hard to imagine why."

"I know, right?" The girl set the milkshake in front of her and started to move away.

"Don't even think of taking away that silver

thingy." Indigo pointed to the stainless container in the girl's other hand. "That's the best part."

A zirconia flashed when she smiled. "I think so too." She set down the container and took Barney's hamburger off the grill, dumping it into another Styrofoam box. "Oh, hey, Priss."

Indigo looked up to see a young woman with black, spiky hair and a widow's peak walking to the counter, holding a baby swaddled in a pink blanket.

"Hi, Sin."

The flamingo-haired girl held out her arms. "You're not leaving without me drooling over the princess." She made "come on" motions with her fingers. "Hand over the goods."

Priss smiled and carefully passed her armload to Sin. "Watch it. The princess just ate. She's likely to burp all over you." She turned to Indigo. "Oh, sorry, you're eating."

"No worries. Nothing could ruin this." Indigo upended the icy metal container, relishing the chunks of strawberry at the very bottom.

Snap, snap. "Hey, Priss, this lady wants to leave a flyer in the window. Okay with you?" The odd girl shifted from foot to foot, cooing to the baby, "Olivia, queen of Bolivia."

Priss's delicate black eyebrows came together. "What of?"

Indigo licked her lips and extended a flyer. "I'm Indigo, owner of The Tippling Widow Winery.

We're now offering yoga classes, aromatherapy and massage. I'm trying to get the word out."

Priss took the flyer and looked it over. "Yoga, huh? That may be just what I need to get rid of the baby fat."

Indigo didn't see any fat on the woman's powerfully built frame but nodded anyway.

"Sure, you can put it in the window." She handed the flyer back. "I may check it out myself. Now, hand over your goddaughter, Sin. We've gotta get to the bar."

Snap. "You're *not* taking her to the bar."

At the look of outraged impropriety on Sin's face, Indigo hid her smile in her milkshake.

Priss held her arms out for the baby. "Oh, don't look at me like that. The regulars just want to see her."

Sin looked the baby in the eye. "Just remember, Princess, sometimes people are a lesson in what *not* to do." She handed the baby over.

Indigo slapped a ten and a five on the counter and picked up her shake and Barn's burger. "Thanks for letting me leave the flyer."

"No problem." Priss settled her bundle in her arms. "You know, you look familiar, but I can't place…"

Indigo ducked her head. "I hear that all the time. I just have one of those faces, you know?" Sliding off the seat, she nodded to Sin. "Girl, you make a mean milkshake."

The sun had almost touched the horizon by the time she arrived at the winery. She had the choice of lugging the mats all the way through the production facility or taking the short route, through the front door. She pulled into the parking lot, "should do" warring with "I don't wanna" in her mind. Was she really worried about the opinion of an employee? No. But she didn't want another confrontation, either. Sondra would fit right in with the harpies of Hollywood.

I refuse to allow her attitude to influence my actions. Indigo pulled into a slot right up front. She had her pick; the lot was empty, save the employees' cars.

Stepping out, she helped Barney down, then pulled the mats from the backseat. "Come on, Barn. We *own* this place." Slamming the door with her hip, she walked as fast as her bulky armload would allow.

Chin high, she strode into the tasting room.

Becky looked up from counting the till. "Oh, let me help you with those." The quarters clattered back into the cash box.

Indigo shook her head. "Thanks, but I've got it. You do your thing." She should have asked how the day's receipts looked, but she didn't feel that strong. She'd find out soon enough, anyway.

Natalie and Sondra stood behind the bar, straightening stock.

Indigo forced her feet to stop halfway to the

door to the manager's quarters and the haven of her office. "Is everything okay here?" She used her owner's voice.

Sondra stared. "Why wouldn't it be? I think we're capable of handling eight customers a day."

She felt herself flush. "Good. Carry on." Why could this woman make her feel like a complete zero with a single sentence? Just as she was trying to work out how she'd wrestle the door open with no hands, it opened.

Danovan's eyebrows shot up. "Hey! I was just looking for you." He held the door with his hip and took the mats.

"Thanks. They're not heavy, just awkward."

Barney trotted to Danovan and sat at his feet. Tail whipping, he sniffed Danovan's jeans.

Danovan looked around his armload. "Come on, move, dog."

"He's missing his—" Face flaming, she grabbed Barney's collar and dragged him back. "He's always liked men best."

"Where do you want these?" His voice was soft as the sympathy in his eyes.

She let go of Barney's collar and followed Danovan down the hall. "Just dump them in my studio."

He tossed a look over his shoulder. "Where is that?"

"The old junk room." She scooted by to open the door for him.

He carried the mats in and laid them by the

door. "Do you want to go over the budget now? I have the numbers ready."

She swallowed the angst, bitter on the back of her tongue. "Let's do it." After all, they might be better than she feared.

They weren't.

Two hours later, Indigo put her face in her hands, her brain feeling as crispy as overdone bacon. "There has to be money for marketing. If there's no marketing, there's no sales increase. If we don't increase sales, we're going down."

Buck up, chickie. She forced her shoulders back, dropped her hands in her lap and glanced out the darkened window of her office. *Failure is not an option.* "We'll have to go over it again."

"Why don't you just lend the business some money? It would only be a short-term loan. Once we get things cranking and the sales up—"

"This business *will* stand on its own." Her voice was as hard as the untilled dirt in the vineyard.

He ran his fingers through his rumpled hair. "Okay. But we've been over it three times already, and I'm telling you, there's no fat in this budget. As it is, if we get mold or a bad insect infestation, we'll have to find money for chemicals. Somehow."

"There has to be a way." She rolled the mouse down the spreadsheet on her laptop. "Let's look at the biggest expenses first. Labor—"

"We've already cut it once. No way The Widow can survive on less."

Sondra. If they let her go, it would solve two problems. Lower expenses, and improve morale—Indigo's, anyway. Sondra seemed to get along famously with everyone else. She opened her mouth to suggest getting rid of Sondra, then closed it. If they got busy, Natalie couldn't handle the tasting room solo, and Becky didn't have the knowledge any more than Indigo herself did.

Hell, I'm the only expendable employee. I'd fire myself, but I'm not collecting a salary. Her tired brain finally spit out an answer. The only answer. "I've got it."

Danovan looked up from his printout. "If you're going to suggest getting rid of Sondra—"

"Don't think it didn't cross my mind." She couldn't help a small smile. "But I don't have the knowledge to replace her. In fact, there's only one position I am qualified for."

"What?" He quirked the eyebrow with the white scar bisecting it, making him look skeptical before she even said anything.

That stung. *He just doesn't know you. Yet.* "Vineyard rat."

The brow developed a furrow. "No way. That's a dirty, backbreaking job."

She crossed her arms over her chest. "So what? You saying I can't do physical labor?"

"I'm not saying that. I'm saying..." He looked like a man who'd stepped in something nasty and was trying to back out of it. "I don't think you'd want to."

"Well, you've obviously gotten the wrong impression of me." She raised her chin.

He leaned back in the chair, crossed his legs. "I'm realizing that."

And the way his gaze lingered on her face like a caress, that wasn't all he saw.

"After all, it's not like Sondra's going to offer."

He choked out a surprised laugh. "Not bloody likely."

"I wonder what her problem is."

"Sondra is like very dry sherry—tart, potent and best sipped sparingly."

"I'd say she's more like cleaning vinegar." Indigo winced. "She sure seems interested in you, though," she said in a teasing tone. "Maybe you should ask her out."

His face tightened to a clench. "I'm not interested in dating. Anyone." His lips moved, forming the clipped words, but his jaw didn't.

She held up her hands. "Point taken."

"Sorry. Bad breakup. Guess I'm still a little... singed." He rolled his shoulders. "I just want to focus on The Widow and getting her back on her feet."

"Now there's something we can agree on. No dating. Focus on business."

He held up a hand for a high-five.

She returned it, then gathered the papers in

front of her. "I now have a small marketing budget. I'll get to work on that."

"I have a contact with a distributor. I'll get in touch with him."

"Wonderful. I'll focus on our local market— retail, restaurants and ways to increase our foot traffic."

"Sounds like a plan." He collected his notes and stood. "Well, it's late. If you'll excuse me." He turned to go.

"Can you meet me in the vineyard in the morning to show me what needs to be done?"

He turned back with a smile so stiff it looked as though it were ironed on with heavy starch.

Her defenses snapped into place with a click. "I did say in your interview that teaching me the business would be part of your duties."

"I'll rearrange my schedule, then." He walked to the door then turned back again. "We'll want to get an early start. It's spring, but it still gets hot out there. I'll meet you, say, seven?"

She'd have to set an alarm to get her yoga in. "I'll be there."

"Don't forget sunscreen. And a hat." Then he was gone. The door fell closed behind him.

She swallowed the bitter taste in her mouth. This was his first week, and he had a ton of work. He was just busy. There was no reason for her to believe he didn't want to be around her.

But that was what she thought, just the same.

CHAPTER SEVEN

A WARM YELLOW glow on her eyelids woke her. Indigo lifted her head from the marketing book she'd been reading, groaning when something in her neck popped. Last she remembered, the clock had just gonged two. She stretched. Yoga, then some toast… "What?" The clock had to be wrong. She snatched her phone to check. Nope. Six-fifty. "Crap!" She jumped up and ran for the bedroom.

As proof that dogs were smarter than humans, Barney remained stretched out on the bed. "We're late, Barn. Get up!"

So much for yoga, breakfast and good intentions. She didn't even have time for coffee. Skidding around the corner to the bathroom, she caught her reflection in the mirror. Hair flat on one side, wild on the other. And the book had left creases on her face. Was that a drool track? "Oh, nice look, Blue." She snatched her toothbrush. The creases would fade, and a hat would fix the hair. *Surely vineyard rats don't need to dress for success.*

Maybe not, but vineyard owners should, especially in front of their employees. So she got to work.

The clock on the mantel was gonging seven

when she closed the cabin door behind her ten minutes later. She'd come back for Barney, since he refused to budge from the bed right now. Shaking a bottle of sunscreen, she squeezed some into her palm and spread the cool balm over her face.

From the vantage point of the porch, the vines looked deserted. But she'd thought that yesterday, too. "Danovan?" Then louder, "Danovan?"

Her answer was the sound of a tractor firing up behind the winery. She snapped the cap closed on the sunscreen and dropped it in a chair. Slapping a hand on her floppy straw hat, she ran down the hill. Just before she got there, a small green tractor turned out of the lot behind the winery. It had a bucket loader in the front and weird, disc-like things hanging off both sides of the back.

Danovan brought it to a halt in front of her and yelled over the sound of the engine, "Hop on!"

She walked to the side. There was only one seat. "Where?"

He extended a hand. She took it and maneuvered to fit onto the tiny platform. The engine rumbled, vibrating through her feet. He positioned her behind the driver's seat. "Stand there." His eyes narrowed, and he reached up to run the back of his finger down her cheek.

She jerked and almost tumbled off the back.

He caught her upper arm. "Easy there." He held up his index finger, displaying a white smear. "Sunscreen, I assume." He dropped her arm, lowered himself into the driver's seat and yelled over his shoulder, "Do you know how to drive a stick?"

"Yes!" She glanced at the pedals on the floor. Harry had taught her, insisting that she know how to drive his Jaguar. But would those skills transfer to a filthy, beat-up old tractor?

"Hang on to my shoulders and watch what I do."

She gripped the seat back instead.

He shifted the column stick into gear. "There's no accelerator. You push this up and down to regulate the speed." When he lifted a lever on the dash, the tractor eased forward.

As they rumbled up the hill, she got a good view of the entire vineyard. Fifteen acres didn't sound like much in LA. But now, faced with responsibility for their care, she felt like a single mother who'd given birth to sextuplets.

You have green thumbs in your genes. Look at Mom. You can do this.

She pushed down the panic trying to slash its way out of her stomach.

You have to do this.

The sun was warm on her back even as the morning air chilled her face. She closed her eyes and took in a lungful of the rich smell of dirt and decaying things. Her shift from Hollywood wife to vineyard rat hit her in a dizzying whirlwind that, inexplicably, lifted her spirits. The future might be uncertain, but today…today was beautiful. Joy, simple and clean as the morning air, blew through her, escaping her lips in a manic cackle. Leaning forward for balance, she raised a fist. "Vineyard rats rule!"

Danovan smiled big and yelled, "I kind of envy you. It's hard work, but this is one of the best jobs at a winery."

They rumbled past her cabin to the end of the road. He turned the wheel, centering the tractor at the head of the first row. "Straw and mulch is put down in the fall to protect the vines from the cold during the winter. It needs to be cleaned up in the spring because it will hold moisture and spread mildew. The rubber pieces in the back of this tractor rotate, sweeping the straw into the center of the row. Then we make another run, push it to the end and dispose of it. Now watch." He pressed a button on the dash and hydraulics whined, lowering the apparatus in the back. He hit another button, and the rotators started spinning, adding a bass hum to the tractor's head-banging song.

She leaned over his shoulder to hear him above the noise.

"The sweeper can damage the vines, so be careful to keep the tractor centered in the row." He lifted the accelerator slide a bit, and they inched forward. "I'll do the first row. Then we'll switch places."

He turned to check the sweepers, then faced forward, his profile a mask of concentration.

Who wears cologne to work in a field? Not that it wasn't pleasant. It was one of those signature scents that fused with the wearer to become something richer, fuller. Palpable. His long, capable fingers nuanced the wheel with constant small adjustments.

Capable. That summed up Danovan DiCarlo in a word. His calm, can-do attitude helped keep her grounded, focusing on the solution instead of the freak-out. So far, she was more than happy with her hiring decision. He was a manager she could rely on.

The capable manager, Danovan may be. But there was still something about the guy that bugged her at odd moments like a snagged hangnail.

At the end of the row, he hit the button to raise the sweepers, then turned into the next row and took the tractor out of gear. "Your turn." He stood and stepped as far out of the way as he could.

It was a tight fit. She squeezed by him, releasing her breath with a whoosh when she fell into the seat. She clamped her jaw tight, took the wheel in a death grip and stared down the row.

"Relax." He touched the back of her hand. "No wasted motion. If you try to muscle it, you'll be sore in an hour. Just flow with it, making adjustments slow and easy." He squeezed behind the seat. "Remember, no wasted motion. You'll need

LAURA DRAKE   121

all your energy. Now, lower the sweepers and put it in gear."

This isn't going to be hard. It's not like when you dented the Jaguar on the Dumpster. You can't hurt a tractor.

Yeah, but she could hurt the vines. Loss of one would mean less product at the end of the season. Worse, it would take a replacement vine two years to produce grapes.

She jumped when his hands closed on her shoulders. "You can do this, Indigo." His voice came from beside her ear.

Time to get it in gear, Blue.

She lowered the sweepers, pushed in the clutch and shifted. Gripping the wheel in one hand, she eased the accelerator lever up...and dumped the clutch. The tractor jerked forward and stalled. And what might have been Danovan's crotch hit the back of her head. "Shit. Sorry."

He grabbed the seat and pushed himself away. "It's okay. I should've been ready for that." He cleared his throat. "You let the clutch out too fast. There's less travel on a tractor clutch than a car, but you still need to ease it in. Go ahead, try again."

Running through the steps, she attempted to channel peace. *Feather the clutch. Feather the clutch...*

The tractor chugged straight at the vines on the

right. She hauled the wheel and headed for the vines on the left.

Danovan's chest bumped the back of her head, pushing it forward. His hands came down onto hers and straightened the wheel. "You're okay."

She head-butted his chest. "I will be, if you don't break my neck. Back up, will ya?"

He released her hands and straightened.

White-knuckled, nose inches from the wheel to gauge her trajectory, she trundled down the row, sticks and trimmings stirring up dust.

When they neared the end, Danovan shouted, "Be sure the sweepers clear the vines, then make a broad turn to come around and center for the next row."

It took her three tries, but she did it. Tractor lined up at the start of the row, she stopped to take a breather, shaking out her hands to relieve the cramps.

"I think you've got it. I'm going to pound end posts." Danovan hopped down. "Yell if you need me, okay?"

She glanced at the dashboard to see if she'd overlooked anything mechanical before he left. "What's that red button for?" Leaning forward, she pointed.

"Don't touch that!"

She snatched her hand back, her heart jackhammering. "What is it?"

His smile was all white teeth. "I'm just messing

with you. That's the button to lower the bucket in the front. We'll use that to clean the aisles once they're swept."

She put a hand to her chest. "You about gave me a heart attack."

"Yeah, but it got you out of your head for a second, right?" He winked. "Relax. Think of this as rat initiation." He turned and walked down the row.

She blew out a breath, tempted to run him over. But when she lowered the sweepers and put the tractor in gear, her hands had lost their life-preserver clench.

HOW CAN THE SUN burn so hot in April? Dano-van shrugged to blot a rivulet of sweat running down his back. His shoulders reminded him how long it had been since he'd done heavy labor. This morning he remembered what he'd forgotten in his sprint for the gold. He'd forgotten how working the vines pared problems down to their essence. Forgotten how he loved the smell of tilled dirt and the gratifying potential of new tendrils. Forgotten how life could change with a shift of focus.

Lifting the mallet, he hammered the next post, feeling the thump in his elbows and the ground's satisfying give in his chest. No impossible personnel problems here. No schmoozing snooty clients. He'd forgotten his first love—creating a beautiful wine from dirt.

Or maybe he'd just allowed himself to be enticed away by doe eyes, a great pair of legs and his own ambition.

"Danovan!" Her voice drifted to him on the small breeze that cooled his face. Indigo stood seven rows away, waving from the porch of the cabin. "I've got lunch!"

His stomach growled approval. Using the tail of his shirt to blot his face, he lifted the mallet and trudged.

Her brown hair pulled back, damp tendrils straggled, framing Indigo's face.

"Did you take a shower?" He put a foot on the edge of the porch and leaned his forearms on his knees.

"I just dunked my head under the faucet to cool off. You could do the same. Wash up. I'll get the iced tea and sandwiches."

"Do you have a hose?"

She waved him up. "Come on in, silly."

"I'm good here, thanks."

She cocked her head. "Are you being all weird because I'm a woman?"

Little did she know, what was weird was him *not* getting up close to a pretty woman. But he needed to keep strong boundaries. *And* his promise to himself. "The other night, you seemed a bit anxious about my walking you back here in the dark. I assumed you were worried about my...

intentions." And the pink on her cheekbones told him he'd assumed right.

"Look, Danovan. We're going to be working closely together. And if we want to turn this winery around, we don't have time for all that Mars/Venus crap. Even if I weren't the owner, you told me you're not looking to get involved with anyone, and I'm not either." She dusted her hands. "So neither of us should have a problem, right?"

He couldn't think of a valid argument that wouldn't bring up his past, so he stepped onto the porch. "Where's the bathroom?"

The room smelled of her. The source of her light jasmine scent turned out to be her shampoo and the hand cream on the sink. *Which you shouldn't be noticing.* He scooped some water from the tap and finger-combed his hair, shivering when the cold drips ran down his hot skin. He couldn't help it if his sense of smell was sharp. His job required it, to detect subtle shades of quality in wine. But wiping his hands on a threadbare towel that had to have belonged to Bob, he had to admit surprise—he hadn't expected such a Spartan bathroom. And as he glanced into the bedroom on his way by, he was surprised by the furnishings there, too. A simple double bed made up with a striped blanket, and a chest of drawers in the corner with nothing on top. Nothing.

Stop noticing.

When he opened the screen door to the porch,

her droopy dog lumbered out ahead of him. Indigo sat sipping iced tea in one of the two chairs, a plate of sandwiches on the table between them.

He sat, and the dog plopped in front of him with a longing look, his tail thumping the boards of the porch.

"Barney, mind your manners. Go play in the vines." She made shooing motions, and the dog wandered off.

Danovan took a long swallow of tea, then rolled the glass on his forehead. "Man, that's good."

"You told me to wear a hat. Why didn't you?"

"I left it on the table and didn't realize until I'd fired up the tractor." He took another long sip.

"Well, I've got sunscreen. You'll need to put some on before you go out again." She put a half sandwich on a plate and handed it to him. "You're getting sunburned."

"Yes, Mom."

She took a bite of her sandwich and looked out over the vineyard. "Spring at the winery is the best."

He should use this time as a teaching opportunity. But he didn't want to talk about Chardonnay. He didn't want to discuss grape varietals. He wanted to know more about her. "So, what was it like, being a Hollywood wife?"

Her head came around, her eyes narrowed, wary.

"If you don't mind my asking."

"It was awful." She lowered her sandwich to the plate. "And wonderful, all at the same time."

"What was the awful part?"

Her sigh held too much world-weariness for a woman so young. "Everyone thinks they want fame and fortune, but they don't know the cost. Living in the spotlight only looks fun from the outside. It leaves no room for being human. The second you step out of the house, you're on, fresh meat for the jackal paparazzi."

"But it was your husband who was famous, right?"

"Yes. I should have been in the background. A nobody. But I wanted to give Harry as normal a life as possible, so I limited the press's access. They didn't like that."

He hadn't known a small smile could hold such sadness.

"So they wrote things about me—about us—that were untrue. Nasty things." Her lips thinned. She pushed her shoulders against the chair back. "But it was worth it." She nodded as if agreeing with herself.

"You loved him, didn't you?"

She speared him with a look. "The surprise in your voice is the awful part I was referring to."

"Sorry." He hid his nose in his tea glass and took a sip. "I deserved that."

"He was the wonderful part." Her gaze on the vines was wistful. "I loved him very much. A love like ours only comes along once in a blue moon. I was lucky."

Silence lay soft on the porch as they ate their lunch. He'd have liked to know more. Like what made a young, beautiful woman fall in love with a man forty years her senior. But he didn't want to intrude on the cherished memories he saw in her profile.

Bees droned, and the breeze played in the dead leaves. He'd never known a woman so comfortable in silence.

"How about you?" Her brown eyes regarded him. "Have you ever been married?"

Shit. He knew these "getting to know you" conversations were always tit for tat. His curiosity had made him forget. *What to say?* His mind was like a frantic mouse working a maze, choosing avenues that ended in blank-wall dead ends or in black stinking pits where he didn't want to go, much less share with her. But she'd answered his question. "I was."

"That sure sounds more to the awful side than the wonderful."

"It didn't have to be. But, yeah, that's how it ended up." Before she could ask the next question, he blurted. "Damn, Memory Lane can be studded with land mines, can't it?" He set his empty glass on the table and stood. "I'd better get back to work. Thank you for lunch."

FOUR HOURS LATER, echoes of tractor vibrations resonating in her bones, Indigo stepped onto the porch of the winery, sweaty, sun-sapped and spent. But for the first time in a long time, an ember of optimism warmed her chest. They'd made progress today. *She'd* made progress today. The rows between the vines were swept and pristine, and thanks to Danovan's tutelage, she'd learned to tie up the tendrils, training them to the wires that would support them as they grew.

She rounded the corner of the front porch. A brightly spandexed flock of bicyclists sprawled in chairs, their charges leaning against the railing. She wiped her hands on her jeans and walked up to them, hand extended to the nearest one. "Hello. Welcome to The Tippling Widow. I'm Indigo."

The lean man looked surprised but shook her hand. "We're just resting a few minutes before we head back to town."

She put on a friendly smile and raised her voice so all the riders could hear. "You're welcome at The Widow anytime." She winked. "Including for wine tastings, weddings and other special occasions. We'll be offering a new menu of services within the next week—yoga classes, aromatherapy and massages." She stepped to a young man in the middle of the group with his back to her. "Wouldn't a massage after a ride feel great? May I?" Putting her hands on his shoulders, she pressed her thumbs into the tight muscles next to his spine, then rolled his trapezius in her palms.

When he moaned, his friends laughed.

"Please spread the word to your wives and friends. The Tippling Widow is back in business." She held the smile all the way to the door. "Enjoy the rest of your ride!"

The cool air kissed her face as she walked in and stood beside the door until her eyes adjusted. Sondra and Natalie were both engaged with three customers at the wine bar.

One more than yesterday. Not a crowd, but it's progress.

Unfortunately, adding one customer here and there was not going to save the business.

"Excuse me, Ms. Blue?" Becky popped from behind the cash register to Indigo's right. "Business is a bit better today." A frown negated her small smile. "Sondra asked us to spread the word in town about The Widow getting better—um, I mean, being…" Red spread from the collar of her white shirt upward.

"I know what you mean. It's okay."

Becky's fingers worried a receipt pad, ruffling the pages. "I had an idea that might help get the word out." She hesitated as if waiting to be cut off. Knowing Sondra, it wasn't hard to understand why.

"Great. I'd love to hear it. It's going to take all of us to get The Widow back on her feet."

"Okay. So I was thinking, we're telling every-one about The Widow's reopening and reinven-tion, but it might mean more if we showed them. You know, like a grand reopening party." Pages snapped faster.

"A party?" *Why didn't I think of that?* She pic-tured tables set on the lawn, with food…maybe a barbecue? Yes, a barbecue. That would be perfect.

"It's probably a dumb idea."

"Becky, I think it's brilliant."

The young woman beamed like a spelling bee winner.

Sondra's leadership style was more Mussolini than Lennon; speaking up had taken guts.

"Becky, you're from Widow's Grove, and you know the culture. Would you be willing to help me plan this event?"

"Oh, yes ma'am, I'd love to."

"Great. And I'm not ma'am. I'm Indigo."

CHAPTER EIGHT

DANOVAN WASHED HIS hands at the sink in the lab. Showing Indigo how to till the soil had taken less time than yesterday's vineyard rat lesson. She'd even perfected changing implements on the tractor. Her rotary harrow tracks were now as straight as his. She learned fast.

Good thing, because she's got a lot to learn.

But he had to give her credit. She was the opposite of what he'd expected from a woman with a 90210 zip code. She wasn't afraid of dirt, hard work or sweat, and it was clear she took this business seriously. She'd refused to lend the winery money, and her tone made it clear she meant it. Though, for the life of him, he couldn't understand why. Surely a widow with her money and contacts could find something better to do. If he didn't know better, he'd think the winery was all she had.

From the questions she asked, it was clear that she was studying the books he'd loaned her, too. Even the drier-than-tomb-dust chemistry text.

He walked to his office and settled in his chair, pulled his cell from his jeans pocket and looked up the phone number he needed.

"Western Wines. How can I help you?"

"Could I speak with Stu, please?"

"Sure. Hold on."

Thirty seconds of classical music later, a drill sergeant voice barked, "Rowland."

"Stu. It's Danovan DiCarlo."

Silence.

"I don't know if you heard, but I'm no longer with Bacchanal."

"Oh, I heard."

Danovan's stomach dropped. Would this shit never end?

Technically, distributors worked *for* a winery, but due to the market's competitiveness, they were as courted as customers. Unless you were as large as his last employer, in which case distributors like Western would fall all over themselves to work with you. There was nothing more coveted than a wine that practically sold itself.

"You shouldn't believe everything you hear. But that's not what I'm calling about. I'm now working with The Tippling Widow here in Widow's Grove, and—"

"The…what?"

He ground his teeth to hold back a smart-ass retort. "The Tippling Widow."

"Never heard of it."

"We're a boutique winery, about fifteen acres, and we've got some really special—"

"We've got no openings for new wineries. Sorry."

Oh yeah, I can tell. "Why don't I send you a bottle of our merlot? I think you'll find it—"

"Won't do any good. We're booked, I'm telling you."

He should keep selling. He should beg.

Bullshit. He wanted to reach through the phone and teach this guy some manners. With his fist. He leaned forward in the chair. "You know, Rowland, I've worked with you for three years, and I've gotta tell you—your customer service skills suck. You should read *How to Win Friends and Influence People*. Maybe you'd have a shot at becoming human someday."

A dry chuckle. "You could be right. But at least I'm loyal. I don't try to screw over my employer."

Click.

Danovan hit End. That was the problem with a modern phone. You couldn't give it a satisfying slam. "Loser."

What was he going to tell Indigo? Well, Rowland had said they weren't taking new clients, so he wouldn't have to lie. He just wouldn't tell her the other part. It was immaterial anyway.

He strode to the production facility to walk off some pissed. He'd imagined the lies the Boldens were spreading, but hearing the actual words seared them like hot metal into his pride. He rubbed his chest, where they burned. It wouldn't do any good to defend himself. Every word out of his mouth would only make him sound guiltier.

Not that he would ever explain to an asshole like Rowland.

People could accuse Danovan DiCarlo of many things, but one thing he *wasn't* was disloyal. Dammit, he'd given his sweat and blood to that family. Maybe a bunch of it he owed to them, but the rest he'd given freely. He'd *earned* his place there.

And now that place was as gone as gone could get.

He made himself shrug it off. There was too much to be done in the present to focus on something he couldn't fix in the past. Better to put that energy into working with Indigo to pull this winery off the trash heap.

He scanned the shipping area, looking for the new warehouse employee. It was past time they began bottling last year's crush.

And anyway, success was the best revenge.

THANKS TO ROSALINA and her cleaning crew, the tasting room patio no longer resembled a Halloween set. Indigo sat at one of the small square tables at dusk, sipping a diet soda and inhaling the luxuriant scent of freshly cut grass. The landscaping service she'd hired had worked all day, but the transformation was worth the money. The roses were trimmed and neat in their new cedar bark beds, and the lawn rolled to meet the road in alternating stripes of Crayola green and emerald.

She could just imagine a bridal party in white, posing next to the pond she planned to build.

Maybe a small stream too, with an arched bridge leading to a gazebo where they'd exchange their vows. She'd arrange folding chairs for the guests in curved rows around it, and—

Barney sneezed.

"What, you think that can't happen?" She rubbed his stomach with her foot. "Better believe it, bud." All it would take was buckets of sweat.

And cash.

She rolled her shoulders to ease the ache between them. She'd really enjoyed her day, running the tractor down the rows, the smell of turned-over earth and worms. Vineyard rat was a physically taxing job but an easy mental one. Everything was black or white; no personnel issues, no worry about her untrustworthy gut. Tomorrow, Danovan was going to show her how to test the soil for nitrogen and water content. Tonight, though, she needed to catch up on the books, much as she'd have liked to avoid it.

As she stood, her phone rang. "This is Indigo," she answered quickly.

"Indigo, this is Jesse Jurgen. You left a flyer about yoga classes at my café?"

It took a few banging heartbeats to get over her surprise. "Jesse, of course. Good to hear from you."

"I wanted to know when classes begin. I've spoken with a few of my friends who are interested."

"Oh, that's great. Um. I can begin anytime you'd like. Does an evening class work for your group?"

"Well, actually, noon would be best. Most of us work, but we can scoot out for lunch. Is that doable?"

It would mean getting up even earlier so she could work in the vineyard, then squeeze in a shower before noon. But at least she'd get her yoga workout. "Yes, I can do that. What day would you like?"

They worked out the details and fees, then hung up. So delighted to have a group of six students, she'd agreed to a Wednesday class.

And tomorrow was Wednesday. She had a lot of work yet to do.

First, she had to do the books and balance the checking account, then the grunt work. "Come on, Barney, miles to go before we sleep tonight, dude."

Two hours later, she and Barney walked to the room next to her office. When she flipped on the lights, the one-way glass windows reflected back the empty room. Well, empty save for the sprawling pile of yoga mats, the rolls of mirrored tiles, a bucket of adhesive and a paintbrush.

Seeing something taped on top of the cellophane-wrapped sheets, she bent and peeled off Tim's business card. A blue ink arrow in the corner made her turn it over. His cell phone number was written on the back, along with a scrawled note inviting her to call anytime.

Harry had had "the" conversation with her in

bed one night. Well, not really a conversation; he talked, and she tried not to listen. His soft voice in the dark said she had to face facts: barring an accident, she was going to live much longer than he. He told her that once he was gone he wanted her to go on and make a new life. With a new man. Even have children someday.

What he said was logical. Sensible. Her brain got the whole circle of life thing. But her heart didn't. He'd kept after her that night until she was in tears. Until she promised she'd try. And maybe someday she would, when her heart got the memo. Right now, it slumbered, dreaming of happier times. With a sad smile, she wadded up the card and dropped it to the floor.

Luckily, the mirror sheets were four-by-four, and the wall height was eight-and-a-half feet, making the math easy. She retrieved a ladder from the production facility and got to work.

By midnight, though her shoulder muscles screamed in a soprano chorus with her back, she had the bottom sheets installed. They were beautiful, but damn, they were *heavy*.

A safe distance away, Barney snored.

"No, Barn, thanks for the offer, but you rest. With your short legs, you couldn't reach anyway." She'd love to trudge home to bed, leaving the top ones for tomorrow night, but that wasn't an option. If she was going to make an impression and pull in more clients, this place would have to look amazing for class tomo—no, today.

What Rosalina had discovered under the grime and neglect had made Indigo smile—a basketball-court-worthy polyurethaned wood floor that leant the room a warm, cozy glow.

And standing here admiring it isn't getting you closer to bed.

She positioned the ladder, stepped up with the bucket of adhesive and prepped the wall for the first sheet. Then came the hard part. She set the adhesive on the floor, hefted a rolled sheet of tiles and climbed the ladder. Once unrolled, it became heavy and awkward. She'd have to center it, not touching the adhesive until it was lined up perfectly. She leaned in, arms shaking under the weight. If she was off at the top, it wouldn't—"Ahhhh!" Overbalanced, the ladder tipped and bumped the wall. Her feet slipped off the step. She hit ass-first. The heavy sheet fell on her chest like a mirrored blanket. "Shit!"

Startled from sleep, Barney howled.

Butt throbbing, she lay stunned.

Barney's nails clicked, and his long face appeared over her.

A bumping sound came from the hall. Then the door slammed open. "What the f— Are you okay?" Danovan rushed over and fell on his knees next to her. "Don't move. What hurts?" His fingers ran through her hair to the back of her skull, where he probed gently. "Did you hit your head? Are you dizzy?"

Barney licked her face.

"Ugh. Stop." She put up a hand to fend off more slobber. "Quit, both of you. I'm fine."

Danovan ran his hands over her arms, feeling for breaks. "Are you sure? Does anything hurt?"

His gaze was clear, but his eyes were puffy, his hair rumpled, and he had a pillow crease on his cheek. He wore sweats but was barefoot. She could see the ghost of a backward UC Davis logo on his faded T-shirt—he'd put it on inside out.

"Only my pride." She sat up and winced. "And my butt."

He sat back on his haunches and ran his hands through his own hair, mussing it further. "You scared the crap out of me. It sounded like we were being invaded. What the heck were you doing?" For the first time, he looked around.

"I'm sorry to wake you." She leaned onto her unbruised cheek and stroked Barney's ears to calm him. "My first yoga class is tomorrow. I have to get this room finished."

"Jesus, woman, why didn't you come ask for help?" He stood and offered her a hand up.

She took it. "This isn't in your job description. Besides, it's late and you work so many hours already."

His body stilled, but his soft brown eyes scanned her face. It was an intimate touch. "I thought we were getting to be friends." He didn't let go of her hand.

Something about his eyes caught her. Though her nerves fidgeted, she couldn't look away. Then, with a start, she realized why. The bones of Danovan's face were hard, but the look in his eyes was soft as suede. There was true-blue caring in those eyes. Only one man had ever looked at her that way—her husband. Her heart knocked her breastbone once. Twice.

She knew what Harry would say. But since he wasn't here, it was easier to ignore him. Besides, Danovan was offering friendship, nothing more.

And boy, could she use a friend.

"Friends. Yes, I'd like that." She smiled. "Very much."

He nodded, as if sealing a pact. "Good." He turned to assess the damage. "Now, let's get this done, so we can get to bed. We'll have another long day tomorrow."

INDIGO'S STEP WAS light in spite of having only four hours of sleep and running a sprayer since sunup. Freshly showered, she jogged down the hill to the winery.

Thank God for Danovan. She never would have gotten those top mirrored sheets up without him. While they worked, she'd entertained him with movie outtakes and pratfalls from her Hollywood life until, punchy with exhaustion, they'd both fallen on the yoga mats, tears of laughter running down their faces.

Behind Danovan's work persona, she'd discovered a nice guy. He seemed interested, sincere and charming. So what was with the tiny finger of mistrust poking at the back of her mind? She was no longer the artless wide-eyed teenager, assuming every friendly person was a friend. She well knew the price of innocence, and she wouldn't pay it, ever again.

But so far, he hadn't been anything but exactly what he purported himself to be.

Maybe she was just jaded.

She jogged past a white shuttle bus in the parking lot. The side of it read, "Parkland Active Retirement Community. Don't just live with us—participate with us!"

Stepping into the tasting room, she counted ten white heads either sipping tiny glasses of wine at the bar or wandering the gift shop. She'd have clapped her hands and skipped if it wouldn't have appeared unprofessional. Still, she giggled inside. Her smile didn't even dim when Sondra stepped from behind the bar and glided over.

"It looks like the word is spreading," Indigo said.

No uncultured hair-flip for Sondra; she did a one-finger slide across her shoulder to send her hair cascading down her back. "Retirees buy only critter wine. They attend tasting tours for a free buzz." She looked Indigo up, then down. "You're not going to approach customers dressed like that, are you?"

Sondra could kill a good mood with two sentences. "I'm leading our spa's first yoga class in a few minutes." She put a hand on her hip. "Did you actually have something you wanted to share besides wardrobe advice?"

"Yes. The sign at the road should be replaced. It's faded and does not show the winery in the best light."

"Thank you. It's on my long list of things that need to get done. Now, if you'll excuse me, I have to get ready." Spine rigid, she did an about-face and walked away. Damned if she'd allow that wine snob to ruin her day. *Critter wine? What the heck is that?*

She moved "wine terminology" to the top of her education list. It would take her years to match Sondra's knowledge, but if she could master the wine snob lingo, she'd have a shot at sounding like a winery owner. Besides, she'd need it for her marketing efforts.

Yeah, I'll squeeze that into my day between aphid assault and aromatherapy.

Passing her office, she stuck her head in. Not wanting Barney underfoot, she'd dropped him off this morning when she'd come down to retrieve the tractor. He lay in his bed, looking like he'd just had a long nap.

"Look alert, Barney. As the official mascot, you have greeter duty in five minutes."

He stretched, stepped out of bed and trotted after her to the studio.

She arranged the mats in rows, put a soothing Celtic CD in her portable player, then opened the transom-style windows to let in the smell of the jasmine blooming beneath them.

"This is the perfect yoga room, don't you think, Barn?"

"Well, I don't know about Barney." Jesse stood in the doorway. "But I like it." She strode in, wearing an eye-searing yellow blouse tied below her breasts, leggings and Keds.

Four women, from young to elderly, trooped in after her. While Indigo took credit card numbers for the class, the ladies stood chattering like excited squirrels.

"Where'd she get those cute mirror tiles?"

"Celtic music. Don't you think Enya is the best?"

"Oh, how sweet, I love bassets!"

"Ladies, can I get your attention? We have a lot to do today, and I know some of you have limited time. Why don't you leave your purses and personal items in a pile by the wall and take a seat on any mat, and we'll get started."

They complied, still chattering.

"Did you know Danovan DiCarlo works here now?"

"The lawn is beautiful, isn't it?"

"Is that really Harry Stone's wife?"

To give them credit, the last was whispered. They settled onto the mats and finally quieted.

She cleared her throat of the butterflies that clogged it. "I'm Indigo, and the furry one with the long face over there is Barney. I'm glad you came out today. I'm the owner of The Tippling Widow Winery and Spa. I have ten years' experience as a masseuse, aromatherapist and yoga instructor." She took a breath and pulled a sentence out of her chest, where it hid behind her heart. "And, yes, I'm Harry Stone's widow."

You could have heard wine fermenting in the silence.

The smile she pasted on felt a bit wobbly, but it would have to do. "Now, I'd like to hear about you. Will each of you please introduce yourselves? Tell me a bit about who you are and what you'd like to gain from this class.'

Jesse spoke up first. "You and I met at the café, Indigo, and God knows everyone here knows me."

"I should hope so. You had a hand in more than one marriage in this room." A long-legged blonde in cutoff jeans and a T-shirt advertising Pinelli Repair and Tow across her breasts scowled at the back of Jesse's head.

"Do not start with me, Sam." Jesse flicked her nails over her shoulder. "We all know how that turned out for you. Anyway, I'm here to fight the middle-age spread before it gets a chance to settle in and get comfortable."

"Smart woman," Indigo said. "Done right, yoga is the hardest workout you'll ever have. Next?"

She looked to the black-haired, doll-like woman with milk-rich coffee skin beside Jesse.

"I am Bina Rani." Her East Indian accent flowed soft and melodious. "I hope to gain tools to aid in relaxation. Between my psychology practice, my husband and my dogs, I need help in finding peace."

"I find that yoga calms me." Indigo smiled. "I'm still working on the peace part, but maybe we can find that together—for an hour, three times a week, anyway."

Priss, the young mother from the drugstore, spoke up. "Oh, yeah, I can get behind that. Olivia and calm don't travel in the same circles." She touched the arm of the elegant older woman beside her. "Not you, Olivia. I mean your hellion namesake."

The elderly lady smiled and patted Priss's hand. "I'm Olivia Preston. I broke my hip about two years ago. I want to increase bone density and improve my balance. The American Council on Aging suggests yoga."

"Yoga can definitely help, Olivia." Indigo stepped to the boom box and turned up the music. "Well, it sounds like you're all in the right place. Let's get started, shall we?" She returned and sat cross-legged on the mat, facing her students. "This is the Lotus Pose."

Before she knew it the hour had flown past.

She'd forgotten how much she enjoyed teaching, and it was nice to work with other people. The last time she'd hung out with a group of friendly women was—her mind skittered away from the Brenda Stone crowd—when she was a kid.

She ended class with her customary palms-together bow. "And may peace follow in your footsteps."

Her students were slow to give up the Shavasana relaxation pose and sit up.

"Wow, that was amazing," Priss said, extending a hand to her mother-in-law.

Olivia took it and was lifted to her feet. "My hip didn't hurt at all."

"God, do I *have* to go home? Can't I just stay and drink?" Jesse rolled her shoulders.

"You're always welcome to do that. The front patio is amazing. And oh, before I forget, The Tippling Widow is having a grand reopening party. I'll fill you in on details as I know them, but please spread the word, will you?"

"A party?" They all laughed at Jesse's squeal. She bounced on her toes. "You're having a party?" She put her arm around Indigo's shoulder. "Girlfriend, we need to talk."

Sam shook her head. "Oh, you've done it now, Indigo. You don't know it yet, but you've just unleashed a force of nature."

CHAPTER NINE

INDIGO HESITATED AT her client's flinch. "Does that hurt?"

"Just a bit, but don't stop. I started spring yard work this week and I'm sore." Carley Beauchamp dropped her head back on the massage table.

Thanks to either her flyers or the little birds in her yoga class, Indigo had booked a few massage appointments the past week. It was only a drop in the bottomless bucket that was The Widow, but it made her feel good to contribute to the revenue. She added a dab of almond oil to her palm and kneaded Carley's calf muscle.

"I hear that Danovan DiCarlo is working here now." Her voice was a bit muffled due to her face being planted in the oval face rest.

"Yes, he's my manager." Her sonar went on alert, pings echoing in her brain. "Why?"

"I'm glad to hear he landed on his feet. I'm a mother of two, and the thought of losing a child... Well, I just can't imagine."

Danovan lost a child?

"How old was...?" Like hairdressers and bartenders, masseuses developed data-mining skills.

"Esperanza— Oh, wow, that is heaven."

Indigo moved down to knead the spot just

below the ball of Carley's foot. "Esperanza, the poor little angel, was only five months old."

"Oh, that's terrible. What happened?"

"Crib death. It wasn't Danovan's fault, but wouldn't you feel guilty regardless, if you were the only adult around when it happened?"

When Indigo rolled Carley's toes in her fingers, the woman moaned. "I wish I could teach my husband to do that. He'd get more sex than he could handle."

"I'm glad it feels good," Indigo said, before moving the conversation back to Danovan. "So he was alone with the baby?" Her voice came out squeaky. No wonder his eyes held such sadness. Poor Danovan.

"Yes. Can you imagine?" Carley's skin pebbled into gooseflesh.

She patted Carley's foot. "You can sit up now. We're done."

Carley pulled the towel around her trim body as she sat. "And it's shameful what the family put that poor man through. To say that he was trying to— Well, suffice it to say I'll never buy another bottle of Bacchanal wine."

The sonar pings were now so close together that they blended to a high-pitched whine zooming around her skull. "What did they say he was trying to do?"

Concern must have shown in more than her tone, because Carley looked away fast, as if just realizing she was discussing this with Danovan's employer. "Um. Sorry. I really shouldn't say. You'll have to ask him if you want to know more." She scootched off the table and laid a hand on Indigo's forearm. "But don't believe everything you hear. Danovan is a good guy."

Once Carley had dressed and left the room, Indigo set the area to rights, wiping down the table, turning off the rainforest CD and dousing the aroma candles. Until she could afford a contractor to wall off a separate room, she was using a privacy screen in the yoga space that she'd picked up at a garage sale. The peacocks that decorated it were a bit tacky, but she thought the fake gold leaf was pretty.

As she tidied everything, her brain sorted information as fast as a veteran postal employee sorted mail. Poor Danovan, losing a baby. Even worse, on his watch. Her mourning heart now ached for him too.

Why would the Boldens speak badly of him? Danovan hadn't wanted her to contact them for a reference...and he must have had more reasons than he'd admitted.

Bull. She remembered the song her mother used to sing. *Believe half of what you see, son, and none of what you hear.* Her brain told her that Danovan was a superb winery manager. Her gut told her that he was the charming, funny, arrogant, frustrating, nice guy he appeared to be.

But your gut is prone to epic failure.

"So? Ask him what you want to know." She grumbled, glancing around to be sure she hadn't left a candle burning. But how do you begin *that* conversation?

She'd keep her eyes and ears open, her sonar on standby.

When she unbuttoned her smock, her phone buzzed from the pocket. She lifted it out. "Indigo."

"It's your party planner." Jesse's perky voice rang in her ear.

"I was going to call you later. The serving staff is getting excited about the grand reopening." Well, two of them were, anyway. Sondra had made it clear that their wine would be better suited to a dressy reception than a barbecue.

"Well, I have good news. The Kiwanis Club will let us borrow their barbecue trailer."

"That's awesome. You've taken the hors d'oeuvres off the menu, right? With no way to estimate attendance, I just can't take the chance. My budget is…firm." More like concrete boots, but she wasn't telling Jesse that.

"Yep. Anyway, it'll be perfect with just cheese trays, you'll see. Now, let's talk about the tables."

A WEEK LATER, sun searing through his shirt, Danovan bent to examine a vine. Aside from a daily walk-through, he'd turned over full vineyard duties to Indigo, only supervising when she had questions or when he had to teach her a new skill.

The most recent lesson had been leafing—strategically removing leaves to allow the budding grapes the perfect amount of sunlight. He brushed a hand over the leaves. They were healthy and perfectly thinned, not a sucker to be found. He squatted and checked the soil at the base of the vine. Just right—enough moisture to sustain the plant but not enough to foster the mildew. He straightened. Who would have guessed a girl from Hollywood would have a green thumb? Well, she had told him she grew up on a commune, but—

Her dog trotted, collar jingling, down the row toward him. Lovely. Why did dogs always gravitate to people who didn't like them?

Barney stopped, turned and plopped his butt on Danovan's foot.

"Get off, dog."

Barney looked up with adoring, bloodshot eyes.

The darned thing was so ugly, you kind of had to feel sorry for it. He leaned down and touched its head. Soft.

The dog leaned onto Danovan's leg and sighed.

Danovan stroked a silky ear.

Barney flopped onto his back in the dirt, his long ears spread, almost touching the vines on either side. He whined.

"You could play a little hard-to-get, dog." He

scratched the freckled belly. "Have a little bit of pride."

"I knew you couldn't resist Barn's charms forever." Indigo's head peeked around the vines at the end of the row.

When the dog rolled to its stomach, his front dewclaw caught on Danovan's wrist. "Ouch! Damn, dog!"

Unaware, the dog trotted to his mistress, who strode the row toward them. "What's wrong?"

Danovan raised his bloody wrist. "He cut me!"

"No way!" She skidded to a stop next to him. "It must've been an accident."

He held out his arm. The cut wasn't deep but had slit the small veins near the surface. Blood trickled down the side of his forearm.

Her air whooshed out. "Oh, Danovan." She leaned over his arm to look closer. The gold highlights in her brown hair caught the light, making him want to touch it. Her clean jasmine scent drifted up, filling his head. His body reacted. *What the hell?* He stepped away. "I'm fine."

"No, you're obviously not. Let me see." She reached again.

"It's a scratch. Forget it." He took another step back, praying she didn't notice the jut in his jeans. "That mutt's had all his shots, right?"

"Of course he has." She put her hand around his wrist. "Come to the cabin. I'll clean it and— have you had your tetanus shot?"

"I told you, I'm fine. Stop fussing." He pulled his arm away, but the skin still tingled where she'd touched. What the hell was wrong with him?

"Okay, if you're sure…" Her confused gaze roamed his face, searching for explanations.

All he knew was that the heat he felt wasn't due to the sun. "I've gotta check on orders before the new warehouse kid ships them."

"Okay." She grabbed Barney's collar. "Come on, you."

The beast had the audacity to wag its tail as she led it away.

Danovan knew he should leave, move on with his work. But something held him in that spot, feet as rooted as the vines beside them.

When the pair made it to the porch, Danovan saw Indigo swipe off her hat and sit on the top step, facing the dog. Though Danovan couldn't hear the words, her wagging finger marked a lecture in progress.

What had just happened?

He'd stepped across the line, that's what. His body had betrayed his own vow.

But a physical reaction doesn't mean I'm getting involved. It's simply a chemical reaction. Instinct. Brain stem stuff.

Indigo looped some strands of hair behind one delicate ear. Though her face's profile was stern, it softened something in him. He took a deep breath and let it out slowly. "You can't bullshit a bullshitter, DiCarlo, especially when the bullshitter is you."

His physical reaction might be instinct, but his feelings weren't. Somewhere along the way, he'd recognized the woman behind his boss.

He admired her. And obviously not just in a professional way. She'd taken on this wreck of a business, rolled up her sleeves and done what had to be done without bitching, without drama. How refreshing was that? His ex was the entitled only child of a legendary winery. Lissette had been sweet, but spoiled. Indigo, on the other hand, might have arrived from pampered southern California, but her roots were more humble, and he'd found her as opposite of arrogant as could be.

She was modest, resourceful and tenacious.

And delightful. And handsome.

Did you really just describe a woman as handsome? But it was true. Indigo Blue wasn't a classic beauty. Her mouth was too wide, and her eyes, with their sad tilt...made him want to protect her.

He snorted. Oh yeah, he was known for protecting women. Just ask the Boldens. He shook his head and finally made himself walk away.

THAT AFTERNOON, HE was working on The Widow's TTB Form 5120.17 when Indigo stuck her head in his office. "How's your wrist? Did you put antiseptic on it?"

"It's perfectly fine. Forget about it."

Her frown told him that had no chance of happening. "Any luck getting in touch with your distributor contact?"

Heat shot from his chest, and the sandwich he'd had for lunch took a slow, greasy roll. "Uh, yeah." He arranged his face, trying for cool and composed. "They're completely booked. Not taking on new clients. I'm sorry."

"It was a long shot anyway." She leaned on the door casing, crossed her arms over her breasts and worried her bottom lip a moment. "Can I ask you a question? It's personal, but I need to know. For the business."

Oh shit. Here it comes. The guilt-worm in his stomach had teeth and was trying to get out. "Um. Okay."

"I heard some gossip, and I just wondered…" Her eyes looked sadder than usual but held a determined glint. "What really happened at your last job?"

"I…" No words followed. Only a picture. A sepia picture of moonlight, pouring over a crib. A crib that held a wax-like doll. A perfect, motionless, beautiful… "I…" His voice cracked under the enormous weight of guilt and grief. "I'm sorry." Turns out, the worm had claws too. He rubbed his stomach. "I'll tell you sometime. Would it be okay if it's not now?" In spite of the writhing in his soul, he made himself meet her gaze. "I swear.

It was nothing that could hurt The Widow. Can that be enough for now?"

"Of course it can. I'm sorry to pry." She pushed away from the doorjamb. "Anyway, I was considering visiting some local restaurants. I'd think our clever name would be a good selling point with the public. Then, of course, once they taste our wine…" Lightening the mood, she rubbed her hands together and smiled. "We'll have them right where we want them."

Her smile went through his professional facade like a car through a plate glass window.

"Of course. That goes without saying."

"But I need some terminology lessons, or I'll look like an idiot in front of the restaurant owners."

"Sondra could—"

"No." Her smile faded. "No way I'm exposing my throat to that she-wolf." She straightened. "Anyway, we can sort this out later because that's not why I stopped by. I'd like to invite you to dinner at my cabin. I wanted to make up for Barney scratching you today."

This is not a good idea. After his reaction in the vineyard this morning, better he kept a professional distance. Even though his brain stem disagreed. He shook his head. "Can't we just forget about it? Move on?"

"I can't. It was a frigging worker's comp injury. You could sue. It's the least I can do." Her teeth captured her bottom lip again.

Damn, she's cute. His brain stem took over the decision-making. "I could sue, huh?" He put his hands behind his head and leaned back. "Maybe I should rethink this." He squinted at the ceiling. "Let's see, dinner or a lawsuit." He shifted his study from the ceiling to his boss. "I guess it depends on what you're cooking."

"Homemade pizza. From scratch."

This was a bad idea. A bad, bad idea. "What time?"

INDIGO HEARD SNUFFLING at the back screen door. "I hear you. You're still not coming in." She'd banished Barney to the screened-in porch. "I know you didn't mean to, but I think it's best to ease you back into the picture with Danovan."

Scooping sauce out of the pan, she used the ladle to spread it on the dough. Her dog's behavior was merely the excuse she'd given for inviting Danovan to dinner. Carley's story still ran through her mind—through her heart. Harry's loss had been devastating for her, but he'd had a full, wonderful life, and she'd shared that life with him for almost seven years.

But losing a baby. Her chest tightened as if to shield a blow. She couldn't fathom the depth of that pain. Poor Danovan.

"Knock, knock." Danovan stood in the light of the front porch, one hand in the pocket of his jeans, a bottle of wine in the other.

An ivory dress shirt looked great against his olive skin, darkened by hours in the vineyard. Her heart tap-danced on her ribs. "Perfect timing. Come, tell me what you like on your pizza."

He stepped in, set the wine on the table by the door and walked over. "What do *you* like?"

"I'll eat anything but fish."

"I'm with you on that one." He peered into each of the small bowls of ingredients. "I don't see anything here I don't like. Why don't you just put them all on?"

"Ah, he likes dump-truck pizza. No wonder we get along." She smiled and turned. He was close. Too close.

His dark eyes took her in. "You look nice." He took a deep breath. "And you smell even better than pizza."

She turned back to the counter. "You're just happy I don't smell like anchovies." She picked up bowls and scattered ingredients over the sauce.

She heard him step away. "I'll open the wine. Where do you keep the glasses?"

She peered into the overhead cabinet. "Uncle Bob only had a couple hundred." She brought down two globed glasses and walked the few steps to set them on the small dining table. "Don't pour any for me, though. I'm having sparkling water."

"Are you kidding?" He held up the bottle. "This is our own Clair de Lune Chardonnay, 2009." He held up a hand at her protest. "I know, you're

thinking red with pizza. But don't overlook a
crisp white."

"No, you don't—"

"Sure, the plum undertone of Chianti is nice
with mozzarella, but supporting the spice actually makes an interesting pairing. Trust me on—"

"I don't drink."

He stopped, mouth open. It stayed that way.

The skin over her collarbones burned.

"I knew you didn't know anything about growing grapes, or the terminology, but you don't…"
He cocked his head as if that would help him absorb the unimaginable. "You're aware you *own* a
winery, right?"

"I *inherited* a winery."

"Yeah, but—"

"Can't a bricklayer live in a log cabin? A horse
trainer can own a car. A corporate CEO might
not wear the pants at home, right?" She could almost hear him thinking, but his eyes gave no clue
as to what was going through his mind. She felt
like a new species of aphid under the hot light of
a microscope. "Why is that a big deal?"

He didn't answer for a few endless seconds,
scanning her face. "What I'd rather know is why
this is obviously a big deal to you, Indigo."

The specimen pin pierced, anchoring her to
the display board. She writhed. In the vineyard
this afternoon, he'd been abrupt when she'd tried
to help him after Barney scratched him. And so

far he'd shared almost nothing of his past. Yet he wanted to dig around her sore spots? Nope, not fair. "Just water, okay?" She turned away, opened the oven door and dropped the pizza on the bottom rack with a clatter.

"I'm sorry."

At his soft tone, she turned.

"It's really none of my business." He crossed to the refrigerator, opened it and took out a bottle of sparkling water. "As long as you have a winemaker on staff, it won't matter that you don't consume the product."

"Glad we agree."

"But you do need to know how to talk wine. And it's a whole different language." He took a small corkscrew from his pocket and proceeded to open the wine. "A whole different culture, actually, but it can be learned. You won't have to know everything about every wine out there, just everything about ours and how they compare in the market." Cork gone, he poured the wine and lifted the glass.

"What's critter wine?"

He chuckled. "Where did you hear that?"

"Sondra told me yesterday that retirees only drink critter wine."

"That's a wine snob's derisive term for wines named for animals, used to attract nonsophisticated buyers to cheap wine."

She had to chuckle a bit at that.

"Oh, yes, there's a bunch of overblown wine snobs out there." He raised the glass, swirled the wine, sniffed it loudly and took a tiny sip, then stuck his nose in the air and adjusted imaginary pince-nez on his nose. "An overoaked swill with a barnyard attack and a fruit-bomb finish." He flared his nostrils and pinched his lips. "Totally spoofilated. A tragic way to treat the grape." The snob melted away with his smile. "This is not unlearnable. It's like anything else. You hang around it long enough and it rubs off on you. You'll do fine, Boss."

She fell into his eyes, snared by the caring look held there. She wanted to linger and rest in the acceptance.

What are you doing? The voice in her head was a splash of cold water.

The oven timer dinged, breaking the spell. She busied her hands, retrieving the pizza.

The charisma inoculation she received in Hollywood needed a booster shot. God knew this man held a gold medal in charm.

Over dinner, Danovan gave her a lesson in terminology, even managing to make it interesting. His wonderful use of description allowed her to understand the difference in wines even if she hadn't tasted them. She'd never be able to hold her own with Sondra, but felt she now had a base to build on.

"That was one of the best pizzas I've eaten." He

eased his chair from the table and leaned back. "I'm stuffed."

"I think the crushed pepper added a hint of *savoir faire* to the sauce—the merest hint of garlic lending a clear, stiff finish."

He laughed. "You've got it. You're a pizza snob, for sure."

"Hey, I'm a quick study, and I have a great teacher."

She stood, but he snatched her paper plate before she could. "You cooked. I'm doing the dishes."

She sat back down. "Oh, yeah, don't strain yourself. The trash is under the sink."

He gathered the plates and utensils. "What was it like growing up on a commune?"

"Not as odd as you might think. No orgies, no navel-gazing, no psychedelic drugs. It was more like a large extended family."

"You told me that your mom is in charge of the farm. What does your father do?"

"I don't have one." She looked down at her clasped hands on the table. "I mean, I guess there *were* orgies back in the old days. Mom didn't know who he was." She straightened. "I never suffered from the lack. Mom is strong, loving and wise. A good role model. And besides, there were men around. Everywhere."

He walked back to the table. "Yeah, but a father is important, too. That's how a girl learns how men should treat a woman. What kind of man she wants to marry someday."

She'd never thought about that. Could that have been why she was so interested in Hollywood heartthrobs as a teenager? Why she'd been so anxious to meet them when she hit the town? Why she'd played so fast and loose when she'd been "accepted" into Brenda Stone's clique?

Do you really want to know?

He carried the glasses to the sink.

"Speaking of fathers…I wanted to tell you how sorry I am about Esperanza, Danovan."

The crack of glass shattering on porcelain made her leap to her feet. "Are you all right? Did you cut yourself?"

"I'm fine. The glass slipped." Danovan's broad back might as well have been a wall. "How did you learn about that? When?" His tone was razor wire running along the top.

"One of my clients mentioned it a few weeks ago."

He stared out the window over the sink, fingering the scar in his eyebrow. "What else did this client say?"

"Nothing. She said if I wanted to know more, I should talk to you." She touched his sleeve. The muscle beneath was taut. She could feel the tension running through it. "As someone who's also dealing with loss, I just wanted to tell you that I'm here if you ever want to talk."

"Thanks."

His tone left her nowhere to go. Subject closed.

He dropped the glass shards in the trash, dusted his hands and turned to her. His expression was—a stranger's. "Indigo, I appreciate the wonderful dinner. But it's late, and tomorrow's a long day."

Irritation and sympathy wrestled in her mind as he walked away. He wanted to know about her, but when she probed, he shut down immediately. She understood not wanting others digging in your past. But that look…

He was giving conflicting signals. And pushing her buttons.

But he'd promised whatever had happened at Bacchanal was in the past. That it wouldn't affect The Widow.

Yeah. Her curiosity and concern was only because of the business. Sure. She walked to the back door to let Barney in, ignoring the small, lonely voice in her head.

CHAPTER TEN

INDIGO DROVE BAREFOOT, but when she parked and slipped back into her heels, her toes whimpered. That wasn't quite true—they'd moved past whimpering an hour ago. They were now in full scream mode. But this was the last and most important sales call of her long day. She'd visited four bars and three restaurants, and though they all met with her readily enough, she hadn't managed to sign any of them.

Thanks to Danovan's terminology lesson and staying up late to study, she'd managed not to sound like a total idiot. But faking it wouldn't make it at the Demure Damsel. No lowly local wine had ever made the wine list here.

Grabbing her purse and sample case, she stepped out of the car, wincing when her feet took her weight. "Toughen up, cupcakes. There's no crying in wine sales." She slammed the door and smoothed the skirt of her suit. Straightening her shoulders and wiping the wince off her face, she strode to the front of the restaurant.

The Demure Damsel was Widow's Grove's only four-star restaurant, holding court in one of the original Victorians on Hollister. If she could get her wines sold here, it would establish their reputation in the local market.

She tapped her way up the sidewalk to the prissy facade that seemed to look down its refined nose at her. The house was dressed in cool sea foam and a soft juniper green, and the fancy fretwork was offset in a bold teal. Beds of perfect tea roses in delicate pastels graced the front of the restaurant, and a weed wouldn't dare set roots in the tiny manicured lawn that looked to be precision-trimmed with scissors.

Indigo swallowed the impending doom at the back of her throat. She might be able to fake her way past a bar owner, but she'd bet her Italian heels that this place employed a sommelier. He'd uncover the kiddie-pool depth of her knowledge in a heartbeat.

This is a job for Danovan, not a beginner like me.

Maybe that was true, but he already had a more than full-time job. Besides, The Widow was *her* responsibility. And if she was ever going to handle the reins, she'd first have to get on the horse.

Knees shaking, she forced her foot onto the first step of the porch.

You've faced down pissed-off paparazzi. You can handle this.

Her guts joined her toes in the whimper chorus.

Five o'clock was way early for dinner at a swank restaurant like this. The crystal place settings and delicate fresh flower centerpieces made the damask-covered tables look like petits fours. Waiters and busboys flitted around them, setting up.

She stopped one. "Excuse me. Could I please speak with your wine steward?"

"Of course, madame. That would be Bernard. Please follow me."

A voice in her head that was probably self-preservation screamed, *Run!*

But she followed on quivery ankles.

You walked the red carpet at the Oscars. You can do this. But that had been Harry's gig. All she'd had to do was hang on his arm and look glamorous. Money could buy glamour.

But it couldn't buy experience.

A dark cubby near the kitchen held a podium, and behind it stood a small balding man with pinched features, a neat mustache and a sour expression. "Thomas, I do not have time for more questions. My shipment is late."

"Madame, this is Bernard, our wine steward."

"Sommelier. How many times do I..."

He trailed off when the waiter stepped from in front of her.

She slapped on a bright smile. "If you'd have bought from a local winery like mine, you'd never have a late shipment."

The waiter, smelling chum in the water, scuttled away.

"And who, pray tell, are you?" Bernard's nose rose, revealing a too good view of his nostrils.

When the kitchen door opened and a busboy walked out, light spilled into their little corner. Bernard's prissy little mouth opened in an O of surprise.

"I'm Indigo —"

"Blue." He breathed.

Oh great, one of those. "Yes. I own The Tippling Widow Winery and Spa outside of town. Do you have a few minutes?"

"But of course, Ms. Blue," he said in an in-church voice. "Why don't we go where we can talk?"

He ushered her across the floor, through French doors and onto the patio where wrought iron tables were scattered amid a small English garden. A place she was sure he didn't usually hold supplier meetings. When he pulled out a chair, she sat, placing her case and purse beside her complaining feet.

He settled next to her. "I am so sorry for your loss—may I presume to call you Indigo?"

She nodded and stifled a sigh. Though the spotlight had winked out with Harry's passing, she still ran into people like this now and again. People who saw her as a Hollywood star, even though she'd never had an audition, much less a role.

"It was so wrong, how you were treated after Harry passed. And that daughter of his." His hands fluttered around his ears, and his eyes rolled up. "Don't get me started."

"I won't, I promise. I've come here today to tell you about some wonderful wine that we're—"

"I have to tell you. *From Here to Tedium* is one of the best films of the past twenty years. And the fact that your husband was able to pull a wonderful performance out of a used-up actor like Peter Horner is just amazing. Harry deserved his Oscar for that alone."

It always amazed her how total strangers were comfortable offering opinions on the lives of famous people—to their faces.

But that was a different lifetime. In this one, she had to sell this man some wine.

She tensed her stomach muscles and allowed her bright smile to dim to sad. It wasn't hard. "That was some time ago, and one tainted with sadness for me. Do you mind if we stay in the present?"

His face fell. He touched her hand. "Of course. How insensitive of me."

She slipped her hand from under his and reached for her case.

He straightened. "Now, to what do I owe the good fortune of your visit?"

This time she barely held back a sigh. He hadn't heard a thing she'd said. "I own The Tippling Widow Winery right here in the valley." She brought out her individual-serving sample bottles and displayed them on the table. "Our wines are well respected, and we've taken top awards at the Santa Barbara International Wine Competition." She didn't mention what year that had last happened. She pulled a sommelier's tasting glass from her case and poured a splash of their Clair de Lune Chardonnay.

He swirled the liquid, sniffed, then sipped. Lips pursed, he took a breath through his nose and set the glass back in front of her.

Her hopes went into free fall.

Bernard crossed his arms and fingered his pointy little chin. "I'm thinking about how we could mutually benefit from an arrangement."

Hope rose even as unease trickled down her spine. "What do you have in mind?"

"I was thinking. Maybe you could encourage your Hollywood friends to frequent the restaurant when they come to visit." He squinted into the distance. "The Damsel could become a gathering place for the famous." A small smile lifted the corners of his mouth. "We could even have a Harry Stone table."

Her stomach rolled. Cheapen Harry's memory so this odious little man would feel important? She had the sudden urge to take a shower. "Bernard. I'm sorry, but that is impossible. The contacts were my husband's, not mine."

"But surely you have friends?"

Heat rose to her cheeks as she shook her head. "I'm sorry. I don't." She gathered her sample bottles and returned them to her case. They obviously wouldn't be needed here.

"A pity." He shifted in his chair. "But maybe there is a small something you can help me with. You see, the owner would like to display my modest collection of autographed stars' photos in the foyer of the Damsel, and…" He lifted the little glass of her wine and held it, like a hostage, in front of her. "Perhaps you have a photo of you and Harry that you'd be willing to autograph for me?"

The buckle on her sample case snapped like a ricochet in the silence. She wanted to give this moron a large chunk of her opinion. She wanted to gag. She really wanted that shower.

But money was pouring from The Widow like an uncorked wine barrel. If she signed a restaurant of the Damsel's lofty reputation, others would follow, giving them a foothold in the local market.

Oh, Harry.

She knew what he would have said. He was a businessman, first and always. He'd tell her to go for it. But even knowing that didn't help.

"If I did…"

His smile was small, but triumphant. "If you did, I'd be willing to cut you a purchase order today."

A half hour later, order in hand, she walked to her car. She should have felt elated. Instead, she felt like lettuce left in the sun.

You got that order because of who you used to be.

No, it was worse than that. She'd gotten the order because of who Bernard *thought* she used to be. The Demure Damsel served exactly zero local wines before she'd walked in, and he'd barely bothered to taste her samples.

Mincing her steps to go easy on her feet, she was tempted to scream right along with her toes. Would she ever live down her former life? Would she ever be seen for what she accomplished in this one? How much longer would this life fit like borrowed underwear?

But this life was the only one she had left.

You've only been at this for two months. You wouldn't expect to sit down at a piano for two months and be able to play Carnegie Hall, would you?

No, but looking at the order in her hand, you'd think she had. Which made her feel like the worst kind of imposter.

In spite of the evening chores waiting at home, she continued driving, her thoughts as twisted as the roads winding through the hills.

She'd managed to snatch the brass ring that every vintner in the Central Valley had grabbed for and missed. She should have been happy. And she would have been, if she hadn't had to prostitute Harry's memory to get it.

She drove until the shadows under the trees spread out to take over the landscape. And kept going.

DANOVAN SAT IN the dark, feet on the railing of the porch, drinking a beer and listening to the crickets. Indigo should have been back hours ago. He had her cell phone number, and even dialed it a couple of times, but disconnected before the call went through. Indigo didn't need him checking on her. Besides, something in the calm of his chest told him she was all right.

The light he'd left burning in the tasting room made a yellow square on the porch, and moths trying to get to it ticked at the screen. He took another sip from the longneck. He'd known Indigo would find out about his soap opera former life eventually. She might not have heard the whole sordid tale yet, but now that she was getting to know the townies, it was only a matter of time.

He should have told her himself. The other night had been the perfect opportunity. But the surprise of hearing his daughter's name on her lips had hit him so hard that his brain had seized.

And what does that say about your character?

In spite of his vow to swear off women, here he sat in the dark, waiting for her to come home. And he was powerless to do anything about it. He'd tried for the past hour to make himself get up and go to his apartment. His feet weren't buying it.

The sound of an approaching car interrupted his self-flagellation. Squinting, he raised a hand to block the headlights sweeping the porch. The car pulled up, the engine shut down and the lights went out.

The crickets ceased their mating songs. The cooling engine ticked in the silence.

After many moments, the car door opened. The interior light illuminated the asphalt and a long graceful leg, as Indigo stepped out. The door slammed, and her heels tapped until she emerged from the inky shadows.

His chest tightened.

The tailored suit hugged her slim figure, and with the sample case in her hand, she looked all business. Sexy business. When she stepped onto the porch, the light from the window fell on her face.

A high note of alarm rang in his head. He dropped his feet and sat up. "What's wrong?"

"I'm just tired." Her purse and case thumped onto the porch, and she dropped into the chair beside him and toed off her shoes. "And my feet are killing me."

Damned buyers probably ate her alive. He'd offered to go with her, but she'd turned him down in a no-argument tone. "I think I have some iced tea in my fridge. Does that sound good?"

"Sounds like heaven."

On the way back, he flipped on a small light before stepping onto the porch. She sat, head against the back of the chair, eyes closed. He held out a glass. "Here."

She opened her eyes and took it. "Thanks."

He sat. "Want to tell me how it went?"

She sighed and handed him a slip of paper. He closed the door then glanced at it. "The Demure Damsel?" He looked up. "You got us in the Demure Damsel?" He glanced at the purchase order again to be sure he'd read it right. "Do you know what a coup this is? They don't *do* local wines. Bacchanal has been trying to get in there for *years*."

This little piece of paper was their golden ticket to the local market. A tide of hope rose in him, a foam of joy floating on top. "You are one hell of a salesman, Indigo Blue." He shook his head and clinked his beer bottle to her glass, where it rested on the arm of her chair. "Saleswoman, I mean."

She gave him a counterfeit smile.

Why didn't she look happier?

He could only imagine the guts she'd had to take on the local market, armed with only samples and a smattering of knowledge.

She was so much braver than he.

"So tell me. How'd you do it?"

"It's real easy when you were married to the biggest Hollywood producer of this generation, and the buyer is a fan." Her lip curled. "You just lay out your husband's body for the guy to fawn over, and he writes out an order."

"Jesus, Indigo." The shock-induced words were out before he could stop them.

"Sorry, but you asked."

He didn't know what to say. He wanted to roar into town and pound the dude.

"Okay, my turn?" She turned to face him. "Why did you run away the other night when I asked you about your past?"

"I...I don't..." He closed his mouth and just sat there like the wordless idiot he was.

"I know why." Her voice was small, childlike. "Because that was another lifetime—one you have a hard time dealing with on the inside. And talking about it with other people is more than you can handle."

"That's exactly right." He turned in the chair to face her, wishing he could take her hand. But he couldn't, and still keep his vow to himself. "That wasn't about you, Indigo."

"I know it wasn't."

They sat for a few minutes, each with their own thoughts. He felt the evening slipping into that familiar black tar pit of depression.

They both needed cheering up. "You know what, we've been working so hard. How about we have some fun? We deserve it."

She looked away. "Thanks, but I just want to relax then get to bed early."

He lifted an eyebrow. "But it's something you need to learn."

She sighed. "Really?"

"Yes. And you'll like it."

She glanced around as if there were an excuse hiding in the corner that she could grab on to.

"If you go to bed now, you'll just lie there and wallow. We both will." He knew he was pushing, but he couldn't let her go without doing something to take some of the sadness from her eyes.

"Okay. But I can't stay up late two nights in a row."

"You won't. I promise. First things first—get changed. You'll feel better after you get out of that suit. Do you have any of those comfortable clothes down here?"

"Yeah…"

He rubbed his palms together. "Then you go get comfortable. I'll get set up here."

She walked away like a robot completing a task.

Ten minutes later she was back, wearing a tight, clingy top and yoga pants, swaddled in a long cardigan fisherman's sweater. Her hair was down, her face scrubbed clean of makeup. She shrugged. "You asked for it. You get what you get." She padded barefoot to the bar.

What he got was an eyeful of more natural beauty than any makeup could mimic. And if he said so, it would destroy the DMZ boundary he'd given himself. But damn…even her feet were pretty. He pulled out a barstool. "I'm going to teach you how to taste wine."

"I told you, I don't drink."

"I didn't say drink. I said taste." When he pat-

LAURA DRAKE

ted the leather stool, she sat. "Judges and serious wine tasters don't swallow. They couldn't, and still discern one wine from another."

She took in the cutting board full of cheese, chocolate, apples and grapes he'd laid out. "What's all this for?"

"I want you to see how wine enhances the flavor of different foods. And vice versa. But first—" He tore off a piece of a crusty baguette he'd nabbed from his apartment. "You need to cleanse your palate."

She took the bread from him, and he tore a chunk off for himself.

They chewed in silence. The light from the pencil spot high in the rafters fell soft on her hair. She already seemed more relaxed, less depressed than when she'd first come in. He chanced a question. "Why don't you drink, Indigo?"

She wrinkled her nose, eyes slitted. "I've seen what it can do."

Had an alcoholic played a role in her life? Her mother, maybe? Surely not. Harry Stone? No, a drunk wouldn't be capable of making films like that.

"Okay, what's next?" He was glad to see that some life had come back to her posture.

He lifted a bottle of their Full Moon Merlot that he'd opened to let breathe, and poured it into a stemless globe imprinted with the winery logo. "Here you go."

She took it but looked dubious. "And what do I do with it once I taste it?"

"That's what this is for." He set a Dixie cup in front of her.

"I spit it out? That's disgusting."

"Not the way I do it." He winked. "Watch." He poured a splash for himself. "First, you look at it. Especially at the edges. Can you see that?"

"See what?" She held her glass to the light.

"You can see the variations in color with the change in depth."

"Oh, okay, I see that."

"Now you swirl it." He demonstrated. "This way you can determine how viscous the wine is. The more viscous, the higher the alcohol content. Our merlot falls pretty high on the scale."

"Does that mean it's good?" She studied the swirling liquid.

"We call it having legs. Alcohol content isn't an indicator of quality. It just means it's a fuller-bodied wine."

"Oh."

"Swirling also allows the aroma to open up. Sniff." He closed his eyes and took in the wine's structured aroma. When he opened his eyes, she was looking at him. "What do you smell?"

"Alcohol. And fruit."

"Okay, good start. Smells are complex, and it takes a bit to detect the subtle ones."

"What do you smell?"

"The fruit is a plum fragrance. A hint of flowers. Violets, maybe?" He sampled it again. "This is an older bottling, so I'm getting just a hint of cedar."

She chuckled. "God, you sound like a wine snob."

"And damned proud to be one. But—" He held up a finger. "Merlot is fruity, so it's esteemed more by drinkers than collectors. A top-of-the-line snob wouldn't touch it."

She nodded. "So you're a run-of-the-mill snob."

His shirt tightened across his chest when he straightened. "I'll have you know that I've judged topflight local contests."

She lifted her chin and sucked in her nostrils. "Groundling."

It was so Sondra that he had to laugh. "Onward, Grasshopper. When you sip, roll it around your mouth to use all your taste buds. Pay attention to the texture and weight on your tongue." He sipped, tasted and held the paper cup against his mouth and spit. "See? Classy, huh?"

"Still yucky."

"Try it."

She did, though he could tell she was self-conscious about it.

"Good. Now this time, take in some air with it. It'll allow you to smell and taste at the same time."

"Without drowning?"

"Watch me." He demonstrated.

"You slurped!"

"I most certainly did not."

"You did. I heard you!"

He gave her his sternest glare. "I know slurping, and that was not it. You try it."

She did.

He pointed at her. "Now *that* was slurping."

She laughed, slapped a hand over her mouth and tried not to choke. She spit it out then waved her hands in front of her streaming eyes. "No fair, you made me laugh!"

"I did not. You are an inveterate slurper." He shook his head. "We may as well stop now. This is hopeless."

A shadow flitted across her face. Then she realized he was kidding and punched him in the shoulder. "You are so bad."

"No, I am the *best*. That's why you hired me." He grinned. "Now, let's taste this with cheese, and then the apples, so you can see what this wine goes best with."

She must have been tired. She spit out every drop of wine, but by the time they'd worked their way through the Chardonnay and two zins, she'd completely relaxed.

He tried to ignore the fact that she looked like an innocent. A gorgeous innocent.

And isn't that just your MO.

The ice-water reminder brought back his focus.

He spit into his Dixie cup. "Try the Lunar Eclipse Zin with the aged cheddar. It's a great pairing."

Elbow on the bar, she swirled the blush wine in her glass, staring as if it were a crystal ball.

"Indigo?"

She continued swirling the glass, transfixed.

"Are you all right?"

When she turned her head, her eyes seeped sadness. "You asked why I don't drink."

He was afraid she'd stop talking if he said anything, so he didn't.

She looked back to the swirling liquid in her glass. "When I drink, I get happy. Everything has a rainbow aura, and I'm like a puppy that loves everyone and can't conceive that anyone wouldn't love her back."

"How is that a bad thing?"

When she didn't answer, he put his fingers under her chin and turned her to face him. "It's okay, Indigo. Tell me."

When her eyes skittered away, he let go.

Well, that's that.

"When I hit Hollywood, I landed a job as a masseuse at a trendy gym and spa." She took a breath that sounded like she hadn't inhaled in a while. "I was making great tips and saving every penny, living in a tiny dump of an apartment so I could buy nice clothes to wear to the clubs.

"See, I was obsessed with the stars. I'd followed every gossip rag in high school. I swear, I knew

more about Madonna than about US history. And
there I was, in the middle of that world, like Dorothy in the Emerald City. I lived in a constant state
of dazzled." She snorted.

"Then, one day, Brenda Stone came in, wanting a massage. I was so nervous my hands were
shaking, but I must have done okay, because she
came back. After all, we had common ground—
I knew every bit of gossip that had ever been
printed about her and her pack. We became—"
she air-quoted "—'friends.'

"Pretty soon, I was hanging out with her group
at the club. I wasn't in the center, mind you, but
the periphery. And I was *so* happy to be there.
I got my picture taken, and it showed up in the
magazines. They called me The Masseuse to the
Stars." She shook her head and sat a few moments,
as if divining the story from the twirling liquid
in front of her.

"Brenda had a party. She was living in her dad's
house, on the bluffs above Malibu. She billed it
the party. When she invited me, I was so excited.
I figured that was my entrée to the *inner* circle.
No more periphery. I took all my savings down to
Rodeo Drive and bought an OMG dress."

He wondered at her wince.

"A scrap of spandex, bloodred and so tight they
sold me double-sided tape to keep from flashing
my girly parts. Tiny crystals scattering down the
front glittered like the Milky Way." Her cheeks

reddened. "That's what I thought at the time, anyway. The last of my money went to matching stilettos.

"I thought I was so hot." Her mouth twisted. "I looked like a ten-dollar hooker."

Her shoulders rose with her deep breath.

"But I fit in with the crowd. The house was stupendous—all white marble and class—just what I'd pictured lying in my bed back home. The huge crowd was sprinkled with young actors and actresses, and tons of hangers-on like me. Well, like I used to be, because I figured that now I'd made it. Brenda introduced me to people. Some of her friends looked at me like I was a curly hair they'd discovered on a canapé, but I was so excited, I didn't notice.

"Then." The word fell out of her mouth, stiff and dead.

She threw her hair back with a parody of a happy smile. "Oh, I was a huge hit. Guys paid attention to me. Like magic, my wineglass was bottomless. I was funny. I was clever. I was a *star*." The fake-happy smile fell from her face like the mask that it was.

"At some point, things shifted. I went from darling to drunk. Savvy to sloppy. Smart to sl— well, you get the idea. But I didn't notice. I was going too fast to notice. This was *my* moment in the spotlight. And I eventually passed out in that spotlight."

She looked into the mirror behind the bar. The woman he saw there was much older than her years, as if this story had added them in its telling.

"When I came to, I was in a rumpled bed, staring at the ceiling. Alone. It took me a few minutes to become aware…" She took a breath. "My movie-star dress was around my neck, and the sheets were…stained." Her upper lip curled from her teeth. "Many times."

He wasn't sure he wanted to hear any more. But if she was brave enough to tell this story, he had to be brave enough to listen. Reaching a hand, he laid it on her arm to remind her she was here, not back in that bed.

"I'd had hangovers before. This was different. It was like my brain was furry. Furry and pounding and blank. I didn't remember a thing." Her deep breath squared her shoulders. She shifted on the stool, straightening. "I was still trying to make my mind move my body when an older man appeared above me. He pulled a comforter over me. I was mortified. But his eyes were so kind. He talked in this calm, peaceful voice. I don't even remember what he said, but he sat with me until I got it together. It was like that voice hypnotized me, because I calmed down. He got me to tell him the little I knew.

"He said someone must have slipped me a drug. A date rape drug. He wanted to call the police." She blew out a breath, her cheeks ballooning.

"I lost it. Crying, begging, probably a little hysterical, I pleaded with him not to. I thought the only thing worse than what had happened, blood and all, would have been if other people knew. I just wanted the whole night to disappear into that blank spot, and if I had to tell someone else about what happened, it would make it real. At the time, I didn't wonder why telling him didn't make it real."

She fell silent, turning the glass slowly in her hands.

Danovan held his face in everyday planes. If she saw his shock, she'd stop. So he sat quietly amazed—by the horrific experience, and the courage it took to talk about it.

And wondering what it meant, that she was telling *him*.

"Harry didn't like my decision, but he accepted it. He took care of me that day…and for the rest of his life." She heaved a sigh. "You see, Harry Stone never saw me the way I was that day—a dirty, used, gullible wannabe. He picked me up, cleaned me off and, for the rest of his life, treated me as if he'd found a diamond in the mud." She slipped off the stool to stand tall, pushing hair behind her ear. "And because he believed it, when I saw that woman reflected in his eyes, *I* could believe it."

For the first time, she looked over at Danovan. "When he died, that's what I lost." She held out her hands, palms up, and looked around the room. "This is what is left." She dropped her arms. "This is *all* that's left."

She didn't seem aware of the two shiny tracks that streaked her cheeks. "And that is why I don't drink."

SHE HADN'T MEANT to talk about it. It wasn't even in her thoughts to do so. And yet, even while *shut up, shut up, shut up* ran through her head like a scrolling banner, the words kept flowing. Until now. What remained of her energy leaked out with the story, leaving her deflated. She turned to Danovan to tell him good-night, and maybe just a bit to see what damage her verbal purge had done.

She froze like a startled rabbit, caught by the look in his eyes. There was caring and sympathy there. But it was the admiration, the twin of the look she'd seen in Harry's eyes, that slammed into her, shattering the fragile mend in her heart. She wanted to run, but the only unfrozen part of her was her heart—it raced, like that rabbit's.

When she looked away to save herself, his fingers on her cheek brought her back. She seized the familiar comfort there, wrapping herself in it—even knowing it wasn't Harry's. A disparate craving fired in her chest at the magnetic tug that made her want to crawl into this man's chest, curl up and relax in safety. Just for a while.

Of their own volition, her hands fisted in Danovan's shirt. Not breaking eye contact, she jerked him close and fused her lips to his. They were warm. Warm and still. But only for a nanosecond before they took her in. She opened to him. There was no "getting to know you" dance of tongues. He plunged in, the ground seemed to drop from beneath her feet and she was falling...

Then his hands clenched her upper arms and he pushed her away, breaking the kiss. Her chest heaved, pulling in oxygen, scanning his face for a reason.

Eyes wide, his breath coming as heavy as hers, he dropped his hands.

She caught a flashbulb pop of emotion in his eyes. Guilt, regret and...was that fear?

He looked away, running a hand through his unruly hair.

Her hand flew to her still tingling mouth. *What have you done?*

Danovan studied his feet. "Indigo, I..."

She didn't wait for the dagger to fall. She turned and ran.

CHAPTER ELEVEN

HE NEEDED MOVEMENT. He needed something to tear up, to make a mess of, to *do*. So the next morning, Danovan chose to clean the wine tanks and the bottling line, because it was a hard, dirty job, made worse as he'd put it off. And especially because he could do it alone.

The steam cleaner's wheels squeaked as he dragged it across the painted concrete floor. Four in the morning might have been an odd time to steam clean, but he couldn't sleep, and he sure wouldn't be disturbing anyone. Reaching the side of the first tank, he plugged in the cleaner, put on his safety glasses, then unlocked the bungs of the tank and lifted the lid.

Engulfed by a miasma of fermenting wine gunk, he turned his head to get a breath. "Oh, Jesus." At this moment he missed Bacchanal's updated technology. Good thing he knew better than to eat breakfast before this job.

You deserve much worse.

Backing away to give it a minute to outgas, he gathered his plastic shovel and buckets.

She'd poured out her guts to him; told him things she probably hadn't spoken of to many, if any. And he still hadn't shared a thing with her.

She kissed me.

Had she done it because she, too, felt the connection between them, or had she just needed a human touchstone to pull her back to the present? The taste of her had lingered on his lips long after she'd run out the door.

Worse, she lingered in his mind, filling his dreams with awful stop-action stills of her terrible night in that bedroom. Not to mention the look of horror in her face last night, before she'd run away.

And that made him want to smash something.

He mounted the step stool, leaned over the edge and shoveled residue. He imagined a fresh-faced Indigo, bursting with youth, innocence and potential, crushed by such ugliness. Now that he knew what had happened to her, he could see the scars of that night: the forlorn cast to her eyes, her skittishness when he noticed her as a woman. And he could understand why she married a man so many years her senior.

The slop made a disgusting squelching sound, hitting the bucket.

Not that Harry Stone was a bad guy. Thank God he had been there. Danovan had no doubt that Harry had loved Indigo, and her love for him was as plain as her grief at losing him. Danovan also knew that there were some sides to love that an eighty-year-old guy couldn't handle. But it was more than that.

And those were the thoughts that woke him.

Not going there, not going there…

The thoughts pounded in his head when he leaned over the side of the tank for the last shovel of gunk.

They had to talk. This morning. Indigo had trusted him with one very nasty, heartbreaking memory last night and after his pulling away from her, she was going to think he thought less of her. And the opposite was true.

He couldn't share with her all the shit that went down at Bacchanal without getting fired, but he found himself wanting to—not because he owed her, but because somewhere between the vines and the sharing, he'd started to *care* about Indigo Blue.

As you started to care about a woman last time. And it almost destroyed you. It *had* destroyed the only innocent party in his marriage—his daughter.

The admission freaked him out. How could he hope to avoid a repeat of his past?

You do something different, that's how. If he'd have been more mature with Lissette, more honest, they might have been able to salvage *something.* He snatched the steam cleaner hose.

The gunk of his past made that full bucket look like ambrosia. *Well, you won't make those same mistakes this time.* As soon as he got done here, he would find Indigo and do something different. Right after a hot shower.

INDIGO HAD SCHEDULED a meeting with the serving staff a half hour before opening. They sat in the guest chairs across the desk from her in their winery aprons. Well, two of them wore the aprons, anyway.

"Round tables for ten will be set up on the lawn. You'll need a level surface for the wine bar, so we'll cordon off the closest edge of the parking lot." She pointed out the window. "The food line will be parallel, on the opposite side."

"I still don't see how wine, silver and white table linens go with picnic food." Sondra didn't need body language to telegraph her disdain. Not with a face like that. "If we're trying to make a good impression on the local market, I don't understand why you won't allocate funds for a nice shrimp cocktail. Maybe crab-cake canapés?"

Indigo frowned. They'd been over this. "That doesn't go with barbecue."

Sondra glanced at the ceiling as if asking for divine intervention. "*Instead* of barbecue."

Indigo didn't have the energy for Sondra. After mortifying herself last night, she hadn't slept well, trying to imagine how she'd face Danovan today. "I don't want a highbrow affair. If we want locals as fans, we need to make *everyone* feel comfortable. And from what I've seen of Widow's Grove, it's more Mayberry than 90210."

"But that's no reason not to try to educate—"

"We're having barbecue." Indigo rubbed one

temple. "Can we move on? We open in fifteen minutes."

Becky raised a hand. "If you don't mind, I'd like to rearrange the gift shop. If we move those clever new corking machines to the endcap, I think they'll catch shoppers' attention."

Indigo nodded, encouraging her to continue.

"And I could make up a wine basket and put it beside the cash register with a sign saying they make great gifts for any occasion."

"Fantastic idea, Becky. You have my approval to move anything that you'd like."

"I've also thought about how to make our wine baskets stand out. You know, for example, an anniversary basket could come with two toasting glasses and one of the bottle stoppers with the bride and groom on them."

Natalie's dark eyes lit up. "Oh, how cute would that be? You could do an 'over the hill' one all in black for birthdays! I'd bet those would do really well on our website." She glanced at Indigo, then down at her hands. "I don't mean to be rude, but the website…"

"Sucks, I know." It had been on Indigo's to-do list from the beginning, but there just weren't enough waking hours in a day. "It's dated and staid, but I haven't had the time or the attention to get creative."

"I wouldn't mind giving it a try." Natalie shot a glance to Sondra. "On my off hours, of course. I took a class on HTML, and I've created a couple of websites for friends."

Indigo smiled her first genuine smile of the day. "I'd love that. I'll pay you for the hours you spend on it, of course. Why don't you mock something up and show it to me?"

Natalie nodded.

This day was beginning better than she'd dared hope.

Sondra folded her slim arms across her refined bosom. "We need to talk about a dress code. For one, it does not reflect well on the winery to have vineyard workers and the like entering through the tasting room."

Her arrogant tone, so similar to Bernard's, poked Indigo's day-old bruises. Sondra had chosen the wrong time to pick a fight. "Becky and Natalie, why don't you get the tasting room ready to open? Sondra and I have some things to discuss."

The ladies stood and, with a last worried look, walked out. Natalie closed the door behind her.

Sondra sat, cool as champagne on ice.

"Do you want to discuss your issue?" Indigo asked.

"I am responsible for the tasting room. It makes a bad impression on customers to have sweaty employees trooping through."

"No, not that, Sondra. I'm referring to your other problem." Indigo pushed her hurt feelings to the end of the long line of her own issues. This was a professional matter, and she had at least as much to lose as Sondra. "I am your employer, and I cannot condone your present attitude." She paused to let that sink in. "Do you want to discuss the problem you have with *me*? You've been rude to the point of insubordination since you walked through the door. I'd like to know why."

For the first time, Sondra remained silent. But her laser stare would have smoked holes if Indigo hadn't been wearing professional armor.

Why quiet now? Holding things in wasn't Sondra's forte. Indigo wanted to poke until Sondra, too, had bruises. And then push her thumb into them. But she was the employer, and a cat fight required equal footing. Apparently Sondra was going to play the "I'm not stooping to answer" game. "I suggest you curb your opinions regarding me and my decision-making in front of the staff," Indigo said. "If you'd like to discuss this in private, my door is open." She stood. "Now, we both have work to do."

Sondra glided out, head high.

And Indigo felt just as Sondra meant her to—the loser. *So much for confronting a problem head-on. I felt better avoiding the problem. Guilt is better than loser.*

"I've been looking for you." Danovan leaned against the open door of her office, hands in pockets.

She shot to her feet, panic careening around her

stomach. She looked for a way out, but since he was blocking the only doorway, there wasn't one. She so wasn't ready for this. Professional armor was useless against the hollow-point ammo she'd given this man, scattered among the smoking nuggets of her past. "I have to get to work. Let's talk at lunch." Head down, she walked to the door and tried to squeeze past him.

His hand on her arm stopped her as effectively as one of those bullets. She had to look at him.

He didn't appear any more comfortable than she. His brows drew together over troubled, reddened eyes. "Please?"

It appeared she wasn't the only one who'd lost sleep last night. Somehow that calmed her panic. That and his hand on her arm. Warmth radiated from his fingers straight into her blood. And she didn't want to confront what that meant, either. She pulled her arm away.

"Let's sit." He gestured to the guest chairs. "I won't keep you long."

Once she took a seat, he closed the door and sat beside her. Too close. Of course, after last night, the other side of the state would have been too close. God, she was mortified. She heard the thunder of her heartbeat in her ears. "Yesterday was… hard. For me. So last night—"

"Was a reaction, I know." He leaned his elbows on his knees, hands dangling. "What you told me last night wasn't willingly given. And that kiss wasn't either, not really."

He smiled, and something in its softness told her he was remembering that kiss. Blood throbbed in her cheeks.

"Look, Indigo, I know you're uncomfortable. But this is a very small business, and you and I are The Widow's only management. There's nowhere to hide. We have to find a way to get past this."

He might not have known it, but by bringing up the business, he'd thrown her a life preserver when she felt adrift in the sea of past and present emotion. *The business.* She snatched and clung. "You're right, of course. I'm sorry to have brought my personal—"

"Sometimes things build up inside. They have to get out. I want to tell you how I know that." He frowned. "No, that's not it. I *need* to tell you. Maybe after that, we'll find a way to move forward without us stumbling over the past every ten minutes." His look told her she wasn't the only one on soft ground. "Will you listen?"

She could tell from the hard line of his jaw that he was set on the telling anyway, so she just nodded. After all, it was a story she wanted to know.

"I may not be a judge, or a lawyer, but I inherited as much ambition as anyone else in my family. I was right out of college, full of knowledge, potential *and* myself. The cum laude opened doors, and I landed a cherry job at Bacchanal."

His fingers clenched the chair arms. "And I don't care what anyone says, goddammit, the old man didn't give me *anything*. I worked my *ass* off for those promotions."

When he slammed his fist, she jumped.

He shot a glance at her then, one by one, his fingers loosened. He rolled his shoulders.

But he's not bitter. She tucked that away to think about it later.

"See, I was a sprinter, on a fast track, and my life was ahead of plan." He hesitated a few heartbeats. "Then I met Lissette." He glanced out the window. "Bacchanal is a family business, and the old man runs it like a feudal kingdom. As the only child, Lissette was the princess of the empire, heir to the throne. She was off-limits, and I knew it. But God…"

He gathered his thoughts, staring out the window as if the words he needed were there.

"Have you ever seen a girl right on the brink of womanhood? So innocent, and yet so bursting with life and yearning for something that she only has a sense of, but wants so badly… Just seeing it captures you. Not in a sexual way, but like a perfect work of art." He raised his hands, palms up, as if trying to hold the vision. "It was as if she lived in an iridescent bubble—frozen in that perfect balance, like a butterfly that only lives a few days, so fragile and fleeting that you have to stop and appreciate it."

The muscles in his face went slack. He looked careworn, older. It made her want to reach out to him, even if only to offer the human contact. She laced her fingers in her lap. She'd given him enough conflicting signals last night—she didn't need to add to them.

"Lissette noticed me noticing her. She didn't want the proper men her father introduced her to. She wanted me." He looked down at his hands in his lap. "I knew better. The 'princess and the commoner' story—that only works in fairy tales.

"I walked away. I tried to ignore her, avoid her. But Lissette...she wasn't used to not getting her way. She was relentless. Everywhere I turned, she was there. Still, I'd have kept my head if it weren't for that damned innocent beauty. It was an undeniable force, pulling me to her. Like I was walking in a trance, and the ordinary world around me no longer mattered. Because, when I was with her, it was as if that bubble closed around us both. The world was shiny and perfect. A place where princesses and commoners *could* live happily ever after."

He snorted, an ugly sound.

Indigo waited, not wanting to hear the rest while at the same time held by the story, the vision and the pain in his eyes.

"But the simple act of touching that bubble shatters it. And there is no going back. There is no forgiveness for ruining something so precious.

You're doomed. Not only in others' eyes, but worse, in your own.

"When the everyday world rushes in, it leaves not a princess, but an ordinary woman. A woman with all the foibles of adulthood and none of the maturity. With the bubble gone from around Lissette, I could see what had been there all along—a beautiful, spoiled, entitled daughter of a rich man."

When he lifted his eyes, Indigo realized with a start that Danovan knew the loss she lived every day. He knew it because he'd experienced it. Hers was for a person she'd known well. His was for a person who'd never existed.

"So when she told me she was pregnant, I asked her to marry me, thinking maybe this was penance I could give for what I'd taken. Her mother cried. Her father hit me. But eventually, they had to give their blessing. Lissette wanted me, and they never could deny her anything." He heaved a deep sigh. "We were married in the biggest wedding the Central Valley had ever seen. A wedding befitting royalty. Sixteen attendants, three flower girls and a full mass.

"I wanted to relocate. I thought that if I could get her away from her family and start fresh, just the two of us, we'd have a chance. But she had no intention of leaving Camelot to live a normal life on a commoner's salary. Not like her parents would have supported that, even if she'd wanted to—they had an heir on the way." He spoke from between clenched jaws.

"I refused to move into her parents' house. She refused to live in town. We ended up moving into an apartment over the garage. That was only the first of a long line of disagreements. We argued our way through the months of her pregnancy. About her parents, her friends, my expectations. By the time the baby was due, we were married in name only. She spent more time in her parents' home than in ours, and God help me, I was relieved.

"But then the baby was born." Wonder broke on his face, remembering. "We named her Esperanza—hope—and that's just what she was to us. She was magical, changing my in-laws from sullen adversaries to soft-hearted, doting grandparents. Esperanza was such a beautiful, happy baby that Lissette transformed as well, into a luminous Madonna. It was a charmed time. And Esperanza brought me hope, too. Hope that Lissette and I could put aside the past and start over. I had plans..."

He seemed to remember she was there. He glanced over, straightened in his chair, and shook his head. "But it didn't last. Things got worse. Much worse. Lissette had turned back into the spoiled, immature person she'd been, and my in-laws again became the enemy. But this time,

Lissette was firmly in their camp, and when Esperanza died, whatever hope was left died with her.

"Along with a piece of me. Maybe the best piece. God, if I could just see Esperanza again. Touch her…"

It hurt Indigo to see him, head bowed, looking broken. She gave up her resolve and laid a hand over his, and they sat in silence.

His voice, when it came, was hushed. "See, you and I are not so different. It's not easy to face your mistakes and dare to hope again. But we're both doing just that."

When he stood, she found herself standing beside him. He took her hand. "I wanted you to know. You're not alone." His fingers came under her chin. He lifted her face. With a simple tilt of his head, his lips were on hers, just as desperate and needy as hers had been last night.

She knew she should draw back. But she couldn't turn away from this raw human longing to connect—she knew it too well. She tried to tell him in her kiss that he, too, wasn't alone. That it was all right to put the past down.

But then all her altruistic thoughts swirled away when her own need rose. Her arms went around his neck, and she buried her hands in his hair. Her breath labored as something in her chest opened. His arms tightened around her, fusing the length of her against him, and still, it wasn't close enough.

What are you doing? You are a widow. Harry...

Shocked to the deepest bruise of her battered heart, she pulled away.

A fleeting look of pain crossed his face. "Indigo, we've both made mistakes. Mine worse than yours. But we've paid for them. We deserve more good than what we've had. I've decided that I'm not giving up on hope." He ran the backs of his fingers lightly down her cheek. "I'm hoping you won't, either."

Did she dare? She knew what Harry would say. He'd tell her it was time to stop mourning and move on, to grab hold of life and savor it, just as he had. But she was afraid. Dare she trust her own misguided compass? Drop her caution and give in to the yearning inside her? Share his hope?

When she was with this man, she wanted to. She wanted to so badly.

She took his hand. "I don't know if I can, but I'm going to try. I promise you, I'll try." She wasn't sure if she was promising Danovan—or Harry.

"That's all either of us can do." He squeezed her hand and didn't let go.

CHAPTER TWELVE

AT CLOSING TIME a week later, Indigo looked up from her computer. Danovan once more stood at her office door, wearing jeans, a tight T-shirt and a hopeful look.

"Hi," she said then went back to typing an email to a potential customer who'd asked about their Harvest Moon Cab.

"We need to go to the fair."

"Hang on one second." She typed her name at the bottom, proofread the email and hit Send. "Now, what were you saying?" She logged out of email and shut down the computer.

"Are you available tonight?"

"Tonight?" Her heart revved.

Smiling, he nodded.

After his revelation last week, the uneasiness between them had lessened. Well, business-wise, anyway. Like horses in harness, they were getting used to pulling together. They'd mowed their way through the should-have-been-done-long-ago list and were working on the should-have-been-done-yesterday one.

And she was beginning to feel comfortable with her duties in the vineyard, too. Not so with her sales duties. She'd signed the Judas photo of her and Harry on the Oscars red carpet and dropped it in the mail to Bernard. She felt like a coward, but she wasn't strong enough to deliver it in person and watch him fawn over it. As much as they needed the business, she half hoped he wouldn't place another order. The thought of walking into that restaurant again made her stomach burn.

"Well?" Danovan shrugged.

She tilted her head and narrowed her eyes. "Danovan DiCarlo, are you asking me out on a date?"

"Nope. This is work. The Santa Maria County Fair hosts the Central Valley Wine Competition every year. The entries had to be sent in months before you took over The Widow, so we're not entered, but we need to scope out the competition." He leaned against the jamb and put his hands in his pockets. "But if you want to ride the Ferris wheel, I could probably be talked into it." He glanced out her window, then to the dog bed under it—anywhere but at her.

She'd never seen him shy before. He was always so in control and sure of himself. "Fine. As long as it's not a date."

"It's not." His smile was slow and deadly. "If you don't want it to be."

She wasn't sure of anything with this man. But her heart gave a silly skip anyway. She really did love county fairs. "It's going to cost you. I haven't had cotton candy in ages."

"I think I can handle that."

"Okay, but it'll be a few minutes. I need to feed Barney, let him out, then change."

THE SUN HAD just set when they stepped out of Danovan's Land Rover and walked across the parking lot of the Santa Maria County Fairgrounds. When they reached the admission booth, she pulled out her cash.

"I've got this." Danovan reached for his back pocket.

She touched his forearm to stop him. "Not a date, remember?" She stepped to the window. "Besides, this is a business write-off."

Grumbling under his breath, he accepted the event pamphlet from the ticket taker, and they stepped through the turnstiles. Once inside, he stopped to study the map.

Indigo took in the scene as people flowed around them. Lights winked on along the causeway and on the rides, lending a magical quality to the deepening dusk. A fresh breeze laced with the smells of popcorn, sugar and gasoline exhaust brushed her face, lifting the sleeves of her blousy top. Laughter, screaming and the *chug-whine* of laboring engines came from the midway ahead. She closed her eyes to absorb the moment. Anticipation fizzed in her blood, and excitement tap-danced in her stomach.

An almost forgotten feeling unfurled, filling

her chest with what felt a little like recklessness. It seemed forever since she'd enjoyed a simple pleasure. The heavy mantle of sorrow and responsibility slid off her shoulders to fall in a black heap at her feet. She knew she'd put it on again later, but for now, she felt lighter. Younger. She bounced on her toes. "Hurry up. What's first?"

He looked up and froze, staring as if he'd been hit in the head and was trying to gather his scattered chickens. His crooked grin spread like sweet butter. "Hold your horses, little lady. Business first." He squinted past the lights, then took her hand, gesturing with the pamphlet in his other. "The exhibitor's hall is over this way."

She remembered the hand that now enveloped hers—large, callused and comfortable. The heat spread up her arm, and when it hit the anticipation in her chest, it burst into a sparkle of happiness. She'd forgotten what that felt like too. She let him lead her past the causeway to the low red barn buildings to the right.

They stepped into the one with the Central Coast Wine Competition sign and found a long cement-floored room with rough wood walls. Tables festooned with wine and unmanned displays from local wineries competed for the attention of the strolling crowd. People spoke in whispers as if they were in church. Serious stuff, this.

Indigo took out her phone and snapped photos, getting ideas for a new show display. The display she'd found in a closet in her office was dated and shopworn.

"Well, Danovan DiCarlo." A fat man in a golf shirt with the logo of the Carbondale Winery on the pocket stopped in front of them. "I'm surprised you'd have the guts to show your face here, after—"

"Yeah, great seeing you, too, Stan." Scowling, Danovan locked onto her arm and propelled her across the room.

"Wait, who was that?" She craned her neck, but the crowd moved, obscuring her view. "What was that about?"

Danovan perused a display. "Stan Barclay. When I was at Bacchanal, we destroyed his Cab in a statewide competition. He obviously holds a grudge."

"Well, that's not very professional." She walked to the next display. *What had that guy been about to say to Danovan?* The nugget of unease that she'd buried in the back of her mind grew, rubbing some of the fun off the evening.

"Oh, but of course." Danovan's sarcastic lilt wore cement overshoes.

They stopped in front of the most elaborate display of all. A floor-to-ceiling booth panorama put you in a vineyard with the setting sun casting a golden tint to the grape leaves, robust bunches of green peeping from under them. In the center, a table draped in casually rumpled gold velvet displayed five bottles of wine, each wearing the distinctive Bacchanal label—and a showy blue ribbon.

When Danovan didn't move, she tugged at his elbow. "That's only because we didn't enter. We'll take them next year."

The grim set to his mouth told her he planned on it.

They walked out of the building. The raucous noise from the midway washed away the refined atmosphere, but not the anger rolling off her companion.

"Next year." Danovan strode so fast she had to trot to keep up. "We'll have a nice display, but one that doesn't take away from the real star—the wine. A slender, dark bottle, showing off the deep, rich berry blush." He traced the form as if it were a woman's body. "Can't you just see it? A gold foil label, heavy black script. DiCarlo Select Merlot."

He wasn't kidding about the ambition part. "Oh, really?"

He seemed to come back to himself. And his audience. "Oh, I didn't mean to...I mean, you, of course, get to name..."

She couldn't step on him. After all, he was working his ass off for less money than he made at his last job. She could pay anyone to do the work, but she couldn't pay someone to care. And Danovan DiCarlo, for all his faults, cared. Maybe allowing him to name a wine he perfected wouldn't be out of the question.

Besides, dreams didn't cost a thing. Dreams were good. She smiled. "No worries. First, let's have a good crush this fall. Then we'll worry about naming our amazing product." She took a step toward the delicious smell coming from the midway, pulling Danovan with her. "Ohhhh, kettle corn!"

A corn dog, popcorn and ice cream cone later, they strolled the games alley, watching the easy marks attempt to win cheap sawdust-stuffed animals for their girlfriends. Indigo took a bite of cotton candy. "Hmm. This is so good it's sinful."

"It gives me a sugar rush just watching you eat it. Don't you know that adults aren't supposed to consume that crap?" He pointed. "Hey, you want me to win you a jelly glass?"

"Nah. It would get an inferiority complex, mixed in with all Uncle Bob's wineglasses. And, in regards to your last point, I'm not an adult. Not tonight. I'm reliving my childhood, and— Oh my God!"

"What?" His head swiveled, looking for trouble.

"They've got a Centrifuge! I love that ride."

He eyed the cylinder and the dizzy teens spilling from the narrow door. "You do?" He glanced to her almost empty cotton candy cone. "You may want to wait—"

"Oh, I'm totally doing that." She dropped the cone in the trash, dusted her hands and shot him a challenging look. "You scared?"

"Honey, Daring is my middle name." He growled deep in his throat, grabbed her hand and marched to the ticket booth.

"Danovan Daring DiCarlo. That has a nice cadence." *Did I just giggle?* Jesus, she hadn't giggled since she was a teen. Well, screw it. There'd be time enough for responsibility tomorrow. Tonight, she was cutting loose.

She noticed the women they passed and how their gazes paused on Danovan as if savoring. *Well, eat your hearts out, ladies.* For tonight, anyway, her hand felt right in his. She'd worry about the rest tomorrow.

Harry. She stumbled a bit, then caught herself. The image of him smiling fondly floated through her mind. She gritted her teeth. Harry would approve. She just knew he would.

Since she'd left Hollywood—no, earlier than that, after Harry died—she'd felt lost, misplaced.

Tonight, for the first time since, she felt natural. Herself. Maybe she was finding her footing again. Maybe the winery could be somewhere she actually fit. *Maybe.*

She shoved the thoughts behind her and tightened her grip on Danovan's hand. Tomorrow would be soon enough for grown-up thoughts. Tonight, she was going to *feel*.

But ten minutes later, she bent over, hands on her knees, wishing she could *stop* feeling. "I think I'm going to throw up." Her stomach was in full gale warning, with ten-foot swells.

Danovan rubbed light circles on her back. "I told you riding that thing wasn't a good idea after all that junk food."

"Please." She swallowed the corn dog, cotton candy, popcorn pollution that crawled up her throat. "Don't mention food."

They stood tucked in a dark niche between rides. The smell of exhaust blew over her in a greasy wave. She fanned her hands in front of her face. *Getting sick does not make a good impression on a first date.* She squinted up at him. "Is this a first date?"

He chuckled and kept rubbing her back. "Not if you hurl, it's not."

She moaned. "Oh, great, no pressure."

"Here, I know what'll help." He took her hand and led her into the darkened field behind the fairgrounds. He stood behind her. "Look at the light on that barn over there. Do you see it?"

"Yes."

"You just keep watching that. You have motion sickness."

She puffed out a shaky breath. "How do you know?"

"My sister never wanted to sit next to a stranger, so she dragged me on every roller coaster within driving distance, growing up." His hands rested, feather-light, on her shoulders. "The best thing is to focus on something that's anchored and stable. Just breathe deep and watch that light."

She did. In ten minutes, the waves in her stomach calmed, and the vertigo sledgehammer quit pounding the inside of her skull. As long as she didn't think about food, she felt better. And the solid wall of him, bracing her back, helped. "I think I'm okay now." She stepped away.

"Good. No more rides for you tonight, missy."

"Believe me, I'm done. You ready to head back?"

"Sure. Let's go." He put a hand under her elbow to help her across the uneven ground.

Once home, he insisted on driving her up the hill to the cabin. The table lamp she'd left on in the great room was a beacon as he walked her to the door. She unlocked it, then turned. "Thanks, Danovan, I had a good time, in spite of—"

His lips cut her off, slanting over hers. It was a tentative kiss for all its brashness. A warm brush, an invitation, before he withdrew to look at her, his eyes full of questions.

It was dark. They were alone. Maybe she could pretend, just a few moments longer, that she was undamaged, young, immune, carefree. She didn't lean in to him as much as just relaxed, allowing the attraction to pull her to him.

Their first kisses had had agendas. Not this

one. She explored his mouth, tasting the alluring sweetness of freedom. He was as addicting as all the sugar she'd indulged in tonight. She craved that rush.

He took her lips as if he owned them, then withdrew, stretching out the cord between them. The drawing strengthened it, so when he returned, they both wanted more.

His hands slipped around her waist, pulling her against him. She put her hands on his chest, reveling in the pliant muscle under the lean scrap of cotton.

The cord thickened to rope, then to cable, as he took her mouth again.

His breath, heavy in her ear, loosened something deep in the floor of her pelvis. Something that had been strung taut for a long, long time. Languid warmth swirled until she felt swollen with it.

She dug her fingers into his cotton shirt and clung as he took—and she gave. His hands in her back pockets held her close, against the rod-hard length of him. She wanted to get closer. Had to get closer. Without asking her brain, her hips twisted against him. The delicious friction pulled a moan from her chest. Her muscles clenched deep inside.

Her mind awoke from its stupor, yanking her back to reality. She broke the kiss and the contact, almost jumping from his arms.

What the hell just happened? She wasn't sure

if she was talking to her mind or her body—
probably both, since there was obviously a con-
spiracy afoot here. "I'm sorry. I feel like I'm giving you mixed messages. I'm—I can't—" Her
words came out in breathless pants.

"I know." He let go and backed up a step. "And
I've got my own stuff to work through." Voice
gruff, he ran a hand through his hair. "I like you,
Indigo Blue. I want you. And I think you feel
something for me. That gives us both conflict,
but there it is."

He took her hand. "But just so we're clear, that
was a date." He smiled. "And when you're ready,
we'll do it again." He lifted her hand to his lips
and kissed the backs of her fingers, a courtly gesture that touched the damaged parts of her heart.
"Okay?"

She stood a moment, fighting a war in her head
that she wanted to lose. "Okay. For now." She retrieved her hand. "I think."

IN SPITE OF the dress, Indigo couldn't pass the vines
without stooping to check the soil and admire the
grape inflorescences. *You've been reading too
many of Danovan's textbooks. They're flowers.*

She ran her fingers over the kelly-green leaves.
"You guys keep up the good work. You're doing
a great job, and I'm proud of you." If someone
heard her talking to the vines, she'd be mortified.
After all, this was a business. But the vines were

living things, and wine making was art as much as science. Who was to say encouragement didn't help? She straightened. "Come, Barney, no time to explore today."

Barney's collar jingled as he trotted toward her, his ears and jowls swaying with his awkward gait.

"You don't want to get dirty before the party." She bent to pet his velvety head. Much as he'd hated it, she'd given him a bath last night, then lit a fire so he could flop next to it. "You're going to be a star today." She clipped the lead on his green collar that matched the company colors. "Let's go. We have a lot to do before the crowd shows up."

I hope a crowd shows up.

Her dressy flats clicked on the asphalt on their walk down the drive to the winery. She'd have liked to wear heels, but they wouldn't be practical. She'd agonized over what to wear, wanting to look professional, since this was her debut event as the owner of The Tippling Widow. But she also wanted to look attractive. After all, they were selling wine, not hardware.

And she sure didn't want Sondra outclassing her.

The butterflies took flight again, brushing the walls of her stomach. Didn't those damned things ever get tired?

Just pretend. Act like an owner, and someday you'll feel like one.

That's what they said, anyway. She touched the

back of her neck to be sure the hairpins were holding. From the front, her smooth coif looked all business. From the back, the curl cascade showed a different side. A soft side that she hoped would catch Danovan's attention. Of course, that had nothing to do with why it took her two hours to get ready. She smoothed her bangs and smiled.

There hadn't been time for more than flirting over the past two weeks in the hustle to prepare for today. She was relieved. The hiatus took the pressure off, giving her time to ease into the idea of possibly dating again. She'd never expected to find another man she'd want, after Harry.

And you still don't know that you have. She remembered the man from the wine exhibit, and his abbreviated comment before Danovan pulled her away.

She shook her head. She knew better, didn't she? Danovan was a master at his job, accommodating, sweet and entirely too good-looking. She was aware of being lulled by his charm and his eyes. But beneath that, deeper, she sensed good in him. Her gut told her to trust him.

So, of course, she couldn't.

But at the same time, pressure built between them. She found herself losing the thread of a business discussion, watching his lips move. Several times, she'd caught him staring at her with a hungry-wolf look that made her shiver—though with dread or excitement, she couldn't have said.

And he'd touched her. Small, seemingly accidental touches. A brush of the back of his hand as they walked side-by-side. When he took her elbow across rough ground. All easily explained, except for the tingle that lingered too long where he'd touched.

She ran a hand over her skirt, hoping that this dress would knock him on his ass. A halter summer sundress, yet conservative, it looked like something Jackie Onassis would have worn—stiff ivory material scattered with yellow cabbage roses. A broad business-suit collar with ivory piping showed off her bare shoulders, tapering to a tightly fitted waist, with a wide belt and a full skirt that brushed her knees.

By the time they walked into the parking lot, Barney was panting. She tied him to the porch railing in the grassy shade. "I'll be right back." She walked into the tasting room.

They weren't opening until noon, when the barbecue began. She admired the custom-made green banners with The Widow's logo in gold hanging from the rafter timbers. Natalie had found the idea online and custom-ordered them. She'd also done a wonderful job revamping the gift shop. The gift basket on the endcap was bound to catch shoppers' interest: a Queen for the Day basket, complete with a tiara and scepter, all done up in pink cellophane and a bow.

Sondra glided over in heels, her navy dress concealed by an apron. *The* apron. "Well, this day has finally arrived."

"You look—nice, Sondra." Surprise leaked into Indigo's considered words, ruining the effect.

"This is practical." Sondra sniffed, but pink stained her cheeks. "I didn't want my dress to be soiled. The minute we're done with the preparations, I'm taking it off."

Indigo wasn't about to kick a gift horse in the mouth. "We're all representing the winery today. I'd really rather you wear it."

"Well, if we're trying to make a good impression…" She shot a look around to be sure she wouldn't be overheard. "You didn't bring that dog, did you?"

This was Sondra, after all. "Of course I did. If you'll excuse me, I need to get him a bowl of water."

They both turned at the sound of a diesel engine. Through the plate glass, they could see a white panel truck pulling up with Peter's Party Supply emblazoned on the side.

Sondra clapped her hands. "Ladies, look lively. The bar and tables are here."

Indigo pushed through the door to the hall. Danovan's apartment door opened. He wore fitted dress slacks, a butter-yellow dress shirt and, when he saw her, a huge smile.

"And who is this?" He took three steps to where she stood, held by his tractor-beam of interest.

"She looks a bit like our vineyard rat, but surely I'm mistaken." His gaze took a long, slow tour of her body. "*This* is a woman."

A furnace clicked on inside her, heat spreading where his eyes touched.

His dark, wavy hair was combed back from his broad forehead, and a two-day growth of beard darkened his jawline, tailored by a razor-line shave that accentuated his full lips.

It should be against the law for a man to look that sexy.

He took another step, bringing him close, but not close enough. When he leaned in, his hair brushed her cheek. His lips hovering at the hollow of her neck, he inhaled deeply, then exhaled. "You even smell fabulous."

She took a breath. "As do you." She closed her eyes. The smell of his soap conjured an image of Danovan naked, warm water running over smooth skin.

His fingers slid down her palms to lace lightly with her fingers. He raised his lips to her ear, so close, but not touching. "Go out with me tomorrow night."

At the brush of his breath in her ear, she shivered. The furnace was now between her legs, the flush spreading upward. "Yes," she said on a breath, agreeing to whatever he might be implying.

He held himself motionless, a heartbeat from her skin.

The vacuum in her chest made her want to lean in to him—on him. She swayed, fighting her own need. When she thought she'd burst with the wanting, he whispered, "Tomorrow, *mia cara*," and stepped away.

She could breathe again.

Fingers still laced with hers, he lifted her hands from her sides. His gaze took one more lingering tour. "*Sei bellissima.*"

She bowed her head, not yet trusting her voice.

He released her hands, breaking the spell.

"I have to…" She waved a hand at the door. "Barney…" She walked on shaking knees to her office.

Behind her, Danovan stepped through the door to the tasting room, whistling what sounded like opera music.

Two hours later, she strolled at the edge of the lawn, a glass of wine in hand—a prop to make her look owner-like and give her something to talk about. She relaxed a moment, letting the crowd noise wash over her. Jesse's husband, Carl, manned a half-barrel barbecue dressed with chicken breasts, hamburgers and brats. The line snaked a good five feet into the parking lot, which had been roped off to traffic. Cars lined the drive and as far down the road as she could see through the oaks.

Most of the round tables were occupied, and the gold tablecloths stirred in the slight breeze. Jesse's centerpieces were a perfect touch: berries, grape leaves and wineglasses. Thank goodness for the mild day. The almost-summer sun might be good for the vines, but it could wilt humans.

But the most gratifying sight was the line at the wine bar. Natalie dispensed complimentary wine while Sondra chatted with the people waiting. Danovan was off leading a group tour through the production facility. Even Barney was busy with public relations, lying on his back in the middle of a circle of kids, getting a belly rub.

The Tippling Widow's grand reopening looked to be a resounding success. She bounced on her toes once, then made herself stop. Owners didn't bounce with joy like a little kid at the gates to Disneyland.

Her yoga students sat at adjoining tables, Bina's bawdy laugh overriding the conversations. She'd brought her husband, Shiv, and at least ten doctors from the hospital where she worked as a child psychologist. Sam Pinelli and her husband, Nick, sat next to them. They'd made quite the entrance, roaring up on matching candy-apple-red motorcycles. Priss and her husband, Adam, had brought his mother, Olivia, who introduced Indigo to several women in her book group.

It looked like everyone had invited everyone they knew. And no one knew more people than Jesse. She stood amid a circle of people, blinding in white short-shorts, seeming to talk to most of them simultaneously.

Indigo wondered why people she'd only known for a short time would go out of their way to help a newcomer. This was more than her friends in Hollywood had ever done. Of course, those were the same *friends* she hadn't heard from since she'd left three months ago. She smiled, relaxing into the sweet acceptance that competed with the warmth of the sun on her skin.

"Indigo!" A man's fussy voice came from behind her.

Her stomach clenched, and before she could stop them, her shoulders rose to ear level. But it was too late to slink off. She forced her shoulders down, the corners of her mouth up and turned around. "Bernard!" She used her fake-happy Hollywood voice, trying not to shudder when he air-kissed her ear. "I'm so delighted you could come!"

Well, the winery owner part of me is, anyway.

"I would never miss a chance to visit Widow's Grove's most notorious resident."

Her lips stiffened to a plastic smile. *Notorious?* She should have known the little worm would have a subscription to the *Hollywood Informer.* She tamped down the urge to advise him that comb-overs went out in the '60s and forced her hand to rest in the crook of his scrawny arm. If she'd survived a harpy like Brenda Stone, she could handle a harmless sycophant. "Bernard, I have someone you just *have* to meet." She steered him across the grass to the wine bar. "This is Sondra, my tasting-room supervisor. I think you'll find you and she have a lot in common."

She dumped Bernard with Sondra, who appeared both delighted at the introduction and stunned that Indigo knew him.

One more round of schmoozing, and then she would snatch a plate of food and sit awhile.

Just then Danovan walked around the corner of the building, trailing guests like the Pied Piper. When he laughed at something one of them said, his teeth flashed white against his olive skin. His face was that of a Roman senator, and he moved with the smooth grace of a dancer.

He scanned the crowd until his eyes stopped on her. The smile that began in his eyes broke over his face in a sunrise of happiness. He might have leading-man looks, but this smile wasn't for a camera. It was for her alone. It whispered a promise—of admiration, respect and hot kisses in the dark. She touched the dampness at the base of her throat that definitely wasn't from the sun at her back.

She spotted a woman standing on the driveway behind Danovan, obviously not a part of his tour group. She was slim, with long, black hair and ample cleavage. Her gaze flicked from Indigo to Danovan, then remained there. A prickle of unease skated across her skin. *Malice*. An odd word, but that was the one that popped into her mind.

"You have good taste. He looks yummy enough to eat in one bite." Jesse stood beside Indigo, arms crossed, following her gaze.

"Don't be silly. I'm a widow."

The blonde rolled her eyes. "Hon, *you* didn't die. Your husband did." Her look softened the blunt words. "You're a vital, beautiful young woman and you deserve to be happy."

Indigo squinted. "Have you been talking to my Harry?"

She snorted. "Hardly. But I'm not blind, either. You and Danovan would make the most scrumptious couple."

"I've heard about your legendary matchmaking skill. I have no intention of becoming a client."

"Oh, hon, I'm too late. You're already off the market, whether you want to admit it or not."

"No, I..." Distracted by the war going on in her head, she stopped, not sure what word came next.

Jesse patted her arm. "I don't mean to sound harsh, but if you let that gorgeous man get away, you aren't as smart as I thought." Raising a perfectly plucked eyebrow, she turned and sashayed away.

Indigo's stomach growled. "The schmoozing will have to wait. I need food now." Unimaginable things always seemed easier with food. She shook off the uncertainty and headed for the food line.

An hour later, she sat at a table chatting with the men she hadn't at first recognized as her bicyclists, having never seen them in anything but spandex.

"So we hit the summit of that fifteen-hundred-foot climb, and we start down the other side. I mean, we are flying. We come to this hairpin turn and Allen, here…"

At a tap on her shoulder, Indigo turned.

It was the slim woman with the shelf of cleavage who had given Indigo the willies earlier. The smile the lady gave the table of men was a pole dancer's come-on. "I'm *so* sorry to interrupt," she simpered, knowing she had the attention of every mother's son at the table. "Would you mind if I borrow Ms. Blue for a few minutes?"

They mumbled assent, eyes lasered to the titty platter, like homeless men at an all-you-can-eat buffet.

This woman didn't look like a potential client, but you never could tell. Indigo stood. "Excuse me, gentlemen." She followed the girl's perky pistoning buns past the porch of the tasting room, to the shaded side of the building. It was quiet here, the crowd's noise only a murmur.

"Can I help you?" Feeling lured and uneasy, Indigo halted.

The girl stopped and turned. "No, but I can help you."

"You are…?"

"Roxy. But my name doesn't matter. I've come to tell you something you should know. Something about your manager."

Indigo tensed as her defensive shields snapped into place. She lifted her chin. "He's a brilliant manager."

"You're new here, sweetie." She flipped her Cher-like black hair over her shoulder. "You probably don't know that his own negligence killed his baby."

In the quiet, Indigo heard her own breath hitch.

"And thanks to his pride and arrogance, he destroyed his marriage."

Who is this woman? Indigo's thoughts screamed around her skull like it was a NASCAR track. "I don't think that's any of my—"

"It speaks to the kind of *man* Danovan DiCarlo is. But that's not your problem." She put a hand on her hip and pointed a long nail covered in purple polish at Indigo. "He tried to take down Bacchanal by giving away their trade secrets—*that's* your problem."

Adrenaline punched into Indigo's blood, making her nerves skitter and her knees soften. *He wouldn't hurt The Widow. He wouldn't. Would he?* She needed to sit down. "Who are you?"

"I'm sure Danovan will tell you that I'm a vindictive bitch. I'm sure he'll have lots of other bad things to say about me. You may even believe him." She leaned in, her narrowed eyes glittering shards of glass. "But is it possible that I could be a vindictive bitch and still be right about Dano-van DiCarlo?" She paused to let her words sink in. "Look, you have a winery to run. And if the rumors are true, that's about all you have. So think about it. Are you willing to risk everything you have on the word of a liar?"

CHAPTER THIRTEEN

NAILED THAT SUCKER. Danovan glanced around his gleaming production facility, proud of every gleaming tank, every dust-free carton of stock, even the cement floor that he could eat a celebratory dinner off of. Sure, he hadn't done all the work. His warehouse rat had about killed himself getting ready. But Danovan had done the hiring and supervising and the steam cleaning himself, so he'd earned some kudos. And after today, there would be plenty to go around. He'd overheard enough conversations leading buyers through the facility to know that The Tippling Widow had made a favorable impression. And from the line at the wine bar, the locals shared that opinion.

With one last lingering look, he walked on aching feet to the door and flipped off the lights, then through the barrel room to the tasting room.

Indigo stood at the bar, taking bottles of wine from Jesse's arms.

He walked over. "Where are the rest of the employees? I wanted to take everyone out to dinner to celebrate."

Jesse waved to the window. "After Carl loads the barbecue in our trailer, we're hitting the road. We're beat."

Indigo thumped the last bottle on the bar then hugged Jesse. "I really appreciate all that you and Carl did today. Not just the wonderful food, but you must have personally called the people in town to be sure they'd come."

"I didn't use a phone, silly." Jesse squeezed Indigo and stepped back. "I have jungle drums."

"Well, it meant a lot to me. Here I am, a newcomer, a stranger, and..." She pulled in a deep breath. "It—it just meant a lot, that's all." Her voice wavered.

Jesse's lips tightened. "Don't you go all soft on me, Blue. Besides, this is going to cost you more than my bill. You owe me a massage."

Indigo gave her a watery smile. "I owe you a lot more than that."

"Oh, hon, you don't owe me spit. I like to see the good guys win. And speaking of that..." She pointed at Danovan. "You do right by this lady now, y'hear?"

"Yes, ma'am, I will."

Indigo turned her back to Jesse. She shot Danovan a disgusted glare, one side of her lip lifted as if he were two-day-old summer road kill.

What the hell did I do? Air raid sirens went off in his head. He had no reason for the guilt gutbomb, but one went off anyway.

Jesse said, "Well, I'm outta here. I'm taking that sexy hunk out there home to bed." She winked at

Indigo. "I'll see you Wednesday at yoga." Waving fingers over her shoulder, she sauntered out.

Danovan had no idea what had changed in the past four hours, but it was clear something had. Something major. His stomach squirmed. "What's the matter?"

With snick of the door closing behind Jesse, Indigo's face fell into hard planes. "Nothing." The compressed line of her lips hardly moved.

"What do you mean, nothing? You're looking at me like I'm a mouse turd on toast."

In her hesitation, time bloated, looming and ugly. Something was wrong. His heart tried to hammer its way out of his chest. *Bad wrong.*

Crossing her arms, she tilted her head as if regarding him for the first time. "If I were to ask them, what would the Boldens say about you? As an employee, I mean."

The gut-bomb expanded to a mushroom cloud. He put a hand to his stomach to try to contain it. "Who talked to you?" He spit the words.

"What difference does that make?"

She took two steps before he grabbed her arm. She turned on him, rancor flaring in her eyes. He dropped his hand. "Who was it?"

"She said her name was Roxy." She spit the words back at him.

Of course it was. He'd known someone would tell Indigo eventually. The rumors were just too juicy not to spread. After the confrontation with

Roxy in the supermarket, he should have known she'd be the one to do it. "Roxy is a vindictive bitch."

A pained certainty spread over Indigo's features before her face fell closed of emotion. "Funny, she said you'd say that very thing."

"Roxy hates me enough to spread half truths to destroy my career. She—"

Indigo moved so fast that when she slammed her palm on the bar, he jumped. The hollow smack echoed off the rafters. "Do you think I give a *shit* about her?" Indigo's face contorted in fury. "Were you even working for them when you applied for this position?" Her eyes scanned his. "No, you were fired, right? I can see it on your face." She almost whispered, "I *trusted* you."

Alarm poured into the toxic brew in his stomach, caustic, burning. Her reaction was beyond his worst imaginings.

"But that's not the whole truth. Let me explain—"

"No. I'm done listening to you. I knew better than to trust my own judgment." She put her hands over her ears and closed her eyes, as if looking at him hurt.

He hadn't realized how much her opinion mattered until she looked at him with such contempt. His mind fibrillated, trying to find a way to make this better. "Indigo, this is not as big a deal as you think. Just let me—"

At his touch on her arm, she recoiled. Her eyes flew open, and the hurt burned off in a flashpoint of heat. "No big deal? If this winery fails, I have nothing. Nowhere to go. No one to go to. And no money to get there, even if I did." Her voice cracked—the sound of ice breaking. "You arrogant ass—this is *all* I have!" Her hand whipped out, and she slapped him. "How *dare* you?"

His cheek stung, but it was his heart that took the worst of the blow.

She stood frozen, staring in horror. Whether the horror was directed at him or herself, he couldn't tell. Then she whirled and ran. The door slammed, and he cringed. She ran past the windows of the porch and disappeared around the side of the building.

What the hell was he supposed to do now? She hadn't said he was fired, but that didn't mean he wasn't.

"Oh, bullshit, DiCarlo." His voice sounded loud in the cavernous room. He had just lost a lot more than a job. And the sad thing was he hadn't realized what he had until now—until it was gone.

You should have told her. He'd known how bad it would look if she found out from someone else. But obviously he hadn't let himself consider just *how* bad it would look. The disappointment in her sad eyes was hard enough to take. But it was the defeat behind it that made him squirm inside.

He'd wrecked her.

And now he had to make it right. Somehow. "God*damm*it!" He slammed his fist into the bar. The pain hit, a searing wake-up call jerking his mind from its downward spiral.

REPERCUSSIONS POUNDED WITH every footfall as Indigo ran to the only safe haven that remained—Bob's cabin.

You can run the winery yourself.

No, you can't.

She didn't know enough yet. Besides, even with Danovan, the two of them working twelve hours a day, they could barely keep up, and the crush was only four months away. She'd have to find another manager.

But you can't afford another one. And if you could, how can you trust yourself to hire another?

Her heavy breath caught on the wad of betrayal in her chest, and she stumbled to a stop, hands on knees, until she could breathe past it.

I'll just sell the damned thing. I never should have attempted this to begin with.

But as she jogged into the dooryard and saw the cabin windows reflecting the last of the sunset, she knew she wouldn't leave The Widow. This was her last lifeline to Harry.

No. Time to stop lying to yourself. Harry is gone. One strangled sob slipped past the taut muscles of her throat before she locked it down.

The truth was that the winery was her last

tether to the best of her life. The golden time, when she'd been safe—safe to be who she was, and it hadn't mattered that the rest of the world thought she was nothing.

Because Harry thought she was everything.

She had tried to hang on to that. To believe she was *that* Indigo Blue. But that certainty had slipped away bit by bit. Like the smell of Harry on his favorite shirt, it faded until now it was just a sad, out-of-place Hawaiian shirt hanging in her closet.

And she was back to being the sad, out-of-place misfit she'd been before Harry picked her up with his eyes.

Climbing the stairs of the porch, she ran her fingers over the worn-smooth wood banister. How many times had Harry put his hand there? Or Bob his? God, how she wished for their wisdom now. She didn't know what to do. There was no one to ask.

She made it through the door but could go no farther. She leaned her back against the closed door, and when her knees buckled, she slid down until she sat, legs splayed, on the floor.

She hadn't trusted anyone to hold her secrets. Until she came here and put her trust in Danovan.

What do I do now?

HE WASN'T GIVING UP. Not again. He was going up there to talk to her. Even if he had to bellow through the door, he'd tell her the whole truth.

Though what he'd do after that, he had no idea.

First, though, he needed to change. It felt like he'd put on these clothes a week ago. Besides, it would give Indigo a few minutes to calm. He strode over and opened the door marked Private. Noticing the light on in Indigo's office, he turned it off on the way by. At the door to his room, he flipped through his ring of keys, looking for the right one.

Metal jingled and Barney walked out of Indigo's office, looked at Danovan, yawned and sat, staring up at him.

"She forgot you?"

Two hours ago, that would have been as unimaginable as her slap. Well, he'd take Barney with him to the cabin. She might not open the door for him, but she'd open it for Barney.

"You want to go see Indigo?"

Barney's tail thumped the floor once. Twice.

Those sad eyes bored into him. How could a dog's opinion make him feel even worse? "You're right. I screwed up. Big time. And I'm sorry. Maybe I can make it right if you'll help me." He extended a hand, slow and easy, just in case. "Please?"

Barney sniffed his fingers then licked them. Danovan smiled, feeling entirely too grateful to the floppy little fleabag. He patted Barney's head and ran his fingers over his surprisingly velvety ears. "Thank you. You're a big pers—er, dog."

Ten minutes later, he was ready. Danovan had found some twine to loop through the dog's collar, but he needn't have bothered. Once out the door, Barney took off, heading for the cabin. Danovan ran after him at the end of the leash, trying to keep up.

They turned off at the end of the vines and Barney stopped in the cabin's dooryard; they both stood panting. Warm light spilled from the window on the covered porch, but through it, he only saw an empty living room. When he'd caught his breath, he looked at Barney. "You're going to help, right?"

Barney ignored him, stepped to the end of the twine leash and tugged.

Serves you right, looking to a dog for help.

He had a bad case of the nerves. Sweating in spite of the chill air, his stomach felt like a bag of popcorn in a microwave. "Okay, we're going. Just give me a second to prepare."

He could no longer imagine living in a place where Indigo wasn't. He remembered her on the tractor, sitting like a queen surveying her kingdom. Her quick intelligence. The way she bit the corner of her bottom lip when she was thinking. Her smile. Her sad eyes looking at him like he *was* somebody.

Somebody she admired.

That was over now, and he didn't know how to get it back. Other than to spill his guts all over the floor and hope she could see through the stupidity and into his heart. Because in spite of everything, in his heart, he meant well.

And standing in the yard like a hound—with a hound—isn't going to make that happen.

But his feet wouldn't move. This was too important. He needed some kind of strategy. His mind sorted and discarded lame ideas while his guts did the jitterbug.

Come on, DiCarlo. You're a problem solver. So get with—

Barney tugged, the twine broke and the mutt bolted.

"Dammit, come back here!" He chased his only advantage onto the porch.

Tail whipping, Barney stood at the door, looking at Danovan as if to say, "You're the one with opposable thumbs. Get the door!"

"Thanks a lot, friend." Danovan grabbed the mutt's collar, fisted his shaking hand and knocked.

"Go away." The voice came from just the other side of the door, but lower, as if she were sitting against it.

"You forgot your dog."

"Oh!" Scrabbling noises, then the door opened, only a few inches. Enough for him to see that she still wore that pretty dress.

No tears. That's a good sign. But when she peered through the crack, the dead look in her eyes frightened him. "Indigo, I…"

She bent a bit and made kissing noises at the dog. "I'm so sorry, Barn. Come on, I'll give you a treat."

Barney would have gone inside if Danovan hadn't had a death grip on his collar. The dog whined.

Turncoat.

"Can I have my dog now?" She didn't look up.

"I need to talk to you."

"I've said all there is to say." She straightened and looked him in the eye for the first time. "Except that you're fired. First thing in the morning, you need to leave."

He stood, mouth open, ready to say something that would change her mind. Words swirled in his brain, but none of them coalesced to anything coherent.

She gave a snort of irritation. "Can I have my dog now?"

"No."

"What?"

"I'm taking him hostage." *You're what?* "I'm—I'm keeping him until you listen to me. And if he bites me, it'll be on you."

She sighed. "Great. His tail is wagging. Obviously he's as bad a judge of character as I."

"Well." He snatched at more words. Anything to keep her from slamming the door on his last chance. "You had your say. I'm keeping him until I've had mine. And bear in mind I've never owned a dog. I don't have any dog food. I think I have some ham in the fridge I could give him, but last I looked, it had kind of a green tinge…"

She gave a ragged sigh. "You're not coming in."

"Okay, how about the porch?" A trickle of hope seeped into his overloaded brain, cool and sweet. *First step.* He tried not to think of the thousand steps to follow; he was on a tightrope over the Grand Canyon. Holding Barney's collar, he backed up to give her space, stepped to one of the chairs and sat. Barney plopped beside him.

She followed, but rather than sit next to him, she leaned on the porch rail, arms crossed. "Ten minutes. Then you'll give me my dog, and we're done."

Time stretched as he tried to gather the words to the story he'd never told before. The full moon created a photo-negative view of the vineyard and made Indigo's dress glow with creamy incandescence. The crickets scratched out love songs in the vines. He let go of Barney's collar, focused on the peaceful scene and let the words come however they might.

"A few months after Esperanza was born, Lissette decided to pick up her life where she'd left off. By life, I mean partying." He shook his head. "When we first met, she'd go to the club maybe twice a month. When she got pregnant, she continued to go but swore she only drank soda, and I believed her. I didn't say anything for fear she'd rebel and go more often." Bouncing his foot bled off some of the jittery energy zipping along his nerves.

"When the newness of motherhood wore off, Lissette found that being a queen was nowhere near as fun as being a princess. She wasn't used to coming second, even if it was to her own baby. I'm not saying she didn't love Esperanza. She did. When it suited her. She wanted to hire a nurse to handle the parts of motherhood that didn't interest her. I refused. We fought. And her best friend, Roxy, was right there to remind Lissette of all the fun she was missing."

He shifted focus from the moon to Indigo. She hadn't moved, just stared at him as if he were a slight danger that bore watching.

"The more we argued, the more she'd go out at night. After last call, she'd come home drunk and belligerent, and we'd pick up the argument where we'd left off. Then she'd sleep like the dead until noon, and I was terrified to leave Esperanza alone with her in the morning. So I'd take the baby to her grandmother, explaining that Lissette needed her rest." A sound of disgust burst from his nose like a sneeze—just as spontaneous.

"Her parents knew what was going on. I tried to talk to them at different times, but I was the bad guy who'd ruined their daughter to begin with. They didn't say anything to Lissette. They didn't do anything to try to help. I guess they figured we could lie in the bed we'd made. But that bed had become a war zone."

Don't think about it. Just say it.

"Lissette wanted to go out that night." He put his elbows on his knees and burrowed his fingers into his scalp. "But I had work to do—we were on a timeline to introduce a new merlot, and the wine had flaws. I told her that I couldn't watch Esperanza and work, too." He took a deep breath and made himself slow down. "She just laughed, said the baby was sleeping, and arm in arm with Roxy, she walked out."

It can't hurt any worse on the outside than it does on the inside.

"I was at my wit's end. I sat in the dark for the longest time, thinking. I'd applied for vintner jobs in Napa, hoping that maybe Lissette and I could start over, away from all the influences that were tainting our marriage. Maybe if it was just us, she'd have to grow up and take on the responsibility of being a mother and a wife. Things couldn't go on the way they were.

"I checked on Esperanza. I set a timer. I checked on her every hour. She was sleeping. Peaceful." His breath was coming faster, breaking his sentences into short bursts.

Don't feel, just say.

"I'd gotten a call that morning. From the owner of a Napa winery who needed a vintner. It wasn't as large or prestigious as Bacchanal, but they were getting good reviews. They had a nice Chardonnay I thought I could improve. I couldn't talk during working hours, so I decided to call him back that evening. If he had a good offer, I was planning to tell Lissette when she came home from the club."

Indigo uncrossed her arms and rested her hands on the railing.

"The timer went off in the middle of my sales pitch." He had to move. He stood, strode to the end of the porch, then back. "I turned it off and continued dazzling this guy with my accomplishments, brilliance and wit." He stopped pacing to spit over the railing. "Oh, yeah, I was brilliant." He continued pacing.

"When I hung up a half hour later, I had a job offer. I was feeling pretty smug. I went to check on—" His voice cracked, along with his detachment. He was back in that room.

"The nightlight was on, but dim. I thought she was sleeping until I leaned close. She wasn't breathing." His chest heaved. His diaphragm was so tight, he couldn't catch his own breath.

"I'm—I'm not real clear on what happened after that. I gave her mouth-to-mouth and CPR, I know that. For a long time. Then I ran for my phone to call 9-1-1. I fell. Hit my head." He rubbed his fingers over the scar above his eye and tried to stiffen the words that had gone all wobbly. "When they got there..." He panted. "The paramedics. It was too late. I knew that. But I screamed at them to try."

She touched his arm on his way by. He kept walking.

"They said it wasn't my fault. That crib death was no one's fault. But I knew. I knew, because I'd turned off the timer. If I'd have gone in—"

"You can't know that." Her voice came soft, out of the dark.

"My baby—" He stopped. Stopped talking, stopped moving. *Look at the moon. Listen to the crickets. Breathe. Listen.*

After a time, the panic stilled a bit. A drop of sweat rolled down his chest. He found his voice. "To my wife and her family, it was my fault. They divorced me faster than I'd known it was legal.

"Her dad fired me the day of the funeral."

It's over. No matter what happens, that's over. You're still standing.

"Danovan, you know it wasn't your fault, right?" Her words came to him, small and sad.

He put on his interview voice. "The point is, my former employer will tell you that I was giving away trade secrets, but he's lying. Yes, the owner of the most respected winery in the valley is going to tell you I did worse than fail at my job—that I tried to hurt his business. But it's not true."

A deformed laugh escaped, an ugly sound. He crossed his arms, tucking his hands safely away. "You're right. I used you, Indigo. Every owner in the area knew me—knew what happened. Knew I was getting screwed. But they didn't have the balls to hire me. They wouldn't take a chance of pissing off their biggest competition, because King Bolden rules this valley."

"W-why didn't you leave? Take that job in Napa?"

Chin up, she stood her ground. He had to give her that.

"Because this is my home!" His pain boomed off the roof of the porch and rolled over the vines. A smoking hole opened in the bottom of his chest and the anger drained out in a gurgling rush through his guts, down his legs and out the bottom of his burning feet. He whispered, "Esperanza is here. I won't leave her."

A strangled sound came from the shadows. He looked close, noticing what he hadn't before: moonlight shone off two silvery tracks on her cheeks.

A churning hunger rose to fill the vacuum left by the story. Every slight he'd endured, every grief-stricken night, every wrong he'd withstood and committed coalesced, filling him with an unwanted craving. He fisted his shaking hands to hold it in—to not reach for her. Because no matter the cost, he couldn't take something that hadn't been offered—something he hadn't earned.

They stood, eyes locked, the tension between them as palpable as the crackle of ozone before an electrical storm.

She broke first. Stretching out a hand, her sad eyes reached into his gut, touching where it hurt. "I want—"

His hands took her bare arms and hauled her to him. When she'd have stumbled, he held her up, taking her with cruel, starving kisses, taking what he could no longer breathe without.

And she gave.

She matched his need, tearing at his hair, climbing him to wrap her long legs around his waist, moaning when he bit her lip. He took a step, resting her bottom on the porch railing. She tore at the buttons of his shirt. He ran his hands over the satin-smooth skin of her legs, from her ankle to the edge of lace at her panties. They were damp.

It almost sent him over the edge. His tongue parried with the thrusts his hips wanted.

He didn't want to think. He was sick to death of thinking. He wanted to feel.

Ripping his shirt from his jeans, she unbuttoned it and pulled it down his arms. He had to let go for just a second, to discard it. But that was too long. He sucked the skin under her ear, at the hollow of her collarbone. "I need you." The words broke from him.

"Take me." Her breath in his ear shot straight to his crotch. His cock strained against the denim prison. She reached down, running a palm over him. "Hurry."

He looped a finger through the lace at the top

of her thighs. The scrap tore easily. Then she was in his hand, plump, moist, hot.

"Hurry." She panted.

"But…I wanted…" His breath came in short bursts, catching on something in his throat. "This isn't the way…I don't have anything."

"It's okay." She leaned back enough to look him in the eye. "Trust me."

He memorized the moonlight on her lust-soft features—he wanted to burn the vision on the surface of his mind, for when he was gone.

Zipper teeth released and her fingers closed around him, tugging. He bucked his hips and moaned. She guided him to the hot center of her.

He needed to plunge, to bury himself in her warmth, to take what she so freely offered. But he couldn't. She was damaged, and this was her first time too.

She whimpered.

"Look at me." It came out a growl from his clenched teeth. He'd made so many mistakes… he wasn't making another. He fisted a hand in her hair and pulled her head back. Her neck, pale and exposed, made him want to bite it.

Her slitted eyes begged him to. "I'm not going to break. Please."

He plunged into her with one violent thrust. She closed around him, a tight velvet furnace.

She made a guttural sound, deep in her throat. It sounded like, "More."

He took the skin of her neck in his teeth and plunged again. And again, speeding up, trying to catch the pulse at his core, always just a bit behind. She strained too, her heels digging into his butt, her nails into his back.

Closer. Frantic, he slid his hands to her butt and pulled her to the top of his hip bones. Her muscles clenched in the most intimate embrace. She screamed release into his mouth. He took it and ground into her, the explosion hitting him like a wall, light bursting on the backs of his eyelids to fall in a shower of sparks.

CHAPTER FOURTEEN

INDIGO CAME AWAKE with a click. From the delicate blush on the ceiling, she deduced dawn was just breaking. The weight on her chest turned out to be an arm. She carefully turned her head. Danovan lay on his side, head on his arm, sleeping. The taut lines of his jaw looked softer in this light. In his sleep-slackened face, she had a glimpse of a young boy.

After hearing his story last night, the niggle of doubt no longer whispered warnings. She understood why he'd lied to get the job. She didn't like it—but she understood. Her gaze snagged on the razor-line scar through his eyebrow. She'd never see it as a sexy flaw to his almost perfect face again. The scar went much deeper. It had hurt to witness his story's telling last night, but all she could do for him was to stand and listen. Take his story, his pain, hoping to ease it.

But what happened after that had nothing to do with sympathy.

She had experienced three kinds of sex in her life. For the first, she'd been gratefully unconscious. The second was Harry.

Harry's lovemaking was like a soaking spring rain.

Danovan was a Category 2 hurricane.

Turning back to the ceiling, she watched the line of sun slowly inch across.

She hadn't known… Cheeks burning, she was grateful for the few moments alone with her thoughts before she'd have to face him.

After the explosion of pain and lust on the porch, Danovan had carried her inside, and they'd spent most of the night exploring the more subtle shades of a storm. He'd awoken her body with mumbled kisses and worshipful hands. She opened to him, and he made her feel…too much.

The emotions he'd churned up hadn't settled with sleep. She felt raw, as if he'd scoured off her protective layer, leaving her exposed. Hurricanes could do major damage.

Danovan was so close she felt it when he took a deep breath. "Good morning, beautiful." He watched her with sleepy eyes and a one-sided smile.

"Um, hi." She rolled away, face flaming, and sat up, holding the sheet to her chest. "I'd better…" Dammit, where were her clothes? She barely recalled him unbuttoning her dress on the way to the bedroom. She shot a glance around the room. Not even a bra? Or her underwear? Not like they'd cover much anyway, but she was not parading in front of him butt-naked.

"Where are you going?" He hissed in a breath. "Oh, God."

At the light touch on the back of her arm, she twisted back to him.

"Indigo, I hurt you."

Bruise fingerprints dotted her biceps. That must have happened when he lifted her...

He trailed fingers down her neck "Oh, shit, Indigo, I'm sorry."

Judging from the small aches, she had bruises there, too.

"It's okay—"

"No, it's not." The guilt in his eyes touched bruises inside her. "Come here." He put a hand at her waist to tug her back into their close-quarters nest.

"I—I've got to get up." There wasn't so much as a washcloth to hide her body beneath. "I've got to do my yoga and get breakfast and feed Barney..." Trying to cover her body with words, she made a dash for the bathroom, not breathing until the door closed behind her.

How did she get herself into these— *Oh, crap*.

The cold reflection of last night in the mirror slapped her. Her eyes were as wild as her hair, her cheeks were scoured with beard burn and loving bruises flowed down her neck. She touched them, unable to avoid knowing any longer.

She'd enjoyed it. Enjoyed everything that Danovan had done to her body. Everything she'd done to his. She forced herself to face the truth in the mirror. She hadn't only enjoyed last night; she'd wallowed in it.

And she felt as if there should be a big red *A* carved in her chest.

Unable to bear the acid wash of shame, she moved to the shower and twisted the knobs.

She and Harry had a good sex life. They'd come together in a soft, loving place. A safe, sheltering place. Nothing about last night had been safe. She stepped in and let the water cool her hot face. Danovan had made her scream.

And she wasn't yet strong enough for that.

If she could hardly face herself in the mirror, how would she face him? Work with him?

Once again, she'd gotten herself into a mess, and she'd have to bumble her way out of it.

Ten minutes later, wrapped in her floor-length dressing gown, her hair in a towel, she stepped out of the bathroom.

Danovan, in jeans and no shirt, sat on the bed, bending to tie his shoe. When he sat up, his chest, stomach muscles and the line of hair that disappeared into the waist of his jeans made her fingers curl with wanting to touch. His hair was as wild as hers had been, and beard stubble darkened his cheeks. But it was the soft look in his chocolate eyes more than the hand he held out that pulled her across the room to sit on the bed beside him.

He took her chin, gave her a kiss then scanned her face. "Are you okay?"

"Sure. Why wouldn't I be?" She tucked away the tail of the towel on her head. "But we've got a busy day, finishing cleanup from yesterday." *Was it only yesterday?* "It really went better than I—"

"I'm not referring to the business."

She tightened the belt of her dressing gown.

"I know that last night was the first time you've been with a man since your husband. If you're feeling a little weird, I think that would be natural." His gaze was making her stomach jump.

Barney walked in, crossed the room and sat, tail thumping the floor, grinning at them.

Saved by a dog collar jingle. "Good morning, Barn." She bent to stroke his ears. "You want some breakfast?"

"Indigo."

His deep voice brought her head up. If he wasn't going to let it go, she'd have to say something. "Last night was…" Nothing she was prepared to talk about. "Look, the winery is at a critical stage. It's going to take everything we have to make this fall's crush a success." She stood. "I think we need to focus on that."

When he stood, he brought with him the scent of their lovemaking. The memory of his fierce eyes and taut face above her weakened her knees with the longing to sink back into that sex-tousled bed.

Focus, Indigo. To pull her mind from her hormone-soaked thoughts, she imagined standing in front of Sondra, her face telegraphing lust when Danovan walked in. That worked.

Until Danovan took her hands, turning her to face him.

To keep him from saying something she wasn't ready to hear, she blurted, "I really would rather the other employees don't know that…that we…"

"That we are in a relationship?" He looked calm, serene, even.

In a… "Danovan, I—"

"Please don't." He put a finger to her lips. "Don't deny us this. It's a good thing. Possibly the best thing, for us both." He squeezed her hands. "If you need time, you've got it. The next move is yours. If you don't want anyone to know, I can live with that. Just please don't say that when we're alone—that I can't do this." He cupped her cheek and kissed her. It was deep and honest and open, as if there were nothing to worry over—nothing to fear.

It made her want so badly to believe.

He stepped away. "Now, about the business. I'm going to make you a deal. Because I owe you."

"You don't—"

"Oh, yeah, I do. I lied. And for you and me to have a chance…" He glanced at the bed. "You have no reason to believe me. I've destroyed your trust, and I couldn't live with myself if you ever wondered if I tried to manipulate—" He looked at the ceiling and blew out a huff of frustration.

"Look. Here's the deal. If you agree, I will stay at The Widow long enough to teach you everything you need to know to run this business."

When she tried to talk, he raised a hand.

"And I'm not taking a paycheck in the meantime."

"But—"

"I've made up my mind. These are the only terms I'll work under. Take it or leave it."

A WEEK LATER, Danovan stood at the bottom of the drive, stretching, waiting. When Indigo had mentioned wanting to get back into jogging, he'd invited her to join him on a morning run. He lifted his foot and pulled it to his butt, feeling the stretch in his thigh. He hadn't run since he took this job, but that was changing, starting today. He hoped she could keep up.

It was weird. In one way, they'd become closer the past couple of weeks. At work they were simpatico to the point of finishing each other's sentences. The open house had doubled the foot traffic in the tasting room, and they'd signed several local restaurants and bars. He sensed in her none of the reticence he had before; she was all in.

But outside of the winery, she was busy. Too busy to go out, too busy to stay in and hang out, too busy to even grocery shop together. Granted, her woo-woo side business had picked up. She'd added another yoga class, and her massage clients were cutting into her evening hours. Even the entire bicycling troupe now lined up for massages after their ride.

And lying in bed at night imagining her hands all over those men was getting old.

Finally, desperate for some time alone with her, he'd suggested running together, even though these morning runs had always been his solitary time. He jogged in place while he waited, trying to stay warmed up. June temps soared during the day, but the mornings still held the damp cool that the vines loved.

He wasn't oblivious. He knew that Indigo had second, third and probably tenth thoughts since the incredible night they'd spent together. She hadn't been ready. He'd known that. But in telling her about the night he lost Esperanza, the emotion he'd stuffed away had come back, concentrated from the compression. Once he got started, it wouldn't be stopped.

You're a selfish bastard.

Indigo was a fragile, still-grieving widow. He'd known it. But it hadn't stopped him from diving into her open arms. He fancied himself an educated, cultured man, yet that night he was little more than a brute. The memory of her bruises made him want to beat the crap out of himself. Since that was a physical impossibility, he'd been doing it mentally.

He wanted to be a better man. He wanted to

be the kind of man who deserved a woman like Indigo Blue.

He looked up at the sound of running on asphalt. Indigo jogged down the hill toward him, pushing a...*wheelbarrow*?

It was a wheelbarrow. And in it, riding like a pasha in a litter, sat Barney.

When she stopped in front of him, laughing, his heart lightened. He put on a mock-stern face. "Really?"

"Hey, Barn and I logged hundreds of miles in the Hollywood Hills, with him in a Radio Flyer."

"Yeah, but everyone knows people in Hollywood are weird. They expect it."

"Dude. Love me, love my dog."

If only it were that easy. He sighed. "Okay, but if anyone sees us, it's going to put a serious dent in my reputation."

"Oh, quit your whining and try to keep up." She took off.

Watching her from behind, he kind of hoped he couldn't. He'd happily chase that athletic body and those sky-blue jogging shorts all day. Until the damned dog sat up, obscuring his view. He sped up to come alongside her. Her hair was pulled back into a high, curly ponytail that swayed as she ran. Her relaxed face made him realize it had been a long time since he'd seen it that way.

"God, it's beautiful here, isn't it?" Her cheeks were pink with the exertion, her lips red.

"Sure is."

Looking straight ahead, she smiled. "I'm talking about the scenery."

"Oh, yeah, that too."

They ate up ground as the road wound between hills the color of corn silk. Live oaks gathered in the hollows, hovering over the road. The sky had lightened, but the sun hadn't yet risen above the hills. His muscles warmed and his body came alive, humming like a well-tuned engine. He pulled in damp morning air, breathing easily. When the endorphins kicked in, he remembered what he'd missed all the months of mornings he'd skipped running, going to work instead.

They ran for a long time to the sound of their shoes slapping on the pavement and the gossip of birds. No cars passed. He decided to take his shot. She couldn't ignore him out here. "Why are you avoiding me?"

Her profile didn't change. "We're in the middle of nowhere. The closest living thing is that cow we passed a while ago." She breathed easily. "We work together twelve hours a day. I'd hardly call that avoiding."

"And yet I'm starting to feel like our night together was my imagination." He got a couple of pants in. "I know I was a bit crazed that night. But I thought… Why won't you go out with me?"

"Do you want to rest?"

He shook his head. "You feel like you cheated on your husband, don't you?"

Her head whipped around.

"It's not a huge leap. You loved him. He's all you've known." He kept his eyes front, hoping she'd be more relaxed if he was offhand about it. "I'm probably very different than him."

He took her silence as assent and hoped to hell he was right.

"I don't mean to push you. I just want you to know that I'm here." He crammed words between trying to breathe. "You take all the time you need. I'll wait as long as it takes." He touched her arm. "But you should know—"

Her brows tented over worried eyes.

"I miss you."

She stopped in the shade. "I think we'd better head back." She put down the handles of the wheelbarrow and squinted at him. "Are you feeling okay?"

Apparently her worry wasn't for his feelings. He stopped and leaned over, hands on his knees, catching his breath. "So now my missing you means I'm having a heart attack?"

"No, no, of course not."

Hope rose when she took his hand, but she was feeling for his pulse. "You just look tired, that's all."

He pulled his arm away. "I'm fine."

She watched him out of the corner of her eye. "I know you are."

Shit. That's it. You're back on a jogging regimen, starting today.

She lifted the lazy mutt from the bucket of the wheelbarrow and set him on the pavement. "Go on, Barn. Want a drink?" She pointed to a small stream that emerged from a culvert under the road. The dog trotted over and drank in slurping gulps.

Maybe he could distract her from watching him take stampeding buffalo breaths. "You know your dog is ugly, right?"

"Hey, just because your ego is bruised, don't take it out on Barney."

"I'm just stating a fact. And why would you want a dog who can't run?"

She put her hand on her hip. "Why would I want a jogging partner who can't?"

"I'm just saying. His snout is longer than his legs, and I think he borrowed his feet from a much bigger dog. He looks perpetually depressed, and—"

"I think he's cute. And at least he has a sweet personality, which is more than I can say for you."

Barney stopped splashing water and sniffed the weeds.

"Barney, come."

Muzzle and ears dripping, he trotted up to the road.

"Sit."

He plopped on his butt, back legs splayed to the side.

Indigo squatted and petted him, making cooing noises. "He just doesn't know you, does he, Barn?" Lips tight, she glared up at Danovan. "You say something nice to him."

"The dog?"

"Yes. You hurt his feelings."

He crossed his arms. "It's a dog. It has no idea what I'm saying." *So why did you talk to him that night?* Desperation, that's all it was.

"Think of one nice thing to say about him. He's waiting."

"Oh, Jesus."

The dog looked up at him and thumped his tail.

"Okay. His ears are soft. Can we go now?"

Her quick kiss on his cheek granted absolution. Her carefree smile hit his soft parts.

They only talked of business, and it wasn't until he was back at the winery and in the shower that he realized she'd never answered his question.

"TONY, DON'T FORGET the stretching I showed you. Keep that up, and you'll nail that Plow Pose." Indigo stood at the door to her studio, ushering out her evening yoga class. "Good night, Karen."

"Thanks, Indigo. See you next week." Karen walked to the door of the winery, but it opened before she reached for the knob.

Danovan held the door for the rest of the students, then limped back into the hallway.

Indigo pulled her sweater closed over the T-shirt that left her midriff bare as she walked to the doorway of her studio. "What happened?"

"Nothing. I'm fine."

"You're obviously not. Was there an accident?"

He walked stiff-kneed to his door and stood flipping keys on his key ring. "No accident. I went jogging on purpose."

She should have known. "Aw, poor baby."

He winced. "Fine, insult to injury. Just rub it in."

Ask him.

He found the key and slipped it in the lock. "Give me a day to regroup, and I'll meet you Friday morning, same time."

She tugged the belt of her sweater tighter.

He opened his door. "You're locking up, right?"

She nodded. *Ask. Him. In.*

He stepped into his apartment. "Okay, well, I'm just going to soak my sore ego in a hot tub now."

"Wait."

He turned.

"Come back in here." She didn't wait to see if he followed, just turned and walked. She'd been avoiding him, his hints and the questions in his eyes for too long. Well, not only *his*. She saw those same questions reflected in her mirror every morning. And now the only question left was did she have enough guts to do something about it?

"Where are we going?"

She led him around the privacy screen to her massage table. "I'm going to go lock up. You take off your shirt and pants."

He eyed the table with a smile. "Will that handle our weight?"

"Massage isn't something I joke about." She crossed her arms, hugging her sides. "You're in pain. I can fix that. Do you want me to?"

"I'm sorry." Danovan's contrite tone said he knew he'd overstepped. "Yes, please."

"Okay, get undressed." She'd taken only a step when she stopped. "You do have underwear on, don't you?"

"Yes'm."

"Good. You can keep them on." She continued walking into the hall, through the door to the tasting room, flipping off lights as she went. *How much to say?* She did want to go out with Danovan. Did want…something. Just not everything. Not the nuclear explosion of emotion and intimacy they'd shared on the porch. She'd never experienced anything like that—like standing at the top of a high place, clutching a railing, fearing not that she'd fall but that she'd throw herself off. The yin/yang of thrill and terror unsettled, even as it tempted her.

And she'd been unsettled ever since.

Locking the front door of the tasting room, she flipped on the porch light and then strode through the darkened quiet to her studio.

Danovan sat in his boxers on the massage table.

She walked to her music player and inserted a rainforest CD. The sounds of a gentle rain and exotics seemed to close in the space. "Have you ever had a massage?" Perusing her large collection of essential oils, she looked for one that would be masculine but soothing at the same time.

"Um, no." The lines on his forehead telegraphed dubious.

"In that case, get ready for an amazing experience." She pulled from the back a bottle of sage and cedar wood oil she saved for special clients. "Just lie on your back."

While he complied, she rolled a towel. When she touched his leg, he jumped. She slipped the towel under the back of his knees. "This will relax your lumbar spine."

"Oh, okay." He looked up at the ceiling with a focused stare and tense hands.

"Danovan, relax." She squirted oil into her palm and rubbed her hands to warm it. The rich earthy scent filled the air. "You know how you're good with wine? How you know a wine's strengths and weaknesses from just tasting it?"

"Yeah."

"Well, this is what I'm good at. I can tell your body's strengths and weaknesses through my

hands. But only if you relax enough to trust me."
She looked down on him. "Can you do that?"

He scanned her face. His shoulders lost their
tight line. "I can."

"Good. Now, close your eyes. Listen to the music
and breathe in the scent. Let your mind wander."

She started at his feet, using hard pressure on
the bottom, squeezing the heel, separating and
pulling the toes. When he moaned, she knew she
had him.

"Roll over."

"Hmm."

"Come on, the best is yet to come."

"In that case…" Danovan rolled over.

"Just put your face in that keyhole in the top of
the table and relax."

His calves were tight and lactic-acid-tender, so
she went slowly.

The music and aromatherapy worked on her
anxiety as well, calming her jittery thoughts. Even
so, she was to his shoulders before she figured
out the right sequence of words to use. "Could
we start over?"

"Oh, yeah. The foot massage was heaven." He
sounded almost dreamy.

"No, I mean…personally." She took a breath.
"See, I'm not very adept at all this. I think we
skipped a couple of dozen steps there on the
porch, and I kind of lost my place."

He would have gotten up, but she pressed his

shoulders back to the table. "I'm not done yet." She worked her way down his biceps, kneading, loosening the tightness in the muscle. Besides, this would all be easier if she didn't have to see his face.

"Is it Harry?"

"Yes. No. I don't know. I think that's part of it. But mostly, I'm just confused. This—thing between us—happened so fast. I feel like we jumped in the deep end, and I don't know how to swim."

This time, when he pushed up from the table, she let him. He sat up and, legs dangling off the side of the table, he took her hand. He turned it over, studying it. "Such capable hands. They're soft, feminine hands, but so strong."

He looked up with an expression that shattered her serenity. He cared. A lot.

"You won't drown. I'll hold you up."

"I don't need some man—"

"Only until you learn to tread water."

He ran his fingers over her palm in an intimate caress that made her shiver. Or maybe it was that gorgeous face of his. Apparently her leading-man vaccination had completely worn off. Heat spread over the skin of her chest. She had no interest in a booster.

"I've seen how fast you learn, Indigo Blue." He leaned over, cupped a hand behind her neck and kissed her forehead. "We'll go back and take those steps we missed." He eased off the table and reached for his clothes. "Starting tomorrow."

His words released the regret that had weighted her for the past week. When she breathed out, it dissipated in the scented air. "I'd like that."

"Thank you for the massage. You were right about that, too." His clothes fisted in his hand, he gave her one last lingering look then turned to go.

She watched him stride away, wondering how a man wearing nothing but boxers managed to look so...imperial.

CHAPTER FIFTEEN

VINEYARD SUMMERS ARE THE BEST.

Indigo adjusted her floppy hat to block the rising sun. Not a leaf marred the pristine row stretching ahead of her. She took pride in keeping the soil tilled and fresh. The pace in the vineyard slowed as the grapes grew. Her work in the vines was now mostly done by hand: tucking the questing shoots back into the vines and leafing around the growing clusters, to assure they received the right amount of sunlight. Mothering the vines in the cool mornings brought her peace—she liked to think that the crush from these grapes would be just a tiny bit sweeter for it.

"And next, singing bluebirds will be circling your head, weaving in the stray hairs for you." She smiled. Lately her life did resemble a Disney movie. The market had good things to say about The Widow's "rediscovered" wines. The staff was working well together, falling into routine days. With the tasting room busy, even Sondra was happy. Well, maybe *happy* would never be a good descriptor, but she snapped less. Indigo's expanding knowledge even made the sales calls less scary.

And she and Danovan were dating. She felt a

silly teenager's thrill at his covert smiles in passing while at work. They were taking the skipped steps slowly. They'd been to the movies, jogged on the beach and gone shopping in Santa Maria earlier in the week, and tonight they were going out for pizza. And so far, all they'd shared at the end of the dates was a good-night kiss.

In their initial rush, she hadn't had time to appreciate Danovan's kissing expertise. She'd had ample time to realize it since. He focused with laser intensity on her face, his dark eyes almost hypnotic, before lowering his head to take her lips, soft, slow and sensual. She relished every single one. But a hollow place had formed in her rib cage that expanded with every night that she watched him walk away down the hill, whistling. She wanted more. She was ready.

Fanning her flushed face, she broke off a runty bunch of grapes and dropped them into the compost bag at her feet.

Maybe I should make the first move.

Her phone buzzed in the back pocket of her jeans. She lifted it and, seeing the number, smiled. "Hello."

"Hey, boss."

It was their code for "Someone's listening—I can't flirt."

Didn't mean *she* couldn't, though. "I'm looking forward to a bit more than pizza tonight. What do you think?"

"I think that would be outstanding." He cleared his throat. "Could you stop by my office on the way in?"

"Is everything okay?"

"Sure. Just have an idea to run by you."

"And tonight, I may have a few things to run by you."

"I look forward to that...opportunity."

Chuckling, she clicked End. Who knew romance could be so playful? In Hollywood pre-Harry, she'd never gotten past the bar scene. Life with Harry had been wonderful and full of humor, but she wouldn't use *playful* to describe it.

Maybe she was too old for this, but she'd skipped steps in her abbreviated love life, and she was taking full advantage of her chance for a do-over.

After a quick shower and change of clothes, she roused Barney from a nap, and they walked down the hill. The parking lot held a few cars, even this early in the day. That was a good sign. She took the rear entrance to the production facility.

"Barney is in the building!" Sean, their twenty-something warehouse rat called from the shipping area, tape gun in one hand, holding a carton closed with the other.

Barney looked up, tail whipping.

Indigo never could resist those sad eyes. "Okay, you go visit with Sean. I'll come get you in a bit."

Barney trotted to the shipping table.

"You're not to feed him Fritos from your lunch, you hear me, Sean?"

"Yes, ma'am, I know. They give him the squirts."

Not how she'd have put it, but... She strode to Danovan's glass-walled office. He sat studying the paperwork spread out before him, his thumbs doing a drum roll on the desktop.

She stopped at the door. "Uh-oh. I recognize that look."

His smile pulled one from her. "That is the look of a genius at work." He waved her over. "I have an idea. A big idea."

She perched a hip on the edge of his desk. "Hit me with it."

Leaning back in the chair, he rested his elbows on the arms and played with his pencil. "The Widow is in the black, which is excellent. But since we're so small, it'll take years to rebuild."

"You knew that when you started here." A ball, small but containing something scary, formed at the bottom of her rib cage.

"Yeah, yeah, but hear me out." His foot bounced. "We could speed up the process with a bigger crush. Your amazing sales skills have increased the demand for our wine. More product equals more sales and more opportunity to grow our reputation."

"That would mean more land—which we can't afford. But even if we could, it would take a couple of years to get it in production."

"That's why I think we should buy grapes."

"Huh?"

"Wineries do it all the time. Some vineyards don't produce their own labels. They just grow to sell to other wineries. Bacchanal buys grapes every year."

"Where are you going with this? You know we don't have the money."

"I know. But assume we did." He pulled a graph from the papers on his desk and held it out. "Here's a projection of revenue if we could double our crush."

But revenue didn't always equate to profit. "That's impressive. But Danovan—"

"I've scheduled an aggressive plan for competitions next year. Our Chardonnay and merlot are going to slay the judges. But our Harvest Moon Cab isn't up to that level of scrutiny. I'm thinking our varietal needs to be changed to create that signature wine I told you about..." He stared off at nothing, tapping his pencil on the desk with a dreamy gleam in his eye.

She waved a hand, beginning to rethink her stopping in. "Ground control to Major Tom."

"Oh. Yeah." He straightened and leaned forward in his chair. "Anyway, if we buy grapes, we can improve the Cab and cut at least one year off our five-year plan. Maybe two."

She studied the cliff-face bar chart. It was a nice dream, but there was less risk in slow, steady progress. "Okay, say we had the money to buy grapes. We don't have the equipment to process them."

"True. We'd need to buy more tanks, expand the bottling line and hire more help in the warehouse." He dug through the snowdrift of papers on his desk. "I've got a budget here somewhere."

"Danovan, have you been drinking the product? We don't have—"

"Here it is." He slid a piece of paper from under his keyboard and handed her the sheet.

It was an income statement. A rosy-lens scenario, with lots of pretty green zeroes at the bottom. Apparently her Disney bluebirds had flown down here, too. "It's pretty and all, but..." She let the paper fall to the desktop and pointed to her lips. "We. Don't. Have. The. Money."

He looked up. "So? We borrow it."

Her heartbeat stuttered then sped up, a tiny tapping at her ribs. She barked out a laugh that sounded fake, even to her. "No problem." She snapped her hair over her shoulder in what she'd always thought of as the Hollywood flip. "I'll strut in and tell them that I'm *the* Indigo Blue, and they'll just open the vault and ask me how much."

His steady gaze was unnerving. "Indigo, you have collateral."

The silence thickened the air, making it stale and hard to breathe. The tapping at her ribs increased tempo. "That's ridiculous. The only thing I own of value is…"

He nodded, his eyes scanning her face.

The tapping became a jackhammer. "You don't know what you're asking." Put Uncle Bob's legacy at risk?

"Yes, I do." He didn't argue. He didn't pull out more hearts-and-flowers spreadsheets. He just waited.

He's got guts, asking me to risk the only thing I have left. I'm not doing this. No one can make me. "Nope, sorry."

His expression didn't change. His wild hawk gaze didn't shift away.

Instead it rammed against her wall of "no." Unease skittered along her nerves on little spider feet. She shook her head. Between Harry's death and the debacle afterward, she'd just begun to stand again, after much struggle. "Everything is going so well. Why put that at risk?" Was she referring to more than the winery?

He cocked his head. Did he wonder the same?

Then the intensity of his gaze diffused. The taut lines of his face softened. He tossed the pencil onto the desk. "I understand."

"I'm sorry." And she was. She hated dousing the fire in him. Without it, he was simply handsome, like a model in a men's clothing catalog. Passion was what made Danovan DiCarlo an irresistible force, in business as well as…other places.

It made him larger than life, and she realized that
was the tractor beam that had drawn her like a
moth to a porch light. She might be immune to
good looks, but coupled with passion…

He glanced out the window-wall to the warehouse, looking pensive. "Indigo, I do understand.
It's too much, too fast." He turned and took her
hand.

Smoky tendrils of heat spread up her arm at
his touch, but it was the softness in his gaze that
convinced her. He did understand. Not only what
she said, but what she hadn't. She squinted in a
half smile, half wince. "I guess I'm just not good
at skipping steps."

"For good reason." He released her fingers and
rose from his chair. "Well, I've got some lab work
to do, and you probably need to start your day,
too."

As she walked out, a cold thought flitted through
her mind. Did his business proposal have strings
attached…to other things? Given her untrustworthy gut instinct, she couldn't be sure. "Are we
still on for tonight?"

"I wouldn't be anywhere else." The warmth in
his smile drove out the chill.

She walked through the barrel room and into
the tasting room. The soaring timbers and picture
windows overlooking the porch and the rolling
green lawn always lifted her spirits.

Natalie stood behind the bar, a bottle of Harvest Moon in hand, laughing at something one of the three women standing at the counter had said. Sondra looked on, wearing what Indigo thought of as her glacier-queen face.

The silk pants were the first clue that the women weren't from around here. Probably LA babes. These were the type of client she'd love to cultivate: chic, sleek and well-heeled.

Well-heeled is right. Those are Sergio Rossi boots.

She walked over to introduce herself. Two steps away, something about the shade of chestnut hair on the closest one hit her in her chest, halting her forward progress. When the woman turned slowly, her profile burned through the covering of Indigo's brain, searing the soft tissue beneath.

Four months hadn't dimmed the cruel glitter in those emerald eyes. "Well. If it isn't Indigo Blue." There was no surprise on Brenda Stone's smooth features.

Indigo was surprised enough for them both. When she left Hollywood, it hadn't occurred to her that she'd see her step-daughter again.

Brenda's swank minions, wearing identical smirks, turned to watch the show.

"I didn't know you owned this little...place."

Yeah, right. Indigo's surprise splintered, and cold trickles of anger seeped through the cracks. She'd had to put up with Brenda in Hollywood, but not now. Not here. Straightening, she put a hand on her hip, grateful that she'd showered and changed into slacks and a silk blouse. "What do you want, Brenda?"

"Why would I want anything?"

The innocent, "oh, Daddy" voice singed Indigo's tender beginning-to-heal scars. "Because you always do. 'Daddy, I want this,' and 'Daddy, I need that.'"

One of Brenda's girlfriends tittered.

The amused cat-with-a-cricket look slid from Brenda's face, revealing her witchy side. "Well, I don't need anything now." When she flipped her hair over her shoulder, the diamonds on her fingers flashed. "I have it *all.*"

It was comical, really. Brenda had always tried to enrage Indigo by waving things in front of her that she cared nothing for. But still, their last meeting stung.

She might have thrown me out of Harry's house, but this is my turf. If she came all this way to play games, then dammit, she's going to get her wish.

She patted Brenda's arm. "Except you never got the one thing you really wanted, did you, dear?"

Brenda shot her a haughty look. "Oh, unlike some, I got *everything* I wanted."

"Not your father's approval."

Brenda actually raised her hand, fingers curled to claws. Remembering her lofty station, she turned her hand, pretended to check her nails and said to her minions, "Let's blow this dump.

If I lowered myself to buy wine somewhere besides Napa, it'd only be from a reputable winery like Bacchanal." Brenda pivoted on her heel and, groupies trailing, sailed out the door. Indigo watched them walk to a white convertible Maserati, pile in and peel rubber.

She shouldn't have said it. It was childish and lowered her to Brenda's level.

But damn, it felt good.

Seeing Natalie and Sondra's stares, she wiped her smile. "I owed her that. The last time I saw her, she insulted my dog." She turned her back and stalked to her office.

Winning a word war with the bitch didn't make up for Brenda pretending to be a friend, then laughing at Indigo behind her back. And it surely didn't make up for Brenda seeing a man as wonderful as Harry as little more than a wallet.

Success is the best revenge.

She banished the stray thought with a shake of her head. Brenda was *not* a good reason to consider Danovan's crazy idea.

Not in and of itself, anyway.

THAT EVENING, SHE PUSHED the loan conflict from the edge of her mind as Danovan drove. She hoped this place was as funky as Sam from yoga class had advertised. "I can't wait. Do you know how long it's been since I had pizza?"

He shot her a look. "Given what I've seen of your eating habits...last week?"

She punched him lightly on the shoulder. "That's a low blow. You've only seen my slips. All the meals you don't see me eat are healthy."

She felt his glance from her scarf-tied ponytail to her ankle boots.

"I'm not being critical. You were a wraith when I first met you. If cotton candy and corn dogs brought you back to a healthy weight, I'm glad."

She ran a hand down her side, feeling for bones. Her clothes had stopped hanging off her a while ago. Between the runs and the yoga, she felt fit and healthy. Could she be recovering from the funk that had begun with Harry's death? Maybe.

A blade of regret pricked her heart.

"Hey." Danovan's large hand covered hers, though his eyes didn't leave the road. "It's okay to feel better, you know."

She started, spooked that he'd read her thoughts. "How do you..." *Esperanza. He knows because he's felt the same.* "Sorry. You're right, of course."

He gave her hand a squeeze.

"Here, turn here," she said.

He wheeled the Range Rover into the parking lot of a strip mall. "Oh, God, tell me we're not going to Chuck E. Cheese's. Kids on sugar-crack give me a headache."

"I don't know, I mean, we could crash a kid's

birthday party for the free cake." She scanned the storefronts then pointed. "There it is."

He pulled into a parking space at the end of the building. They stepped out and headed toward the last unit, boasting a sign that read Yukon Pizza.

"What does pizza have to do with Alaska?" He held the door open for her.

"Got me. I've never been here." She walked into a wall of warm air laced with the smells of yeast and spices. Voices and laughter overrode the jukebox she could barely see in the dim recesses, blaring "The Lion Sleeps Tonight."

Ahead stood a serving counter with a perky blonde teen behind it. The restaurant continued to the left and back, with small, plastic gingham-tablecloth-covered tables littering the sawdust-covered plank floor.

The decor left no doubt as to the theme. Cross-country skis hung from the ceiling, framed mountain landscape posters adorned the wall and mining lanterns hung from wooden ceiling beams, providing dim yellow light. Indigo's attention was pulled everywhere at once—a flag of Alaska spread across the ceiling in one corner, a kayak propped in another, and in the very back, she could barely see... "Is that a stuffed polar bear?"

"Yeah." The girl behind the counter said, "I think the owners ran out of room in their house for all their crap."

Danovan pointed to the wall where a foot-long trout sporting a mink cuff was mounted on a plaque. The placard said that the Arctic Trout grew fur in the winter, causing problems in the spring when the rivers got stopped up with all that shed hair.

She laughed. "Reminds me of the Jackalopes I saw in an Arizona tourist trap once. A jackrabbit with pronged horns coming out of its head."

After they'd ordered their Roadkill Pizza, the girl handed Danovan two mugs—his beer, her soda—and she passed Indigo a plastic basket of unshelled peanuts. Danovan led the way to a relatively quiet corner and they sat.

He scanned the memorabilia on the walls. "You know, this place is kind of like Chuck E. Cheese's for adults."

"Yep. So, how much money would we need?" She blurted the question she'd thought about all afternoon onto the table.

Startled hopefulness broke over his face. "You're actually thinking about my proposal?"

"Not really." She shelled a peanut for something to do with her hands. "Well, thinking, maybe." She tossed the hull on the floor and raised a finger. "But that's light-years from *doing*, okay?"

"Of course." The corners of his mouth lowered, but that didn't wipe away the hopefulness.

"What would we need to buy?"

He grabbed a napkin. "Do you have a pen?"

She pulled one from her purse and handed it over.

"I have the exact figures in my office, but I can rough it out. First we'd need grapes. I have a grower in Napa who I've bought from in the past. He has consistent, excellent quality. Adding the market price and shipping—" He jotted a figure. "Then we'd need more fermentation tanks, barrels, bottles—" He wrote another figure. "Add the warehouse labor—" He made a line and tallied, then slid the napkin across to her.

The total was two zeroes more than the balance of her personal account. And though the winery was in the black, the cash flow had yet to catch up. The salty taste of worry mixed with the peanut she'd swallowed. "This adds risk. What's wrong with waiting and letting the winery fund its own growth?"

"Providing we sell out the additional wine we produce, the payout on the entire loan is seven years."

"So the risk is—"

"Negligible." He spread his hands, palm up. "Because you have me." He flashed her a car salesman's smile.

She shook her head and grabbed another peanut. *Why are the handsome ones always arrogant?*

"I'm kidding." He dropped the smile and lowered his forearms onto the table. "Well, at least half kidding. You're new to the industry, so you don't know my reputation. Whatever else the

Boldens would say about me, I am an excellent winemaker." He looked her in the eye. "It's not bragging if it's fact. Wine I make will sell out. You can take that to the bank."

That's exactly what you're asking me to do. The only thing Danovan stood to lose was a ten percent share of nonexistent profits. When it came to debt, the "we" shifted to "me."

And "me" doesn't make good decisions.

She held his gaze, studying. *But he does.* Danovan had done everything he'd promised. He'd taught her the basics of the business, the terminology, how to tend the vines. His guiding hands touched every aspect of The Tippling Widow.

And they were now in the black.

"I'll tell you what. I'll go and talk to a lender." The bitter taste of salt from the peanuts backed into her throat. "If they turn me down, it takes the decision out of my hands anyway." *When they turn me down.*

A waitress stepped to the table and set down a bubbling platter of gooey, delicious carbs.

Indigo shoved aside the subject and her worry to take in a huge lungful of heaven. "Have I mentioned how much I love pizza?"

SHE WAS REALLY considering it. Sure, the bank might turn her down. Even if they said yes—he wasn't deluding himself—she might decide not to take it. But a restless sparking of possibility stirred in his chest, like the change in the air before an electrical storm. He felt antsy and hyper-aware of his surroundings. Their heels, clicking the pavement on the hill to the cabin. The stirring of leaves and the smell of growing grapes came to him on the warm breeze, woven into the clean scent of her perfume.

God, he'd come to love that smell.

Her hand slipped into his. Lissette's had been tiny. It fit in his like a young girl's, making him feel protective, masculine. But Indigo's hand was long-fingered, slim and strong. More like his own. Equal to his own.

She'd make a great partner. When he realized the voice in his head was referring to more than a job and a period much longer than an affair, his fingers clenched.

"What's the matter?" Indigo asked, her face at his shoulder only a pale blur in the dark.

"Nothing." He forced the muscles of his hand to slacken. "I was just thinking that it's nice to be with someone who doesn't need to fill silence with chatter."

She squeezed his hand, and they walked on.

He approached the thought more slowly this time. *Love? Is that what you're talking about?*

Silence echoed back. *I wasn't referring to* your *chatter. A little help here.*

Nothing.

They turned in at the path that led to Indigo's

cabin porch. A warm light inside made the stirring curtains glow at the window. A long nose appeared in the crack. "Looks like you have a welcoming committee." He took her elbow at the stairs.

She chuckled. "Yeah, Barney founded my fan club."

He stepped in front of her. "But he's not the only member." When he cupped her cheek, lifting her chin, she moved willingly into his embrace. Her arms twined around his neck and her hands up into his hair. He tasted the coffee they'd drunk on her lips, the sweetness of the night on her tongue. Her body molded to his—or maybe his did the molding. Regardless, the result felt strong, solid, somehow right. Her kiss was sweet, full and fine, like expensive port.

Until she whimpered.

The kiss morphed to the laughing burst of Moët & Chandon as bubbles shot through his blood to his head, leaving him dizzy. His tongue delved her depths. His cock was a steel rod, throbbing an insistent demand that matched his racing heartbeat. *Now. Now. Now.*

The dog whined and scratched at the door.

Stop.

He broke the kiss and, hands on her upper arms, pushed her away. "Your first fan awaits." He stepped back.

"What's wrong, Danovan?" She sounded as confused as he felt. "Is it me?"

He dropped his hands. "It's not you. It's just that us working together and...being together messes with my head sometimes." He ran a hand through his hair. Mixing business and pleasure was a bomb that had destroyed his last life. "Look, I want you. That's obvious. But I've also asked you to put a lot of faith in me with the winery, and I know that's pretty scary for you. I don't ever want you to think that I used this—" he waved a hand, indicating them both "—used *us*, to influence your decision."

She tilted her head, and only one side of her mouth lifted. "I can't decide if you're sweet or the most egotistical man I've ever met."

Yeah, join the club. He hadn't felt this conflicted, this unsure of himself since...well, ever. He just shrugged. "You are in my blood, Indigo Blue." He ran a finger down her throat, to where the first button of her blouse halted his progress. "You make me burn." After a long look, he made himself take another step away and turn. "Sleep well."

He heard her open the door and murmur to the dog as he walked away.

Either he'd just done the most decent, noble thing ever, or the dumbest. His brain argued the former, his body the latter.

CHAPTER SIXTEEN

GUTS SHAKING, AND HOPING it didn't show, Indigo strode into the soaring-ceilinged icon that was the Silversafe Bank of Santa Maria. Her business heels clicked on black-veined marble as she tried to lock her shoulders back and surreptitiously tug down her skirt at the same time.

If he turns you down, the decision is made. If he approves it, you can still say no.

Halting before the desk of what the walnut-and-brass nameplate advertised as Vice President of Administration, she slapped on a stiff, but hopefully businesslike, smile. She shifted her briefcase and stuck out her hand to shake. The probably-a-secretary-in-spite-of-the-title lady on the other side of the desk looked startled, but after a moment, shook Indigo's outstretched hand.

"I have a two o'clock appointment with Craig Zimmer." Her phone buzzed its incoming-text buzz. It was from Danovan.

Call me as soon as you can.

I'll call on my way out.

She stared down at the brown roots of the VP's blond hair as she checked her computer. "Ms. Blue, yes. I'll let Mr. Zimmer know you're here."

Too fast, Indigo found herself on the other side of a huge kidney-shaped desk of the Senior Business Loan Officer, a fit, too-young-for-the-gray-hair man who looked like he played tennis at a country club in his off-hours. She swallowed and sat.

"What can I do for our most famous resident?" His smile held a business line, but his tone said "spoiled dilettante."

Great, one of those. The simpering Bernard was an example of one reaction to her past. This was the other—someone who looked at her like she was gum on his wingtip. *Strike one.*

She held his gaze and pushed her shoulder blades closer together. "Hardly. My late husband was famous, not I."

"I'm sorry for your loss." His mouth displayed sorrow, but his eyes weren't buying it.

"You may or may not be aware, but I am the owner of The Tippling Widow Winery in Widow's Grove."

"I am aware."

"Well, we'd like to expand our operation. I'd like to buy grapes to double our crush." She leaned down and flipped open the top of her briefcase. "This will of course require the purchase of capital equipment and labor to handle the increased production." She lifted out her ammo—spreadsheets, colored pie charts and bar graphs. She'd tweaked Danovan's numbers to reflect a slightly less rosy view. She didn't want to oversell. If the banker didn't think this was a smart risk, that would be good enough for her. She handed the papers to Mr. Country Club. "You can see that to keep costs down, we'll purchase quality used equipment. I would also hire less experienced applicants who want to learn the business."

Her phone buzzed again.

Call me. Now.

She couldn't. Her churning gut might be unreliable, but even she knew that this gas-filled bag of ego would be offended if she took a call. Or even texted back. Danovan had more experience to handle whatever the emergency was, anyway.

The executive studied the charts with squinting scrutiny, his lips pursed. After a few agonizing minutes, he looked up. "I wasn't aware that you were an experienced vintner, Ms. Blue."

She squished the crickets partying in her stomach and folded her hands in her lap. "I'm not. Well, I wasn't. I'm what you'd call an apprentice vintner. Danovan DiCarlo is The Widow's manager. He's teaching me and is responsible for the day-to-day operation of the production facility."

The creases in the banker's lips deepened. "Ah, Danovan DiCarlo."

Strike two, from the look. "Are you familiar with Mr. DiCarlo's expertise?"

He looked away. "I am familiar with Mr. DiCarlo."

Which wasn't an answer to her question. At all.

Her blood flash-heated to a boil. She wouldn't sit here and listen to this judgmental ass, even if it meant losing the chance at a loan. "I'm aware that there are rumors being spread about Mr. DiCarlo by his former employer due to a personal disagreement on a non-work-related matter." She grabbed her briefcase, stood, lifted her chin and tried for imperious. "I assure you, his expertise as a manager can be ascertained in our current financial statements, which are page twelve of the completed loan paperwork you have in your hand."

He placed his hand on the paperwork and leaned back in his swivel chair. "I will review your application, then submit it to our loan committee along with my opinion, Ms. Blue. I should be able to get you an answer within the next few days."

"Thank you." She turned and sailed out of the office before he could offer her his hand, since she wasn't sure she wanted to shake it anyway. She unlocked her car and got in, then dialed Danovan's cell phone.

"DiCarlo," he barked.

"Well, Silversafe Bank is probably a washout. I couldn't call until now. What's up?"

"Are you still in Santa Maria?"

"I just got out of the meeting with Mr. Country Club. Do you need anything at the store? I've got to—"

"Indigo, you'd better… Get off the road, dammit!"

The urgency in his tone twanged her nerves, sending vibrations to her gut. She heard car horns blaring in the background. "What's wrong? What happened?"

"I'm on my way to the vet. I think you'd better meet me there."

"Oh no! What's wrong with Barney?" Hearing the surge of his car engine, her heartbeat surged to match it. "Which vet?" *Oh God, not Barney. I can't lose him, too.* Slamming the door, she started her car.

"Ynez Valley Vet Clinic, outside of town. You know where it is?"

She hit the speaker button, tossed the phone onto the seat next to her, rammed the car into gear and floored it. "I'll find it. What happened? Is he okay?"

"He's…just hurry, okay?" *Click.*

Shattering all speed limits and swearing at pokey law-abiders, she listened to the clock ticking in her head and thoughts of ever-increasing disastrous scenarios, all starring Barney.

Arriving at the clinic, she might have damaged the transmission, throwing the car into Park before it stopped. While it still rocked, she was out and running for the glass door of what looked like a doctor's office from the '60s. Large aluminum-framed windows looked into a reception area sparsely populated with owners and pets. Barreling through the door, she ran to the Formica-clad desk. "Barney—my dog. A bassett? Where is he?" She stopped, unable to get enough air past the blockage in her throat to say more.

The wide-eyed teen receptionist pointed to a door, and Indigo slammed through it to a hallway. She had to slow to look in the small windows of the doors on either side. In the second on the left, she recognized Danovan's broad shoulders leaning over an examining table. But not the red-haired man across from him.

She stood frozen, hand on the door, unable to push it open to a future she couldn't face.

Danovan shifted, revealing a long, brown ear. A grief-tipped blade sliced her chest. *You have to be there for Barney.* The door felt weighted with lead when she pushed it with a shaking hand.

"We won't know—" The young vet looked up.

Indigo took the two steps to the spotlighted table where an IV line snaked down... A sob coughed from her chest.

Wet with sweat, a too-still Barney lay, eyes closed, foamed saliva drying on his muzzle.

"What happened?" She'd pushed out air hard enough to allow her to shout, but all that came out was a breathy whisper.

Danovan ran fingers over Barn's slicked flank. His eyes were bottomless—haunted.

She looked to the vet. "Is he going to be all right?" Then wanted to snatch the words back. *Why ask if you can't handle the answer?*

The vet fiddled with the stopcock on the IV. "The next two hours will tell. This should flush some of the poison—"

"Poison?" She whipped her head to Danovan. "What happened?"

"I was on the tractor, spraying fungicide for black rot—"

"Why? That's my job!"

He glanced at her, then away, as if unable to look at her hurt. "You were at the bank. I wanted to do something to help you. He must have been following the tractor."

She strained to hear past a gale of panic.

He stroked Barney's ear. "I turned at the end of a row, and saw him…" He scrubbed a hand over his eyes as if he could erase the vision from his brain. "It never occurred to me that he'd follow me."

In a blinding flash, molten anger spattered her guts. "Get away from my dog!" She slapped at Danovan's arm. "You never liked him!" She put her hands on Danovan's chest and pushed. He took a startled step back. Pain burned through her guts to her core. It was everywhere. She had to get away from it. "You've killed my dog!" She followed him, slapping at his chest.

Danovan stood, hands clenched at his sides, taking it.

"Hey, stop now." The vet stepped around the table and put a hand on her arm. "If he hadn't gotten here as fast as he did, your dog *would* be dead. The important thing now is Barney. Let's focus on him. Okay?"

The anger rushed out of the holes it burned in the bottom of her feet. All her energy went with it. Jesus. What had she said? She stepped back to the table, leaned her hands on the edge and tried to stop breathing like a buffalo. She could barely see the rise and fall of the dog's shallow breaths. *Oh, God, Barney.* When the cool plastic of a chair touched the backs of her knees, she released her grip.

Exposed by the surgeon's light, Barney looked so vulnerable. She dropped her chin on her fist on the table. She stroked a finger over the freckles on Barney's muzzle, hoping for a twitch that didn't come. "I'm sorry to freak out. It's just that Barn is all I have left of my husband." She glanced up at the doctor. "Please. I can't lose him."

"This should counteract the pesticide, providing he didn't ingest too much. We just have to give it time." He glanced at Danovan. "I have other patients. If you two are okay…"

"We're fine, Doc. Go ahead." The weight of Danovan's hand dropped onto her shoulder.

She shrugged it off. "I'd rather be alone."

The door opened and closed.

She took Barney's oversized foot in her fingers, stroking it. "You have to get better, Barn." She waited a moment for the aching tide to recede from her throat and behind her eyes. "It's you and me, bud, remember? Dad's—" The ache surged. "—gone." It came out strangled and wet. "We have to…" She took a breath. "Oh please, Barn. Don't leave me, too." She laid her head on the table and put her arms around as much of her dog as she could reach as the tide swamped her.

Sometime later, the door clicked open behind her. She palmed her eyes but didn't turn.

"I'm not leaving." Danovan's deep voice came from behind her. "I understand what Barney means to you. If you're not ready to leave Harry behind, I understand that too. But I'm not leaving you alone. Not now."

She felt blindly for his hand, took it and squeezed. "I didn't mean what I said. I just went crazy…"

He slid a chair next to her and sat. "Forget it. It's a natural reaction."

She turned her head, and the ruin on his face jerked her from selfishness. *That same thing happened to him after Esperanza died.* In their grief, the Boldens had blamed him, too. "Oh, God, Danovan. I'm so sorry."

"I'm sorry, too." He took a deep breath. "Look, I know this isn't the time, but I have to say it. I know you're not ready to close that door…to leave Harry behind." The weight of sorrow was heavy on his face, adding years. "And that's okay. I just want you to know that I'm here, Indigo. As a friend, if that's all you can handle right now."

"But Harry *is* gone." She shook her head slowly. "See, that's the thing about denial. You can't live there forever. Whether I want it to or not, the sun keeps coming up every morning, carrying me further and further away from him." She ran a finger down Barney's ear. "All I can do is try to adjust to that receding distance every day. I'm starting to think that's how grief works. Tiny steps, every day. You can't speed them up, and you can't slow them down."

"I *hate* that." He dropped his chin on his fist on the edge of the table.

"Me, too." She put an arm around his shoulders and they sat in silence, watching Barney breathe.

CHAPTER SEVENTEEN

A WEEK LATER, Indigo watched the sun go down through the sweep of windows as her class filed into the yoga studio.

"Barney, poor baby!" Jesse dropped her gym bag and crouched at the dog bed where Barney lay, tail thumping, anticipating adoration. "Does the vet say he's going to be okay?"

"After a really scary night, he woke up fine. The vet kept him for two days but said he'll make a full recovery, thank God. He's almost back to his old self."

Priss walked in, dropped her bag and bent over the basket. "Oh, hey, you okay, dude?"

Indigo's phone rang, and when she read Silversafe Bank on the screen, she nearly dropped it. "Ladies, sorry, but I've got to take this. I'll be right back."

She left Barney in the center of a crowd of spandex-clad women, rolled on his back in bliss, receiving tummy rubs as if they were his due. Stepping around the screen to her massage area, she answered in her winery-owner voice. "This is Indigo. Can I help you?"

"Ms. Blue, this is Craig Zimmer at Silversafe Bank."

"Hello, Mr. Zimmer." She swallowed, not sure which she dreaded more: approval or rejection.

"I'm calling to inform you that the board has approved your loan request. I'll have the loan docs prepared and ready later in the morning for you to sign."

"Oh." She cleared surprise from her throat. "Yes. Um. Thanks for letting me know. I'll be in touch soon." She hit End before she could say anything stupid. *What the heck are you going to do now, Blue?*

She pushed down her shoulders and pulled up her virtual big-girl panties. *You're going to calm down and go teach yoga. That's what you're going to do.*

Walking around the screen, she clapped her hands. "Okay, let's limber up with some Cat-Cow stretches, shall we?" She clicked on the speakers and took her place at the front of the room. The sound of soothing piano music to an accompaniment of ocean waves poured over her. Maybe an hour of this would quiet her jangled nerves. The women assumed the position on their hands and knees. "Don't forget your focused breathing, ladies."

She'd pushed the loan to the back of her mind since it was out of her control. Sure, she knew on some level that approval was a possibility, but the shock that reverberated through her was proof that she'd believed the answer would be no. And the queasiness in her stomach told her she'd been hoping for a no. She didn't want to be the ultimate decision-maker.

"Olivia, don't go too far into the Cow—remember your hip, dear."

But now it was on *her*. She had a decision to make. And no idea of how to make it.

"Okay, let's transition to Pigeon Pose…"

An hour later, class was over.

"Hey, Carley, are we still on for this weekend?" Priss asked.

"Of course we are. Olivia, are you coming to Hearst Castle with us?"

"Sure, providing you're not driving that boat of a convertible. It messes my hair."

Sam closed the flap to her backpack, and lifted her motorcycle helmet from the floor. "Hey, Jesse, how about throwing an end-of-summer party in September?"

"Only if you're buying a new dress for it, sweetie."

"Oh, come on. Nobody cares if I come in jeans."

Jesse batted her eyelashes. "Maybe not, but you're not getting through my front door in them, Pinelli."

Indigo forced the words out with a huff of breath. "Jesse, can you stay back a minute? I need to ask you about something."

"Sure, doll." She rounded back to her friend. "I mean it, Sam. I'm sure your husband would appreciate seeing you in more than those danged overalls you've pulled on over your yoga pants. You'll thank me later. You know you will." She waggled her fingers at her grumbling friend as Sam walked out the door.

Indigo switched off the music and waited for the last stragglers to leave.

"What is it, sweetie? You look worrieder than a bunny at a wolf conference."

Indigo chewed her lip and tried to think of how to word this. "How did you make the decision to quit that once-in-a-lifetime math scholarship at Princeton to come home and propose to Carl?"

Jesse leaned a hip against the table. "You know, I thought I'd have to make good on my threat to throw myself off the Pismo Beach Pier before he agreed."

"How did you make a huge decision like that?"

"Are you thinking about that Roman god of a manager of yours?" She tipped her head, and a sparkle came to her baby blues. "Should I start planning a reception?"

"What? No!" Blood pounded to flood Indigo's face. "Have you lost your mind?"

Jesse winked. "Hey, you two are all alone out here at night, with the moonlight and the grapevines… Pretty romantic setting. Stranger things have happened."

"Why do you think everything is about a man? My God." She fanned her face to cool it. "This is about the business."

"Hon, you've been married, for cripes sakes. You've made big decisions before."

Yeah, but that was easy. Harry chose me.

"You're serious, aren't you?" With a focused squint, Jesse watched Indigo fidget. "Darlin', you're a woman. You just have to trust your intuition. End of story."

Indigo threw up her hands. "But I can't trust mine. That's the problem!"

"Why are you so afraid to make a mistake? Good lord, I've made a ton of those. Everyone does."

"Yeah, but—" Indigo fumbled with the music remote and dropped it.

"You are a mess, aren't you, hon?" Jesse bent, picked up the remote and set it on the table. "Okay, here's what I do. First, I figure out what is the absolute worst that can happen. I'm talking downright Armageddon. And if I can live with that, then I'm good to go." She spread her hands in a ta-da gesture. "See?"

What would she do if she lost the winery? She'd been so worried about the possibility, she'd never looked beyond it. "I'll try that. Thanks."

Jesse lifted her gym bag from the desk. "Are you gonna tell me what this is all about?"

"I will, once I've made my decision. Promise." Indigo followed Jesse to the door.

"Well, once you've made *that* one, you're going to have to decide what to do about that gorgeous manager of yours." She speared Indigo with a look. "If you let that one get away, you'll regret it for the rest of your life."

"Jesse—"

Jesse tapped a long nail to Indigo's lips. "Just think on it, that's all I'm saying." She turned, and with a waggle of her fingers, sashayed out.

Armageddon. Indigo looked around the room. Could she live with losing the winery? It was not only her livelihood—besides Barney, it was her last link to her happy days with Harry. She had fond memories of The Widow even before she'd come to live here. And now she couldn't imagine living somewhere that she didn't wake up with Uncle Bob's cabin wrapped around her. Watching the sun on the vines as she waited for the water to heat for her first cup of coffee. Seeing Danovan's eyes when he looked up from his desk…

Whoa. Wait a minute. When had Danovan become part of that picture? Part of her dream? She didn't know. But there he was, pointing out a lever on the tractor, squinting at the swirling blush in a glass, holding her hand at the vet's.

And here she'd thought a bank loan was her biggest problem.

She stooped to pet Barney's smooth head. "Is he getting to you, too, Barn? Is that why you followed him on the tractor?"

The dog's sad eyes tore something in her chest, opening a yawning hollow. She fell to her knees and hugged Barney, burying her face in the warm fur of his neck. "Are we traitors if we let go of Harry?"

Her mother's voice echoed from deep in her mind. *Go to a quiet place, put on some soothing music and open some lavender oil. Just trust. The answer is inside you.*

She walked around the screen to the massage area. She might not have the answer yet, but at least she had the tools to dig for it.

IT WAS DARK by the time Danovan held the back door for his warehouse rat. "Thanks for staying and getting those orders out, Sean."

"No worries, boss. I can use the money. I'm taking on an extra class in the fall."

"I'll see you tomorrow afternoon, then." He closed the door behind Sean and locked it. He'd been against the idea, but Indigo had been right to hire a part-time college student. Sean was cheap, flexible and smart, and he was doing a great job.

Flipping off the lights, he followed the beacon of his office light through the shadowed warehouse. The deskful of paperwork didn't hold the attraction it had earlier.

Where's Indigo? He hadn't seen her since morning.

He turned off his office light and followed the next dot of brightness: the exit sign over the barrel room door. A security light was the only one in the tasting room full of shadows. Indigo had probably already left for the cabin.

On the way to his apartment, just hoping, he pushed open the door to the yoga room. It was dark, but the cloth privacy screen at the end of the room glowed with flickering candlelight. He stepped into the scent of lavender that took his mind back to Indigo's massage. Took his body back, too. He shifted his thickening cock, then crossed the room to peek around the screen.

She sat, legs crossed, on the massage table, in yoga pants and a sports bra, eyes closed. The backs of her hands rested on her knees, palms open, fingers relaxed.

The candlelight played over her smooth, tawny skin. She looked like a Hindu goddess.

She looked like an angel.

A sound came from the corner. Barney lay, tail thumping on his dog bed, gazing at Danovan with adoration. He was beginning to see why people kept dogs. He'd almost killed Barney, but the animal bore no grudge. He wished humans were so forgiving.

Indigo's eyes opened, and her smile shot to his heart. "My thoughts must have conjured you. I was about to go find you in a few minutes."

He stepped to the table, drawn by the open look of simple happiness on her face, reminding him how seldom it was free from worry. "You keep looking at me like that and you'll conjure something else." He cupped her cheeks and lifted her face. "You're even more beautiful in candle-light."

The day he'd come for an interview, he'd been in free fall—his life and his career heading for the rocks beneath the cliff he'd fallen from the day Esperanza died.

But instead of crashing, he'd found himself. He found the man he wanted to be, had always been, reflected in her eyes.

He didn't have to lean down. He tried to convey his gratitude with a soft, slow touching of lips. Before his body could force him to the next step, he backed away. The moment was too fragile to let passion tear it up.

She favored him with a beatific smile. "The banker called."

The peaceful bubble burst. Not for the first time, he cursed the ambition that drove him. He took her hand and ran his thumb across its smooth back. "You know, there're worse things than spending the next five years growing the business together."

"They approved the loan."

His heart stuttered then sped on, a frantic snare drum in his chest. "We don't need—"

"I'm going to town tomorrow to sign papers."

He tightened his core, trapping the eagerness before it could hijack the moment. "Maybe you shouldn't."

Her brow compressed, and she tipped her head. "You're an alien, aren't you? What have you done with my vintner?" She waved a hand in front of his face. "This is your chance, Danovan. 'DiCarlo Select Merlot,' remember?"

He couldn't say no while looking into the expectancy shining on her face. Wrenching himself away, he walked to Barney and squatted. The dog rolled on his back for a belly rub. "The wine will still be there when we can afford it. It's too much to risk." He scratched and Barney whined with pleasure.

"Oh, I see. There's that arrogance again. You assume I'm doing this for you?"

He looked up. "You're not?"

She unfolded her legs, dropped them off the edge of the table. "I left Hollywood by my own choice, but most people thought I turned tail and ran." She leaned her palms on the edge of the table. "Even here, I'm still living in the shadow of that damned town. I'm tired of people making assumptions. I'm sick of having to appear to be whatever people think Indigo Blue ought to be." She lifted her hands, then slammed them onto the table's edge. "I'm ready to do what *I want* to do. And you know what? Tonight I realized that what I want to do is kick some butt." She nodded as if agreeing with herself then turned to him.

"So? What do you say, partner? Feel like kicking some butt with me?"

"Oh, lady, do I." A chinook wind of ideas, plans and joy swept through him. With the two of them united, anything seemed possible.

He gave Barney a last pat, stood and took the two steps that separated them. "But first…" Stepping between her legs, he ran his hands down the bare skin of her back, reaching down to cup her buns. "I have different plans for this butt, if that's okay with you?"

THIS WAS RIGHT. She *knew* it.

Harry had tried to tell her, but she hadn't been ready to listen. Tonight she listened and understood. Reaching for something else didn't mean she had to let him go. Harry would always be within her. Cherished, honored, remembered.

Her smile rose from joy in her chest. "I thought you'd never ask, DiCarlo." She wrapped her arms around his neck and pulled him into a hold-nothing-back kiss.

It felt good to let herself go, to do what made *her* happy. And damn, this made her happy.

His arms came around her, one hand sliding up under her hair to cup the back of her head.

Happy. And hot. And hurried. Wanting his skin under her hands, she pulled at the placket of his shirt, trying to loosen the buttons and pull it out of his pants at the same time.

He broke the kiss and, breathing heavily, leaned his forehead on hers. "Slow, Indigo. No skipping steps this time. We're all alone." His eyes, so close, seared her with intense emotion.

Exactly what emotion, her nonworking brain couldn't identify.

He rubbed her nose with his. "And we have all night."

A whimper broke from her throat. "Not when you look at me like that." His hands stroking her thighs didn't help either. She leaned in and took out her impatience on his willing mouth. Wrapping her legs around his hips, she pulled his granite erection right where she wanted it—almost.

"Damn, woman, that's not fair." He moaned and ground against her.

She crossed her arms, and with one smooth pull, the bra was gone. "Told you I was going to do what I want from here on out." She leaned back on her hands and shot him a saucy look.

His appreciative eyes were all over her. "I'm going on record as being heartily in favor of that decision." He lowered his head to take her nipple in his mouth. When he sucked, it lit a fuse that burned, fast and hot, direct to her core.

The recent days and weeks had drifted up while they took slow steps. She now realized those drifts of days were a mating dance—making what waited at the end that much sweeter. That much more urgent. "We have all night. But I need you now." She panted in his ear. "Please, don't make us wait any longer."

His hands tightened on her thighs, and he made a sound deep in his throat. His teeth grazed her nipple.

"Yes, that."

When he straightened, the tightness in his jaw told her that she wasn't the only one who'd been waiting for this.

She unlocked her ankles from around him and rocked from hip to hip, pulling down her thin spandex pants.

He'd undone only two buttons on his shirt when she grabbed his jeans and unzipped them. "Wasted motion, DiCarlo. Wasted..."

He brushed her hand away, pulled himself free and entered her with one long thrust. "Is this what you want?"

"Yes." Her muscles spasmed and heat pulsed, melting her. When she could no longer support her head, it fell back, and he sucked the base of her throat like a starving vampire.

The table was just the right height. He held her hips tilted, allowing perfect access to her pulsing core. She locked her legs around him, her thighs spread in as wide an angle as years of yoga allowed.

He withdrew so slowly it made her squirm. He hesitated, right at the edge of her, so long she had to look up. The dark, smoldering look in his eyes almost sent her over the edge.

"You. Are. Mine." He slid in, so fast and deep she felt their hip bones touch.

She moaned and raked her nails down his back, frantic with need. He grasped her hair, pulling her head back, his eyes demanding she not look away. "Tell me."

Just as she felt a twitch deep inside that signaled the knife's edge of release, he withdrew, and even her heels in his buttocks couldn't hold him close.

His cock pulsed at her beginning, but still he held.

"Please." She whimpered.

Tell me. His eyes demanded.

She let go, of the fear, the worry, the grief that had held her separate from him—from the world. She no longer needed that wall. She was safe here in his arms. Staring straight into his eyes, she said, "I am yours."

He thrust, deep and fast, but they were both coming before he got to the end of her, an orgasm that began when she looked into his eyes. They both cried out, and he pulled her off the table to rock her, riding the shockwaves of electricity that pulsed between them, perfectly matched.

When their breathing calmed, he cradled her, whispering small sweetnesses in her ear.

She buried her face in the hollow of his shoulder as the last storm-surge wave of emotion leaked onto his shoulder.

CHAPTER EIGHTEEN

One month later

AUTUMN IN THIS VINEYARD *is going to be the best.*

Danovan walked the row of vines at daybreak, stopping every fifty feet or so to sample a grape's sugar/acid content. The seeds were still green and bitter, but the cool, moist mornings were ideal to set the fruit.

Thank God they hadn't had one of those blazing hot summers that could raisin the fruit on the vine. The rising sun's intensity burned through his shirt, reminding him that it could still happen. They weren't out of the woods yet. He pulled off a cluster, dropped it into a baggie and, with a marker, noted where in the vineyard he'd picked it.

Hard to discern exactly when harvest would begin, but his best guess was the last week of August or the first week of September. The vines would decide. This must be how a woman felt nearing the end of her pregnancy. There was so much to do to prepare. Even more so this year. The new-to-them equipment had been delivered, installed and steamed to sterilization. Sean had cleaned the bottling line, and new bottle shipments were arriving daily, though cases of them already lined the walls of the warehouse. He'd ordered grapes from his Napa contact and had gotten a great deal, even with the shipping costs.

He rubbed the small of his aching back and straightened. Smiling, he took a deep breath of the aroma of ripening grapes.

Life is good.

At the sound of a screen door opening, he turned to the cabin. Indigo, in a silk robe, stepped barefoot onto the porch. Her hair was rumpled from bed, and she had the heavy-lidded look of just waking.

"Hey, sleepyhead, daylight's burning!"

She crossed her arms and squinted into the hammered sun. "Maybe I wouldn't sleep so late if you didn't keep me up all night."

He let out a self-satisfied chuckle. "I didn't hear you complaining last night."

"Too sure of yourself, DiCarlo. You've got to work on that."

"Maybe, but then I'd be perfect, and I'm told that can get irritating."

After that first night, when Indigo let him get close for the first time, they'd stayed wrapped together, snugged tight. He rarely bothered to sleep in his apartment anymore, unless they both decided not to climb the hill at the end of the day.

She was a constant surprise. Each day he found himself stumbling over new layers of Indigo Blue. He'd known her sadness, but now she showed him her joy, her love of life, her youthful optimism, her soul-deep sparkle. He hadn't known the love of a strong woman would make him stronger.

The past month had been the best thirty days of his life.

He cut through a break in the vines. "Why don't you hop in the shower, Indigo, and I'll make coffee?"

"Oh, for cripes…" She reached for the screen door. "Come on out, Barney."

The dog made an awkward shuffle down the stairs and hit the dirt running.

He barreled into Danovan's legs. "Ooof." He bent to ruffle Barney's ears. "I know you slept well. But does it always have to be on my feet?"

Tongue lolling, Barney looked up at him.

Damn dog is so ugly he's cute. "Come on, Barn. Want some eggs?" He took the steps and set the grocery bag half full of grapes on the weathered boards.

Indigo stood, arms crossed. "I keep telling you, human food isn't good—"

His kiss stopped her.

Then it stopped him.

But the sound of a car pulling into the drive below halted what would have happened next. Annoyed, he looked up to see Natalie's Camry stop in a parking space.

Indigo stepped out of his arms and put a hand to her hair. "Oh, jeez, we must be really late now."

"Speak for yourself. I was working until a rumpled sexpot walked onto the porch and distracted me." When she was about to protest, he stopped her with one more kiss.

His phone buzzed from the back pocket of his jeans. "Damned interruptions." He patted her firm butt. "Hop in the shower. Coffee's coming up."

On her way to the door, she put an extra roll in her hips that made him want to ignore the phone and chase her back to bed.

And her wink before she stepped in told him she knew it.

"Imp." He pulled out the phone. "DiCarlo."

"Danovan, it's Will, from Cedar Cellars. I have bad news."

His stomach took a high dive. "Don't even tell me our grape shipment is going to be late."

"Worse. There are no grapes to ship."

His stomach fell, landing with a splat on the porch. "What?" He put a hand on the rail to steady himself.

"Mildew. We've gotten a lot of rain up here. We've been spraying for weeks, but nothing's worked. I'm facing a total crop failure."

The pain in Will's voice made it impossible to yell at him. But Danovan still wanted to. "What the hell am I going to do now, Will? It's way too late to buy elsewhere—everything's been contracted."

"Damned if I know. I've got my own problems. If it helps, I'm more pissed than you are about it."

"I know you are. I'm sorry as hell for your loss, Will." He paced the porch for something to do. His mind outran his feet. "Look, I've got to go and figure out plan B. Best of luck to you, okay?"

"And to you, Danovan. Sorry."

Click.

I could try Danbury out in Temecula. Or Gray Horse. But the odds of them... He was halfway down the steps when he stopped short.

Indigo. She had put the winery up for collateral to handle capacity that they no longer needed. He winced as the weight of the winery slammed onto his shoulders. She'd gone into debt on his say-so. Their grapes looked good so far, but even a bumper crop wouldn't fill all those empty bottles in the warehouse.

He couldn't tell her.

He turned back, mounted the stairs and headed in to make coffee as if the world hadn't just imploded.

Somehow, he would make this right. Fast.

IF THE CRUSH is good, maybe next year we'll put in the little stream over there, and the arched bridge that will lead to the gazebo where couples will say their vows.

Indigo sat at her desk, staring through the window at the emerald expanse of golf-course-worthy lawn rolling down the hill to the road. The groundskeepers were doing a great job. If she weren't so busy, or so dignified, she'd go out and roll down it. She imagined Sondra's horrified expression. Maybe she'd find time this afternoon…

Her Cheshire Cat grin reflected in the clean window. The woman staring back at her looked like she had it together. Competent. Accomplished. Happy.

And maybe a bit smug.

Her grin widened. Nothing wrong with a little smug. Being in love with Danovan was like playing. He made what had always been awkward for her, easy. Her reflection frowned. Okay, so she hadn't told him about the love part yet. But it was complicated, what with her being his boss, them trying to keep their affair secret from the staff…

Okay, so she was afraid. She had reason to be. What if telling him changed things between them? He seemed as infatuated as she, but he hadn't said the *L* word yet, either.

"Ahem."

Only Sondra could make clearing her throat sound cultured.

Indigo swiveled her chair. "Come in."

The woman shifted from foot to foot in the doorway, her fingers working the tie of her green apron. "I need to take Friday off." Her chin jutted. "I haven't taken a day off since I returned, and I have an appointment that cannot be rescheduled."

"Of course. You're allowed a vacation day now and again."

Sondra's lips pursed. Her gaze roamed the room. She looked like she'd been expecting an argument and, in the absence of one, wasn't sure how to proceed. "Natalie will need help during the busy times. Though Becky is learning, she doesn't yet have the expertise—"

"Of course, I'll keep an eye out and jump in if it gets busy."

"You?" She said it as if a toddler had proposed doing surgery. "I'd thought that Danovan would assist."

Indigo's jaw tightened so fast her teeth clicked. "Danovan is busy preparing for the harvest." She'd be damned if Sondra would ruin her mood. She leaned back and forced her muscles to stand down. "I'm fully capable, Sondra. I may not know everything yet, but I know *our* wines." Stinging, she couldn't resist a small one-up. "After all, I've signed many local clients. Including the Demure Damsel."

"I'm not convinced our wines had much to do with that sale." Sondra managed to appear innocent even while she looked down her nose.

Indigo flushed. From irritation or embarrassment, she wasn't sure. Maybe a bit of both. "Well, that sale helps pay for the vacation day I just allowed you, so I hardly think you're in a position to complain, are you?"

Sondra's spine lost its rigid line, and a haunted

look of animal fear flashed across her face before her usual haughty mask fell once more.

"I'll be sure everything is in order before I leave on Thursday." She turned and stalked out.

What is going on there?

BEHIND THE CLOSED door of his office, Danovan leaned his elbows on the desk and dialed one of the last contacts he had.

"Sorry, Danovan. I've got nothing. All my grapes are contracted."

He wasn't surprised. It was the answer he'd heard thirty times in the past three hours. He'd even stopped wasting time giving his name and his story about the tenth call. "Do you know of anyone who has any for sale?" It worried him to buy grapes from an unknown entity, but at this point —

"Where are you located, again?"

"The Central Valley. Why?"

"Right. Well, somebody at my local co-op told me a guy named Winters down your way had some grapes to sell. Something about a small winery that went belly-up. You know him?"

Danovan flipped through his address book.

"Winter Wines—Reese Winters, owner."

He'd skipped that name on purpose the first time through. After his failed attempt at an interview at the winery months ago, Danovan knew there was zero chance that Winters would cross the Boldens, despite being sympathetic. And selling grapes to a winery where Danovan was employed would be considered high treason by his former in-laws.

"I do know Mr. Winters. And he knows me. Thanks for the tip." He clicked End.

He dropped his head in his hands. He'd have to tell Indigo. God, he'd rather clean a Porta-Potty after an outdoor rock concert. In August. With his bare hands.

But she was the owner. His boss. She had the right to know. He put his hands on the desk and, sighing, pushed himself to his feet. It wasn't that she would fire him. He didn't think she'd hold it against him—in their professional *or* their private lives.

And that made it even worse.

He imagined telling her. The sadness would return to her eyes. The grief-stricken waif he'd met the day of his interview would return. Only this time, it would be *his* fault.

True, she'd made the ultimate decision; it was her signature on the loan documents. But he should have known she'd heed his advice. He was her teacher. Her mentor. And he'd told her the risk was negligible. Their previous five-year plan now looked golden. In hindsight.

"Shit." She was right. He was arrogant, always believing he knew best.

Cleaning a Porta-Potty was too good a job for him.

Some wunderkind he was. His firing from Bacchanal was a fart in space compared to making the walk to Indigo's office to tell her this news. When his knees went spongy, he plopped back into his chair.

Add cowardice to his list of faults. He *couldn't* bring more sadness to her eyes.

There just *had* to be another way.

Winters.

Something about that name sent a buzz of possibility down his spine. There was an answer there somewhere. He felt it. And his instincts were always right.

Well, almost always.

An hour later, he pulled open the tasting-room door. The plan he had cobbled together would work, if…

If stood behind the bar, chatting with a customer. When Sondra looked up, he held up a finger and tipped his chin.

She excused herself, wiped her hands on a cloth and walked over. "Yes, Danovan?"

He glanced around. "Is Indigo in her office?"

"She's giving a *massage*." She said it like *blow job*.

He felt his ears heat. "I don't think—" He bit back the rebuke that wanted so badly to roll off his tongue. "Sondra. I need your help. It's important."

"You do?" Some of her flint chipped off with the words, and her eyes lit up.

He'd have to be careful—if he stepped on her toes, he was dead in the water. "I'm taking a chance by talking to you. By even asking. I wouldn't do it if it weren't so critical. But I know you want the winery to be a success, so…"

"What is it?"

"I need you to call a supplier and negotiate a contract for a load of grapes." He glanced around to be sure no one was close enough to overhear. "And I need you to keep this between us."

She crossed her arms. "Why?"

He forced himself to meet her stare. It wasn't easy with all the squirming that was happening in his brain. He'd suspected she wouldn't do it without knowing everything. But he'd hoped. "Because the supplier won't sell to me."

She tipped her head back. "Ah. The Boldens."

Holding her gaze got harder. "The Boldens."

"Why don't you have your girlfriend call?"

His mouth dropped open, but nothing came out.

"Oh, come on. Did you really think no one knew? You two have been mooning around like a couple of hormone-drunk teenagers for a month now."

He swallowed. Well, he was too deep to back out now. He spit out what he'd hoped to keep in. "If shit comes down, I don't want Indigo implicated."

Her eyes slitted. "Oh, but I'm disposable?"

He was shaking his head as she said the words. "No, no. It'd all be on me. I'd see to it."

She studied him. "And why should I take this risk of getting fired if she finds out?"

Here came the trickiest part of all. He glanced at his feet. "Because I think you need this job. Now, more than ever. Like I said, it's in all our best interests that the winery does well and, trust me, we need these grapes."

When he heard her *tsk* of irritation, his brain stopped squirming. He inhaled the first deep breath he'd taken since he left his office.

"All right, Danovan. Tell me what I'm to say."

INDIGO LOOKED UP when Danovan walked into her office. "I'm starving. What would you say to lunch at the Farmhouse? I'm buying."

The look of veiled caution on his taut features stopped her prattle *and* her hunger. "What's wrong?" In the few beats of silence, she felt her pulse, like hummingbird wings, brushing the inside of her wrists.

"I've got bad news." His lips lifted to a small smile. "And good news." He crossed to the guest chair and sat. "The grape supplier called me this morning. Total crop failure. He can't fill the order."

The loan! She remembered all the pretty, shiny equipment in the warehouse. And her collateral to buy it. "Shit, Danovan—"

He held up a hand. "The good news. I found

another supplier. Better news. Same price. Best news. They're local. Lower shipping costs."

She fell back in her chair and put her hand over her jolting heart. "Jeez, you scared me. Next time give me the good news first, will you?"

"Sorry to alarm you." He slid a few pages across the desk to her. "He faxed me the contract. Go ahead and sign it, and I'll fax it back. Then I'll let you buy me lunch to celebrate."

"Nice save." She scanned the paper in front of her. "Just let me read it first."

CHAPTER NINETEEN

INDIGO SCRUBBED A water ring off the tasting bar with a cloth, watching a senior couple wander the gift shop. They were the only customers in the place. Friday was the tasting room's slowest day. That was probably why Sondra chose to take it off. She didn't trust anyone with *her* baby.

Indigo let go of the irritation when her stomach growled. "Hey, Natalie, what would you say to ordering pizza? We've never had a company lunch, and I'd say this is the perfect day for it."

Down the bar, Natalie's eyes lit up. "I vote yes."

Indigo had enjoyed the morning. It was great to interact with the customers, and she'd gotten to know Natalie and Becky better, since Sondra usually stood guard over them, as well. The elderly couple strolled out the door and down the porch steps to their car. "Better yet, let's have a picnic on the porch."

"But if customers—"

"I'll order an extra pizza, and we'll invite them to eat with us." She lifted her hand for a high-five. "See how easy that is?"

Natalie slapped her palm. "Think Sondra could take every Friday off? You're more fun." As soon as the words were out, her eyes widened and she slapped a hand over her mouth.

Indigo kept a straight face as she pulled her phone from the front pocket of her winery apron. "It's easy to be a substitute. It's the teacher who has the tough job." She hit speed dial for Yukon Pizza.

While she waited for the restaurant to pick up, an older man with a thick torso and a shock of white hair walked into the tasting room and headed for the bar.

"Yukon. Best pizza in the lower forty-eight. Can I help you?" the voice on the other end of the phone finally said.

"Yes, I'd like to order a couple of pizzas for delivery."

Natalie laid a coaster and a tasting glass in front of the man. "What can I pour for you, sir?"

"Thank you, miss, but I'm not here to taste. I'm looking for Indigo Blue."

His florid face almost matched his red polo shirt. The logo read Winter Wines. *Our new grape supplier.* "Um, I'll have to call you back." She hit End and pasted on a customer-service smile. "I'm Indigo. Can I help you?"

"You sounded different on the phone. I'm Reece Winters."

The string tugged, and the memory popped out. "Oh, Mr. Winters." She walked around the end of the bar. "You and I didn't speak on the phone, but I'm glad you stopped by."

"Well, if we didn't, someone's pulling both our legs. I could have sworn she said her name was Indigo." He shook his head. "Anyway, I figured since you're local, I'd stop by and countersign that contract in person." He put out a broad hand for her to shake. "I'm hoping this can be the start of a long, mutually beneficial relationship."

Shifting the phone, she took his hand, listening to the bells jangling in her mind.

He mixed up two phone calls. It happens.

"Would you like a tour of our production facility? We're pretty proud of our new equipment. Afterward, if you have time, you can have lunch with us."

"Sounds great."

She turned and handed her phone across the bar to Natalie. "Will you order a couple of pizzas? Just hit redial."

Natalie smiled. "You're trusting me with the toppings?"

Distracted by the bells and the dangling threads, Indigo nodded.

Mr. Winters glanced around and up at the soaring timbers. "I can't imagine why I wasn't aware of your winery."

Indigo led the way through the door to the barrel room. "Well, Uncle Bob, the previous owner, produced only what he grew. But we have plans to—" The door of the warehouse was pulled from her hand.

Danovan looked as surprised as she. Until he glanced behind her—then he looked much more surprised. He flinched and his eyes darted, as if looking for an escape route.

The bells morphed to the claxon of air raid sirens. "What is it, Dan—"

"DiCarlo." A growl came from behind her. "What are you doing here?"

"Danovan is my vintner and our manager." She looked back to Danovan. "You two know each other." It wasn't a question. She didn't know how or why, but this was going to be bad. She could almost see white bolts of electricity arcing between the two men. Caught in the middle, the bolts shot down her nerves, snapping and popping. Or maybe that was her own dread. Either way, when it hit her nerve endings, it sizzled. And burned.

"I think we've both been had, miss."

"Reece." Danovan had the doomed look of a firing-squad victim.

"So this is where you washed up." Mr. Winter's florid face edged toward a startling shade of eggplant. "I told you about the Boldens. You knew I couldn't sell to you, so you had some woman call me."

She heard the *scree* of his teeth grinding.

"I'm right, aren't I?"

Danovan's voice went up an octave. "Forget me. You should be talking to Indigo. She's the owner."

But Winters refused distraction. "I understood your youthful ambition and the mistakes that come from it." His hands fisted. "What I won't abide is a liar. Especially one who puts my livelihood at risk." He reached in the back pocket of his pants, pulled out a few folded sheets of paper and tore them in half. "I'm not selling grapes to you."

When he handed the torn sheets to Indigo, Winters's eyes were sad. "I'm sorry, miss."

He turned, stalked away.

Indigo jerked from her frozen state. "Wait, Mr. Winters. Can't we talk about this?"

Without a backward glance, he walked out the front door.

Taking her new life with him.

She kept her back to Danovan. She didn't want to see him. "What did you do?" Her words sounded as dead as the place they came from, deep in her chest.

The silence at her back had the tint of stunned.

It didn't matter what he said, anyway. It was done.

She walked away.

TEN MINUTES LATER she didn't have to look up to feel him standing in her doorway.

"Just tell me." She had no right to the shock that echoed in the hollow places inside her where her happy dreams used to live. After all, he'd lied to her before. But in wanting him, she'd forgotten. Explanations, even reasonable ones, didn't erase a lie. The dead space in her chest expanded until it was hard to inhale around it.

It was too late to matter, but she had to see if he was lying, still. She raised her head.

His handsome face was haggard, as though he'd aged in the past few minutes. "There's not a spare cluster of grapes in the state. I even tried Oregon and Arizona. I called Texas, for God's sake." He tore his hand through his hair. "But then I did the math. Shipping costs would have killed us. It would have cost more to get them here than we'd have made on them. Winters was the only one with extra capacity. And I knew if he knew I was involved, things would end up...well, like they have."

"Why did you have *some woman* call? Why didn't you come and tell me?"

He stepped in. "I'm really sorry, Indigo. I was doing my best to find a solution."

She remembered the warning bells earlier. A coating of frost covered the walls of the dead space. "Who was the woman?"

"What woman?"

"The woman who called Winters."

"Oh." He seemed to pull himself from distraction. *Probably trying to think up some spin on the truth to get him out of this. After all, it worked on me before.*

"Um. I'd rather…I'd rather not say."

"I have no doubt of that." She crossed her arms as if the flimsy barrier could protect her. "Who was it?"

His eyes were on everything but her. "Sondra. She didn't want to. I—convinced her."

She had to keep going, in spite of the dart in her heart. "I see. So given the choice of trusting the owner of the business affected by this setback, you instead went to an employee who you know I've had problems with." She nodded. "Makes perfect sense to me."

"Indigo—"

She held up a hand. It stopped him. "Do you have such little faith in my ability? In me?" She hated the pain that leaked out in the last word. She slammed her lips closed and waited.

His shoulders slumped. Barney's basset face had nothing on him; Danovan was the picture of heartsick.

An hour ago, that would have mattered.

"Indigo, I knew how you'd worry. You never wanted the loan, not really. You did it because I wanted it. You trusted me." It came out in a rush. "I couldn't fail you again."

"We could have worked through it. Together. Danovan, the only way you've ever failed is in not coming to me. Talking to me. I was right not to trust you. With my business or my—with anything else."

LAURA DRAKE   333

He looked at his feet. "It was mine to fix."

"*Yours*? Really?" Her nerves, crispy from the lightning strike, crumbled before a blowtorch of anger. "Who the hell do you think you are? It wasn't yours to fix. You don't own The Widow. I do."

"I know that. I've never—"

"You should have trusted that I could handle the 'worry.'" Her fingers clawed the air quotes. The blowtorch roared, burning her illusions like a brush fire in a drought. "I'm not another little fairy princess who's going to break under strain."

He took a step back as if she'd slapped him. "That's dirty. Bringing up Lissette—"

"You betrayed me. The fact that you didn't trust me is all I need to know of what you think of me. As a businessperson *and* a woman."

"Indigo—"

"Don't you get it? I didn't need a savior. I needed a partner." The fire's fuel was almost gone. She tasted bitter cinders at the back of her throat. "Now I'm going to lose the winery. I'll leave with less than I had when I came here." She snorted. "And I'd thought leaving Hollywood was my lowest point." She shook her head. "It seems I keep finding new lows. When will I learn?"

The walls went up, his expression shifting from subtle shades of vulnerable to guarded. From guarded to impenetrable, as evidenced by the iron in his jaw and the glint of steel in his eye.

"I've done nothing but try to help. You have the right to be upset with my choices. But I've never been disloyal. To you or any employer—or to any woman. You have to believe that."

He hesitated to see if she'd argue.

She didn't.

He didn't so much straighten as tighten. A boxer preparing for a gut punch. "You need to fire me." His words fell like chips off steel.

"What?"

"Do us both a favor. Fire me." His lips twisted. "I'd quit, but that would be disloyal, wouldn't it?"

The pile of ashes in her chest collapsed, smothering an ember of hope she hadn't realized was still there—a hope that he'd come up with an answer that would carry them through this crisis. An answer they both could live with.

Proving that you're still waiting for a man to make everything okay for you, Blue.

Only sheer pride kept her shoulders straight and allowed her to hold his stare. Apparently it was the only thing that survived the fire. It was all she had left. "Fine. Gather your stuff and get off the property. I don't need you."

WINE WAS FINE, but this was a night for his old buddy, Jack Daniel.

Danovan sat at the bar of the crowded pub, sipping the only friend he could buy. In the dim light of the faux Victorian lamps, he watched the ornate mirror behind the bar, observing the Friday-night crowd with an anthropologist's eye. When he squinted, they blurred to a kaleidoscope of color and sound. That was nice.

He'd felt this way since his debacle this after-noon, as if he'd been inside a bell tower when the clock struck twelve. His ears rang with the reper-cussions. The sound and vibration still resonated, echoing back and forth. Even the air around him felt different—close, safe. He kind of liked that bell. It kept out the world and whatever came next. He was grateful, for now, to exist in this space between.

You did everything you could. She'll be okay now. That blunt pain was one of the vibrations he felt spreading through him like a deepening bruise. But his friend Jack Daniel was helping with that. Danovan signaled the bartender for an-other.

"Well, look who's slumming."

At Roxy's chalkboard screech, he turned and the bell around him cracked and fell away. Lissette stood beside her friend, fine crystal next to coal.

"Go feed your flying monkeys, Roxy, I'm not in the mood." He threw back the shot.

Her nose wrinkled. "Pond scum." She turned away and smoothed a too-short dress over her hips. "Come on, Lissette, let's troll. There're a couple of cute guys at that table."

"You go ahead. I'll be there in a few."

With studied nonchalance, Roxy stalked away.

The sight of his ex brought the past crashing into the present. Her sweet perfume filled his head with flashbacks. The cool spring evening she'd taken him to the boathouse and seduced him into ridding her of virginity—not that he'd needed a huge push. The morning he'd picked himself off the floor after informing Lissette's father that she was pregnant. Lissette, fragile in white, walking down the aisle toward him. Her mascara-smeared face screaming drunken insults. The baby they'd created, bathed in moonlight from the window over the crib. More echoes.

Lissette twirled the straw in her Metropolitan and smiled. "You look like day-old road kill, dude. What happened? Did the Hollywood doll wise up and leave stiletto punctures up your back?"

He signaled the bartender for another. No use lying—this was a small town. "Let's just say I'm currently unemployed."

Her almost-white brows lifted. "What did you do? Oh, wait, don't tell me. You did what you always do—you walked around acting like the savior of the universe, making imperial decisions, thinking you know what's best for everyone and everything." She lifted her drink in a mock toast. "Admit it. I'm close."

He clicked his empty glass to hers. "Dead-on, as always. With the facts *and* the switchblade sarcasm." He put both elbows on the bar. "If you'll

excuse me, I'm really not in the mood to play tonight, Lissette."

"Aww, I'm sorry, Danovan." She slipped onto
the seat beside him. "I don't mean to be a bitch.
Really."

"I'm not touching that one, either." When the
bartender walked up, Danovan pointed to both
their glasses.

For a few moments, other conversations flowed
around them.

"I moved out," she said in a little mouse voice.

That sunk into the self-pity cotton he'd wrapped
himself in. "From your parents'?"

"About time, don't you think?"

And he wasn't going *there*, either. "Did you
move in with Roxy?"

"Nope. Got a place on my own. I have a job,
too, you know."

He turned to look at her, first making sure his
mouth was closed.

She laughed. "Yeah, I know. Kind of shocked
me, too. I'm working at an antiques store just
down the road from here. It turns out, I like antiques. It's a nothing job right now, but I'm learning, and I hope to become the manager someday.
Maybe even a buyer."

His ex—responsible? Working like a commoner? "Well good for you, Liss." Wow, if that
was possible, what else was? "I don't want you to

take this the wrong way, but at the risk of sounding arrogant, yet again…I'm proud of you."

She ducked her head to hide her blush. "Yeah, well, after Esperanza—I mean, after—" she waved a hand "—then you were gone. My parents tiptoed around me like I was a mental patient. There was really no one left to look at but myself."

She focused on her fingers, folding the edge of her cocktail napkin. "I was rebelling against my parents even before you came along, but it was so much more fun when I saw how pissed they were that I was dating you."

"Oh, thanks for that. I wasn't feeling low enough."

"Aww, Danovan, I didn't mean it that way. You were so sweet, taking on Daddy for me." She touched his sleeve. "I loved you when we married. I was just too young, and probably too spoiled, not to screw it up." She sighed and went back to her cocktail napkin folding. "I know you won't like hearing this, but you were a lot like Daddy. Always trying to make the world safe for me. So I think I just transferred my rebellion from him to you."

Who is this woman? Not the woman he married, surely.

"I screwed up so many things. There's so much I'd do different now. But it's too late."

Her big china-blue eyes turned her statement into a question. He just looked back.

She made a sad, disparaging sound. "Yeah, I thought so." She put on a bright smile that didn't come near to reaching her eyes. "But, hey, I'm a princess, right? I've got that going for me."

The world had shifted today in more ways than he'd realized. "Ah, Lissette, I'm sorry."

"That's okay. I earned it." She waved the subject away. "What if you went back to your Hollywood lady and told her that you're an idiot and you're sorry?"

He just shook his head. "She already knows both those things."

Lissette slid off the barstool. "Well, I better find out what trouble Roxy has gotten us into." Leaning over, she brushed her lips across his cheek. "You take care of yourself now, you hear?"

CHAPTER TWENTY

INDIGO SAT BEHIND her desk, chair swiveled to the window, waiting for Sondra's car to pull into the lot.

Her mother had always told her to do the dirtiest job first.

She reached for her coffee cup, noting the fine shake in her fingers that came from too much caffeine and too little sleep.

At first, after the showdown with Danovan yesterday, she'd been an automaton, doing what she had to do to get through the wasteland leavings of the day, her brain on autopilot. Once the employees left for the day and the doors were locked, she couldn't avoid thinking any longer.

Staring at the wooden ceiling over her bed in the single-digit hours of night, she had imagined her life as a railroad line. Most of the time you rocked along, enjoying the scenery. Major events were like station stops—pauses in the trip. She'd survived a couple of derailments along the way, but she'd naïvely assumed they were behind her. She'd trusted her gut and watched the tracks retreat into the distance ahead.

But yesterday, the tracks had disappeared from beneath her. And she hadn't seen it coming. It took several hours of staring at the twisted ruin to absorb the shock.

Looking down the track behind her lent a different perspective. She could now see that Harry had taken the role of the father she'd never had, teaching her, guiding her. Protecting her. He'd picked her up and given her back her self-worth, only wanting her love in return. And she had given it readily. She had loved him, with a fierceness she hadn't known was in her. She could only hope he'd known that.

Then she'd come here and hired Danovan. He'd agreed to teach her the wine business. But he'd taught her much more. He'd taught her a different kind of love. A passionate, lighthearted love between two equals.

Except he didn't quite see it that way, did he?

She hurt. Not only because he wasn't the man she had believed him to be, but also because she'd let him in. And now the space that Danovan had occupied inside her ached like a missing limb. But she couldn't afford the luxury of indulging in her heartache right now. No more pretty illusions. She had to clean up this latest wreck and begin laying new track.

So she'd spent the night plotting a disaster recovery plan.

And today, she'd begin implementation.

She was waiting when Sondra stepped into the tasting room and pulled her key from the lock.

"You couldn't turn down a chance to take over, could you?"

Sondra whirled to face her, startled. "Whatever are you talking about?"

But she knew. Indigo saw past the surprise to the thoughts racing behind the woman's eyes. She recognized the look, because Danovan had that same look yesterday. "I think it's time you and I stopped playing games, don't you?"

Sondra pulled in a breath, inflating her imperious suit. "Whatever. It worked. And you're welcome." She took a step toward the tasting bar.

"Oh, no, you don't." Indigo dropped an arm—a railroad crossing bar. "Why do you assume that? If it worked, I wouldn't know about it, would I?"

"Winters knows?" Her shoulders caved a bit as the air leaked out of her suit.

"He was here yesterday. Had a little visit with Danovan, tore up the contract and handed it to me before walking out."

"Oh."

"Why did you do it?"

More air leaked out in her snort. "Well, I didn't do it for *you*."

"I'm naïve, not delusional." Indigo tightened her gut and asked the question she should have asked months ago, but she'd been too afraid. "You've had a stick up your butt about me from the very beginning. Before I prepare your last check and take your key, I'd like to know why."

"You're *firing* me?" Sondra threw her shoulders back and rose to her full height. The suit inflated in spite of the leaks. "You can't fire me. You need me."

"Nope. I realized yesterday that I don't. I may not know everything, but I know enough to hire a suitable replacement. One with a better attitude."

"Oh, really?" Her mouth took a bitter twist. "Fine. Fire me, then. It means nothing to you." She threw up her hands. "You want to know what I have against you, Little Miss Hollywood? You marry an old man to become somebody. Then, when he has the good taste to die, you take your 'poor me' show on the road and waltz in here not knowing wine from goat piss. You bat your eyelashes and expect everyone to fall over themselves, teaching you. Well, that may work on men, but it doesn't work on *me*." Sondra stood, hand on hips, her cheeks a deep shade of rosé. "You have everything."

Every slight, every insult, every assumption people had made about Indigo gathered, forming a squirming hot ball of outrage. "How dare you?" Indigo leaned in until she was nose to nose with Sondra. "You don't know shit about me. I have nothing. You get that? All I had when I got here was what I'd earned with my bare hands as a masseuse and a yoga teacher. That's what paid your salary until I went out and increased sales." She spread her arms. "This place is it. It's all I have.

And after your stunt was exposed yesterday, I'm most likely going to lose it, too."

When she stuck a finger in Sondra's face, the woman flinched.

"And don't you *ever* insinuate that I didn't love my husband. Think what you want of *me*, but Harry was a saint of a man, and I'll be *damned* if you or anyone else will wipe your feet on his memory." Her finger had somehow morphed to a fist, and she shook it in the startled woman's face.

All the air had whooshed out of her. She stood, glaring at Sondra, chest heaving.

Sondra stood glaring back, breathing just as heavily. Then, slowly, her face changed, seeming to collapse in on itself. Her shoulders rounded and hunched. "You can't fire me." Her voice quivered, as did her bottom lip.

Sondra dropped her head back, and tears traced down the sides of her face. "I have less than you!"

Indigo would have been less surprised if Sondra had stripped off her clothes and danced on the bar.

"Do you want to know where I was yesterday? In court. Divorce court." She dropped her face in her hands and sobbed. "My husband left me. Left *me*, for a woman half my age…a little chit who does the weather on the local news channel." She sniffed. "She couldn't tell you her name without a teleprompter, much less the *fucking* weather."

Indigo's brain tried to assimilate the fact that

Sondra had just dropped the f-bomb. "I didn't even know you knew that word."

Sondra let out a watery chuckle and ran her fingers through the mess of mascara under her eyes. "Well, then, it seems we both learned something today."

I sure have, anyway. The ice queen had melted to a sodden mess. Sondra's red nose, blotchy skin and ugly cry proved there was a human in there somewhere. She touched Sondra's elbow. "Come to my office. We'll get you cleaned up and then we can talk." Sondra would be mortified if anyone saw her like this.

After the loan of mascara and a mirror, and several tissues later, Sondra looked more her old self.

"I really need this job. My husband has cleaned out the bank accounts, and…" Her voice wavered.

"You're not fired. Providing—" She handed over another tissue. "Providing you can accept my supervision. I'll want to hear your advice, but once I make a decision, I expect you to respect it and carry it out. Even if you don't agree."

"I understand."

"I know you understand." She held Sondra's eyes, surprised at how, today, it seemed easier to do. "What I'm asking is if you can accept my authority." She was never giving up control of something she owned, ever again. To anyone.

Sondra nodded and blotted under her lower lashes. "I can do that."

"Good. Then I think we'll make a strong team." Indigo flipped on her computer. "Now. Do you know anyone you can recommend as a new manager?"

"What?" Sondra snapped out of her personal drama and to attention. "Where's Danovan?"

Indigo tapped a key, and the monitor came to life. "I fired him yesterday." She found her accounting software icon and double-clicked.

"Are you out of your mind?" Her cut-glass diction made it clear the ice queen was back.

Indigo lifted an eyebrow.

"Sorry." She cleared her throat and smoothed her hands over her thighs. "Can I ask why you let him go?"

"By not discussing the problem with me, he put the winery in jeopardy."

"Oh, I see. He stepped on your little—" She closed her eyes and took a breath, then opened them and tried again. "It's your decision to make. But you said you wanted to hear my advice, so I'm going to give it to you. Will you listen?"

Indigo tapped in the password. "If it doesn't take too long. I have an important errand."

"Danovan DiCarlo is the best vintner in the area. In a few years, he'll be the best in the state. It was blind luck that you got him to begin with— he can do much better than a small operation like this. Surely you know that."

Indigo pulled up their cash-flow statement then

turned her attention to Sondra. "I really don't have time for past history."

"Fine. Let's talk about the present. He didn't tell you about the grape situation because he didn't want you implicated if things went bad."

"That wasn't his decision to make. I should have been informed. I could have been upfront with Winters—about everything."

Sondra folded her hands in her lap. "And what would you have done if that didn't work out?"

"What I *would* have done isn't the point. The point is, he didn't give me the opportunity—"

"He's in love with you, you know." Sondra stood. "At least, he *was*." She turned and strode to the door, her mantle of aloof firmly in place. "I have work to do. You do what you feel is best."

A half hour later, Indigo was on the road.

"Firing Danovan wasn't a personal thing. It was business." Saying it out loud helped, even if there was no one in the car to convince except herself.

They'd obviously not been discreet enough, if Sondra knew they'd been…dating. "Okay, so she knew. But there's no way that she could know something that *I* didn't know. That Danovan loves me?"

Unless he told her.

"You do not believe that."

He told her about the grape fiasco, and he didn't tell you.

"Maybe, but Danovan wouldn't do that. Besides,

that no longer matters. I'm about to go into *the* most important meeting of my life. Do you think we could focus on *that* for a minute?"

Silence. Apparently she'd actually won an argument with herself.

For now.

"Oh, shut the hell up." She turned in at the wooden sign decorated with a horse-drawn sleigh amid snow-covered hills, and the words Winter Wines arching over it. She'd done some homework since meeting the man yesterday. This was a much larger operation than The Widow: seven times the size of their vineyard and twice the production. As for the grapes he didn't use himself, he sold most of them to Bacchanal.

And now her. She stepped out of her car and slammed the door. She stood tall, tightened her sphincter and, guts shaking, tottered in high heels through the gravel lot.

Thanks to a video tour posted on their website, she knew where the offices were. So when the woman in the white apron behind the counter asked if she could help, Indigo told her, "I have an appointment with Mr. Winters," and then kept walking.

"Let me just page him for you." She reached for the phone.

"I know where the office is." She breezed by with a wave, hoping the woman wouldn't call her bluff. Or see the shake in her hand.

Better to beg forgiveness than ask permission.

She pushed through the swinging door to a hallway of offices. The white shock of hair she glimpsed in the window of the second one supercharged her heartbeat.

Glancing at the ceiling, she mouthed a silent, heartfelt plea then knocked.

"Come."

She opened the door, strode in and stuck out her hand.

Mr. Winters's lips shifted from a budding smile to a thin line as red spread up his neck. He put his hands on the desk and pushed himself to his feet. "Miss, I can't—"

"Mr. Winters, you and I didn't get a chance to talk yesterday." Indigo left her hand awkwardly suspended between them, telling herself if he took it, she'd at least have a shot.

Come on...

When her hand disappeared into his broad one, she could breathe again. "I will only take a few minutes of your time. I know you are a busy man." She retrieved her hand and sat.

"Miss—"

"Please, call me Indigo."

"Ms. Blue. I don't know what we have to talk about. I cannot sell to a winery that employs Donovan DiCarlo."

She forced a smile. "Then we don't have a problem.

Mr. DiCarlo no longer works at The Tippling Widow, as of yesterday."

His bushy white brows rose, and the chair squealed when he leaned back. "Is that a fact?"

She leaned forward. "Mr. Winters, I hope to have a long, satisfying business relationship with you. And that cannot be founded on dishonesty. If I say something, you may rely on it being the truth."

He steepled his fingers and studied her.

She made herself still. On the outside.

He sighed. "He's not a bad guy, you know. He just has some things to learn."

It was her turn to sit back, fumbling with how to respond. "Sir, I don't think…"

His easy smile didn't simplify matters. "Call me Reece, please. If we're going to do business, we should be on a first-name basis. Now, would you like a tour of *my* facility?"

"I'd love to see your grapes, Reece." Some of the tension of the past twenty-four hours whooshed out with the words.

An hour later, pride dancing in her stomach, she was on her way home. The summer wind tore in the open windows and sunroof, lifting her hair as if it, too, was dancing. "I did it. I actually, by God, did it!" She pounded a fist on the steering wheel.

She'd held back in the fear of a misstep for so long that releasing it, she felt weightless. She wanted to hug Barney. She wanted a milkshake for dinner. She wanted to party.

Too bad you fired the only person you'd want to party with.

"Well, I can guarantee that *you* weren't on the guest list. And frankly, you're starting to freak me out. I don't think this is normal."

Probably not. I'll go away if you stop denying the truth.

"Truth is, I just saved The Widow." She swiped the hair out of her smile. "Me. All by myself."

Now who's being arrogant? You had help.

"I don't see anyone else in this car."

The nightmare scene from yesterday floated through her mind, along with his words.

"I've done nothing but try to help. You have the right to be upset with my choices. But I've never been disloyal. To you or any employer— or to any woman.

"You need to fire me."

"Do us both a favor. Fire me."

"I'd quit, but that would be disloyal, wouldn't it?"

His eyes. Belying his biting words, his eyes were soft. Sad.

Loving.

"He *wanted* me to fire him." Denial blew out the sunroof. "He knew that firing him was the only way for me to get the grapes. To save the winery. So he goaded me into it."

And he trusted that you were smart enough to figure it out. Not bad for an arrogant ass who wants to make all the decisions, huh?

He'd been trying to help her in the only way he could.

That soft, loving look burned like the deep cut of a razor blade. At first there is no pain. But then blood sheets down, and you know it's going to hurt soon. A lot. And for a long time.

He'd trusted her when she hadn't trusted herself. Since she'd come to the winery, she'd been whining that people didn't respect her authority. The truth was, the authority was lying in front of her the whole time, and she had been too scared to pick it up. When she hadn't, Sondra and Danovan picked up the power and used it. For their own purposes, to be sure, but also to help The Widow.

To help her.

She waited for her smartass conscience to comment, but it had gone back to sleep.

The newly painted sign for The Tippling Widow came up on her left. Slowing, she turned in and hit the buttons to roll up the car windows and close the sunroof. She didn't feel like partying anymore. She wanted to bury herself under the bedcovers, snuggle with Barney and pour out her regret into the pillow.

Because, even knowing all this, it didn't matter. She and Danovan were over.

What happens to teachers when the students graduate?

They move on to the next students.

Danovan had done what he needed to do—what he'd promised to do. It was time for her to honor his teaching and do the same.

Six weeks later

DANOVAN RAISED HIS clippers over his head, both to signal the driver and to use his sleeve to blot the sweat stinging his eyes. "Carlos, bring the tractor down this row!" He shouldn't have to work the vines, but thanks to the bumper crop, there wasn't a spare hand to be hired in the Central Valley.

Not that this job was glamorous to begin with. He was little more than a harvest supervisor during the day and a security guard at night. He was the only regular employee of the defunct vineyard, and a temporary one at that—this job would end when the vineyard sold.

This was the winery that had been contracted to buy Winters's grapes but had been shut down by the bankruptcy court first. He knew he was lucky to get this job. The CPA firm handling the receivership was based in LA, or else they'd have been warned off hiring him by anyone in the valley.

He clipped another bunch of plump, perfect Concords and dropped them in the bin at his feet.

Too bad he wouldn't get the chance to turn these beauties into wine.

Such a shame.

The vineyard had been bought two years ago by a couple of lawyers from Westwood—a pair of wine aficionados who liked sampling wines much more than the reality of producing them. Poor management had run it into the ground. If only he had the money, he'd buy it himself. But if he had money, he wouldn't be here; he'd be at The Widow, using the money to pull The Widow out of its jam.

Now his job was to simply get the grapes in, turn off the lights and lock up.

That's what happens when a newbie tries to run a winery.

For the hundredth time today, a freeze-frame picture of Indigo surfaced in his mind. Sometimes it was so strong he expected to see her walking down a row toward him in her floppy straw vineyard hat and the special smile she wore only for him.

Unlike this winery's recent owners, Indigo had known enough to know what she didn't know, and she hired experienced people to teach her until she could run it herself. She was the exception.

Jesse and Sondra had recently told him that, in spite of the craziness of harvest, Indigo was doing fine. He hadn't doubted that she would. She had the tenaciousness of a kid who'd spied a candy bar in the checkout line.

"Ouch, dammit." He stared at the small bloody spot on his finger where skin used to be. Served him right for daydreaming.

When the tractor hauling large fruit bins labored slowly past, Danovan dumped his fruit into it. The phone in his pocket buzzed. He set down his bin, checked the display and answered. "Hey, Sis. Let me guess—it's raining there?"

"Duh. It's Seattle. Why ask?"

Just hearing the lilt in her voice lifted his spirits. "To remind you how bad it is, so you'll move south."

"Nah. I got used to being miserable, growing up with you. I wouldn't know how to function any other way."

Of the three of them, he and Stacy had always been closest, though some distance had grown between them in recent years as they each got on with their own lives. "So you don't care that it's a gorgeous, sunny eighty-two here, and not a cloud in the sky?"

"See? Miserable. You make my point, Danno."

He chuckled and shoved the clippers in his back pocket. "If you didn't call about the weather, what's up?"

"The family took a vote, and I was elected most likely to survive this phone call, so…"

He put his finger in his other ear to hear over the tractor. He didn't like the sound of this. In spite of being scattered across the country, his family had remained close. That could be both good and bad.

This was going to be bad. "Why am I afraid?"

"We, the fam I mean, made an investment yesterday."

"And you are calling to rub it in? You know I have no money for—"

"No, dumbshit. *You* are the investment. We're buying the winery you're managing."

He felt the heat rise in his neck as his ego plummeted. The sun blazed hotter. Sweat popped on his forehead. "No."

"Yes."

Goddammit. He'd known they were concerned about his latest setback, but he'd now become the family charity case. "That's just great. I'll recommend a manager you can hire."

"Danovan, don't be dumb. What better investment could we make than a winery that you're in charge of?"

He took a deep breath. He wouldn't kill the messenger. His sister probably wasn't aware of the knife she'd jabbed into his guts. "Look, Stacy. I'm done with the Central Valley. When this harvest is over, I'm heading to Napa."

"Tucking tail and running, huh?"

Scratch that. She knew about the knife. The option of killing the messenger was back on the table. "Screw you, Stace, and the rest of the investors. Where do you get off, going behind my back…? Find a new charity case. I'm just fine."

"Don't you dare hang up on me, Danovan DiCarlo." She hesitated a moment to be sure he hadn't. "Do I need to remind you of how you all bailed me out?"

Stacy was a brilliant forensic CPA, but her investigative skills didn't extend to her love life. Three years ago, the family had loaned her money to divorce her cheating husband, and they'd set her up in her own practice across the country from the loser.

"Looking back, I don't know what I would have done…" The last words choked off.

He didn't have the heart to call the pity card. "Oh, hell, don't you go all soft and blubbery, or I *am* hanging up."

"Shut up, hardass." She released a damp chuckle. "Just think about it, will you? You have a couple of weeks until you need to make a decision."

He ran his hand through his sweaty hair. "I'm not going to change my mind."

"Oh, and Danno? I love your stubborn, prideful ass."

Click.

This had to be the bottom of the ocean. Could a grown man sink lower than having his family bail him out without him even knowing? A wave of vertigo washed over him, tilting the horizon.

"Hey, Joe, keep things moving, will you? I've gotta get out of this sun."

"Sure, boss."

He trudged to the end of the row then headed for his car in the lot. He had to do some shopping anyway, and the chore would have the added benefit of air-conditioning.

His family meant well. But even so, he felt betrayed. Powerless. Small. A man took care of himself—it was his job to get out of his own messes.

He stopped still, ten steps from his car.

This is how Indigo felt when you went behind her back about the grapes.

Well-meaning people taking your power might have a better outcome than when your enemies did it, but the feeling was the same.

Shitty.

He unlocked the door of the seven-year-old sedan he'd traded the Range Rover, even-up for. His wheels sucked, but it was worth it, not having a payment over his head.

This newly simple life did have its advantages. After the initial panic, he found he kind of liked drifting through the days, not looking ahead, trying not to look back, his only concern the immediate needs of the vines and his body. Once he got used to this new way of life, he'd found it oddly peaceful.

At least, he thought that feeling was peace.

Sliding into his oven with plastic seats, he fired the engine and cranked the AC.

He *thought* he'd changed. Become more humble and appreciative of the small things.

But how could he really know for sure?

INDIGO EYED THE grapes jiggling by on the shaker conveyor, picking out green ones and bits of stems. God, these grapes were beautiful. And thanks to Reece Winters, they had all they could process. She was mixing her crop with Winters's to assure consistency of the end product since The Widow's were higher quality.

Thanks to Danovan.

She picked up a grape and bit into it. Bittersweet. Just like her life lately. Everywhere she turned, he was there: in the driveway, showing her how to drive the tractor; kneeling in the soil, teaching her how to test for moisture; at the bar, instructing her on wine-tasting etiquette.

In the bedroom, teaching you other things.

God, she was seriously considering a lobotomy. As if her own memories didn't haunt her enough, the voice in her head was driving her mad, saying things she couldn't afford to think.

Like the difference between Harry's love and Danovan's, on a physical and emotional level. And the realization that, though Harry had nurtured a young, naïve Indigo, Danovan's love was more what she needed now.

She'd spent a month licking her wounds before she could admit that, even though Danovan took way too many liberties professionally, he wasn't like that on a personal level. He was always respectful and supportive, never grabbing anything she didn't freely offer. He'd followed close, yet let her lead. She missed him at her back.

But he came as a package deal, and professionally, she couldn't trust him.

She sighed, running her hands over the grapes he'd so loved, wishing he'd had a chance to work on that signature wine he'd always talked about.

Oh, well, he'll have that opportunity in Napa.

Jesse had told her recently that Danovan was moving on. How could that fact hurt and make her happy at the same time? He needed to start over somewhere new. Somewhere he would be judged on his brilliant talent and not what happened at Bacchanal.

Or here.

"Indigo, there's a problem with the crusher," Sean yelled over the sound of the machinery. "Oh, and Marco stopped in and told me they need you to test sugar on the next section of grapes."

"Okay, hang on." Her brain shifted two gears as she rearranged her afternoon. Again. "I'll work on the crusher. Go find Vern and ask him to test the grapes." Thank God she'd kept the old man's résumé from when she'd interviewed managers in the beginning. At seventy, he couldn't handle the physical labor, but his fifty years of experience in the wine business had proved invaluable.

Yeah, but he's no Danovan.

She had to admit, this time, that part of her brain was correct. Vern had been upfront that, though he knew it all, his expertise was more as a vineyard manager than a master winemaker.

Something would have to be done about that soon. Maybe she could contract with someone out of Cal Poly.

Wiping her hands on a rag, she walked to the crusher. Damned thing would have to be replaced next year; there was an electrical short somewhere.

Thanks to the bank loan, she'd been able to hire the extra help she needed for harvest, but most days she still needed four clones of herself.

A half hour, a broken nail and a skinned knuckle later, the crusher chugged along, spilling pulp and juice into the fermenting tank.

"Indigo, pizza's here!" Becky yelled from the doorway of the barrel room.

"Grab Sean. I've got to get cleaned up." She had one more reason for giving Becky the task of retrieving the warehouse rat. From the looks she'd seen between the two of them, there was a romance budding there.

She wiped her grease-and-grape-stained hands on her jeans. She'd just wash her hands now and jump in the shower in Dan—the manager's quarters later. Vern had a fragile wife at home, so he hadn't been using the apartment.

Thank God for her regular employees. They'd

really stepped up over the past month. Indigo had instituted a weekly team meeting on Fridays over lunch. If she didn't know the answer to a problem, they worked out the solution together. Even Sondra had been helping, staying in touch with their commercial customers while Indigo was tied up with the harvest.

She headed to the warehouse restroom and washed up for lunch.

By the time she made it to her office it was draped in pizza and employees.

Becky plopped a piece of "the whole Yukon" on a plate and handed it to Indigo when she'd dropped into her chair. "Yukon says they're giving us the ten-percent frequent customer discount from now on."

"Great. The way Sean eats, there won't be any profits left otherwise." She took a bite of heaven.

"Hey, I'm not eating more than my share. That's Sondra."

Sondra cut her pizza with a knife and fork. "I hardly think anyone's going to believe the word of a warehouse rodent."

Even Vern laughed.

Indigo put the slice down and wiped her hands on a napkin. "Okay, guys, let's come to order here. I have a promo idea, but I need your opinions."

"What's up?" Natalie asked.

"Well, I'd like to do something fun to celebrate

the crush and thank everyone who's supported us this year. I'm thinking about a grape stomping."

Sean shoveled another piece out of the box. "Is that sanitary?"

"Since when are you concerned with sanitary?" Sondra squinted down her nose at him. "It's old-school. That's how wine was made before all these machines."

"That's how we did it when I started out," Vern said.

"I think it's a clever idea," Becky said.

"Great! But we don't have much time. I'm thinking if we use the last grapes picked, we could do it in two weeks." Indigo glanced at her calendar. "But it'll be smaller than our last party. I don't want to invite the entire town. Just our best customers and a few friends."

Sondra put her plate aside and dusted her hands. "You can't plan it. You have too much to handle with the crush." She glanced at Natalie and Becky. "We could handle it, though."

"Would you?"

The serving-room staff lit up, and everyone started talking at once.

Indigo kept most of her smile inside, proud of the team she'd lucked into. The team they'd become.

Yeah, but you're missing the most important one.

I have what I have, she answered herself. *Stop peeing on my parade.*

CHAPTER TWENTY-ONE

THE SLOPING DRIVE of The Tippling Widow was lined with cars all the way to the road.

This was a bad idea.

Danovan drove slowly, scanning the sides of the road for a parking space. If there wasn't one within a reasonable distance, he'd take it as a sign and keep going. Forget Sondra's invitation. He'd only agreed to come after she'd questioned his courage. And his intellect.

But he really did want to see for himself that Indigo was doing well. Maybe then he could stamp "done" on the Central Valley and head to Napa.

Oh, bullshit. You can con other people, DiCarlo, but it's pretty pathetic when you try to con yourself. This was simple selfishness. He just had to see her. He was starved for those sad eyes, that wide mouth, that odd mix of tough and vulnerable that had drawn him in from the start.

"Oh, screw it. I'm out of here. She doesn't need me messing up her life again."

A sedan-sized slot appeared on his right. He'd checked the rearview mirror, braked and cranked the wheel before his brain had time to veto. He barely managed the squeeze without bumper-kissing, shut down the engine and pulled the key.

Then sat, listening to the tick of the cooling engine and the *hurry, hurry* tugging at his guts. He'd stay lost in the crowd. She'd never know he was there.

He got out, locked the car door, and hiked.

"Sweet Home Alabama" blared from the hill, getting louder as he got closer. He needn't have worried about staying lost; there must have been about a hundred people filling the parking lot, the porch and the lawn.

He slammed to a halt.

But Indigo was easy to spot. She was the one standing in a wooden tub, up to her slim calves in grapes, dancing.

She wore cutoff-way-short jeans and a hunter-green T-shirt with the winery logo in gold emblazoned across the chest. Arms over her head, she snapped her fingers. Her hips gyrated. Her breasts swayed. But it was the look on her face that made his chest seize midbreath.

She danced, eyes closed, her head thrown back like a sun-worshipping goddess. Her mouth curled in a smile of pleasure so strong that it mainlined into his blood. He'd seen her in exquisite joy like that before. In bed. Over him. Under him. He used the back of his hand to wipe dampness from his upper lip.

This was one big mistake, dude.

Seeing her like this threw the desolation of time stretching behind him into sharp contrast. And worse, the time stretching before him. He was a drunk who'd been sober for two months and one day. Now he'd not only fallen off the wagon—it had rolled over him.

When the song ended, everyone applauded. Indigo opened her eyes and scanned the crowd. When her gaze met his, it stopped. The light, sexy smile that had once been meant only for him lit her face then fell off, as if for a moment, she too had forgotten the past two months and a day.

Sobered, she took Natalie's offered hand, acknowledged the applause with a curtsy, then strode to the foot-washing station set up a few steps from the tub.

Now Sean, dressed in the same uniform but with much longer cutoffs, stepped into the tub, and the speakers blared the brass riff opening of "Dancing in the Street."

Danovan was so damned proud of her. Emotions warred in him: pain, regret and sadness. But mostly pride. She looked fit and healthy. She'd been knocked down by a sucker punch, and yet she picked herself up and went on.

A hand landed on his shoulder. He jumped.

"Well, what are you doing about this problem you have, Danovan?" Jesse wasn't smiling.

"I'm leaving, that's what. I should never have come." He stepped out from under her hand.

"She's a robot since you left, you know. Efficient, sure, but there's nothing behind the eyes."

"Well, she needs to be a robot right now. Better

if she could be two of them, with a bumper season like this."

Jesse sighed. "That's not what I meant, and you know it."

He wasn't staying for another lecture. "I'd only make it harder, Jess, and that's the last thing I'd want." He turned and walked away.

"For her? Or for you?"

Both. Head down to avoid questions from well-meaning people, he kept walking across the crowded parking lot and down the drive.

"Danovan! Wait up!" Indigo ran across the grass barefoot, hair streaming behind her. She stopped a few steps from him, breathing harder than she should have been from a twenty-yard sprint.

"Indigo." Even knowing he shouldn't stare, he drank her in; no telling how far to the next oasis in the vast desert of a future without her.

She watched him, too, but her eyes were wary. She tucked her thumbs in the belt loops of her shorts. "I just wanted to say thank you."

He snorted. "For what?"

"For everything. For teaching me. For caring." She tipped her head. "How did you know I'd figure it out, about Winters?"

"Because you're smart. I haven't been right about much the past year. But *that* I was sure of." He took her in, memorizing everything about this moment. "I was an idiot a lot of the time. I don't have all the answers. And you never needed saving, anyway." He closed his eyes to break his stare and made himself turn. "I've gotta go."

He walked to the bottom of the drive.

"Hey, DiCarlo!"

He looked back. She stood, one hand on her hip, the sun picking up highlights of blond in her glossy, dark hair. "Yeah?"

"I have some contract work that requires a master vintner. You want it?"

The thought of being around her again, hearing her laugh, seeing her come around a corner toward him… He knew he should say no. But then, he'd proved long ago that he wasn't a strong man. "Call me. We'll talk."

"JUST MAKE THE call already." Jesse had stayed after yoga class to drive her point home with a railroad spike and a sledgehammer.

"I'm going to." Indigo hit the pause button on her iPod and Enya was cut off midtrill.

"I don't see a phone in your hand." Jesse slung her yoga bag over her shoulder.

"Look, seeing Danovan yesterday mixed up stuff in my head, and I've got to sort it all out."

Jesse's eyes did a slow roll. "Oh, please. What is there to sort out? You miss him. You need him—"

"No. That's the point. I do *not* need him." She straightened the stack of massage flyers on the desk.

"Oh, really?"

"The crush is almost over. Now we've just got to—"

"Oh. Honey." It was never a good sign when Jesse crossed her arms. "You didn't tell me you were taking a vacation to *denial*. I'd have taken you shopping for a new swimsuit."

"I'm not. I don't need him. Not in business— not in my personal life." She shifted the flyers to the other side of the table. It was true. She was proud of her team, and in spite of the zillion small catastrophes, they'd done it—the grapes were in. Standing on her own was freeing. Exciting. Rewarding.

Hollow.

She dropped the flyers. "But I *want* him." The little girl voice came from the empty place inside her.

"Well, hot damn. I was beginning to think there was no hope for you."

"Do not mock me, Jess. This isn't easy."

"Oh, hon, I know it isn't." Jesse patted her arm. "You just trust that woman's intuition of yours. It'll never steer you wrong."

Oh, yeah. I'm so good at that.

"Well, give me a hug. I've got to get back to feed the tourists."

Indigo was enveloped in a perfumed hug. "Thanks, Jess, for caring."

Jesse backed up and pointed a carmine talon in Indigo's face.

She held up her hands. "I know. I'll call. I promise. Soon."

When Jesse left, Indigo grabbed her gym bag and stepped across the hall to the manager's quarters. She needed a shower but didn't want to take the time to jog up the hill. She unlocked the door. Besides, it was time she started...

His smell smacked her in the face. His belongings were gone, but he lingered—in his scent, his to-do list thumbtacked to the wall by the dining table, the chemistry book he'd loaned her that sat on the bedside table.

Just standing in his space made her ache.

"No wasted motion, Blue. And *this* is wasted motion." She made herself stop stroking the book and lay it back on the table. "And wasted emotion."

But the shower was worse. She imagined the last time he'd been here. Pictured his tawny skin, water sluicing the soap away, exposing long, lean muscle...

Her nails bit into her scalp. She lightened up on the scrubbing. They'd never made love in this shower. Now she wished they had.

"No, no you don't. Quit messing around, Blue. You've got a zillion things to do today."

Including making that phone call. After all, if she were secure in her independence, this call would be easy. She ducked her head under the spray. Danovan DiCarlo was the best man for the job. End of story.

"This is a business decision. Nothing more." She was too busy perusing trade journals these days to read fairy tales.

An hour later, she made herself stop staring out the window and pick up the phone. It was clear that if she didn't get this out of the way, she'd get no work done today.

Professional. You're going to keep this professional.

"DiCarlo."

"Hello. This is Indigo Blue."

His warm chuckle made her face heat. "I think we're a bit past formal names, Indigo."

"Um. Yes. Well. I've called to offer you some consulting work. I'm looking for—"

"How are you? You looked happy yesterday. Are you?"

His soft tone frayed her determination. "The harvest has gone well. I'm very satisfied…" She gave in to the tug in her chest. "I'm fine. And you?"

"I'm good, actually. Turns out, you and I are going to be neighbors. Unbeknownst to me, my family bought this winery. I've decided to stay and run it."

Her spirits fell. And rose. Her shoulders simply slumped. "Oh. Then you'll be too busy for contract work."

"Actually, since the crop was sold before I took over, I do have time. But I don't think it's a good idea."

Her spirits were on a wild mouse ride. They plummeted. "This could benefit us both, Danovan. Will you at least listen to my proposal?"

He hesitated so long that she checked her phone screen to be sure they were still connected.

"I guess it won't hurt to hear it."

"Thank you. I hired a good manager, but tweaking wine isn't his forte. I thought about calling Cal Poly, but this is too important to trust to someone I don't know. I'd like to contract with you at an hourly rate to come on site and fine-tune our products."

"I don't know. That would be...difficult for me."

You're not the only one. "It would be strictly business."

"Yeah. That's the difficult part."

She had expected he'd turn her down, so she'd come up with a sales proposal. "Oh, come on. Do you really think you can go a whole year without playing in the lab? Without digging into pH levels, volatiles and sequestrants? Danovan DiCarlo, not touching a spectrophotometer for a year? Impossible."

"I always did love your spectrophotometer."

Hope pulled her forward in her chair. "You should. You bought it. Cost the moon, too."

"Indigo, I want to. But I can't. You know why."

She did. Habits were hard to make, and once made, hard to break. Especially him. But the wine needed tweaking, and he was the best man for it. That trumped her petty personal worries. Time for the big guns. "What if I offer you carte blanche to create your own signature wine?"

"What?" The tone in that one word told her that their spirits were in the same car on that wild mouse.

She knew she could count on his ambition. "You can use some of the grapes we bought from Winters. You'll be free to experiment, create and name the wine anything you'd like. It would still be a product of The Tippling Widow, but I'll split profits on its sale with you. Fifty-fifty."

"I can do anything? No oversight? No pressure?"

"Yes." She knew she had him. Her professional tone belied her fist pump.

He chuckled. "You're evil. You knew I couldn't turn that down."

"I'm just a good businesswoman."

"I've been telling you that from the beginning. I'll be out on Wednesday."

She hung up, her stomach weightless from the drop. "Now all you have to do is stay professional."

Oh, yeah, you can do that. She hadn't known the evil part of her brain could chuckle.

SIX WEEKS LATER, Indigo locked up after Sondra and went in search of Barney. Well, that was her excuse, anyway. She knew very well where he was. Every Wednesday when Danovan was in the lab, Barney could be found there, camped out in the corner. At first she'd tried to keep him out, but when Danovan said he appreciated the company, she'd laid a blanket down for the little traitor to sleep on. He'd always liked men best.

Turned out they had that in common.

There was some kind of selective amnesia going on in her brain, brought on, she was sure, by the evil part. With every week that went by, it got harder to recall why they had broken up.

Oh, yeah, that's right. Danovan DiCarlo can't be trusted.

She flipped off the lights and walked through the barrel room to the warehouse. It wasn't just that he'd lied to get the manager job. It wasn't only his lie by omission about the Boldens. Or the debacle with Reece Winters. But *all* of those were symptoms of the same illness—a Superman complex.

She didn't need a rescuer. And if she needed one in the future, she'd do it herself.

But he's changed.

Go away. There's not enough empirical evidence to support that theory.

But she had to admit, the evidence was piling up. Little things, like him not having an opinion on anything except the lab. Over the last few weeks not once had he tried to help. He was professional and polite, both friendly and distant at the same time. He came in, did his work and left. She couldn't find a thing to complain about.

And frankly, that was getting irritating. Was she the only one finding this difficult?

Well, it was for the best. Someday she'd be ready for a relationship. But until then, better she got settled with this new independence she'd paid so much for.

The lights of the laboratory reflected on the painted floor as she walked to the glass-fronted room. It was empty.

Movement in a corner caught her eye. Danovan sat on the floor, ruffling Barney's ears.

"Who's a big guy? Who's the Superdog?"

An adoring Barney licked Danovan's chin.

"Yeah, that's right. Barnabas Blue, that's who."

She crossed her arms and leaned against the doorframe. "Am I interrupting?"

They both looked up with smiles. Luckily, only Barney's included drool.

"Ah, Indigo. We were just coming to find you."

"It's really a shame that you dislike dogs."

"It is. Luckily Barn's not a dog. I have this

theory. Barney's some alpha guy, reincarnated as a bassett hound to get some rest." With one last pat for Barney, Danovan climbed to his feet.

"Oh. I see. That explains it, then."

He was different today. More relaxed. More open. More…Danovan. And in spite of her arguments, it was melting the frozen lump in her chest. Who could resist a man cooing over a dog?

He brushed off the back of his jeans and walked to the table. "I have a surprise for you."

The soft curve of his mouth and touch of his warm chocolate eyes made her heart patter like a crushing teenager's.

Stop it. You're a business owner.

Speak for yourself.

"You're done calibrating my wine?"

"Better than that." His eyes sidled away, and he fiddled with a knob on the centrifuge.

Surely he couldn't be done with his wine yet. He'd be back next week. Wouldn't he? "You're not done with your signature wine, are you?"

"Well, that's what I need to talk to you about." He swirled wine in a glass beaker. Round and round.

The longer time stretched out, the more nervous she got. And witnessing his nervousness bumped it to a higher power.

"What is it? Is something wrong with it?"

"I don't know." Staring at the swirling red liquid, a line formed between his brows. One perfect, one scarred. "I won't know until I ask. But then it'll be too late."

She straightened from the doorframe. Whatever it was, she would be ready to meet it. "I can take it. Tell me. Is my wine faulted?"

"What?" His head snapped up. "No, no, nothing like that."

She put her hand to her panicked heart. If Danovan DiCarlo was worried, she was terrified. "You're freaking me out. Please tell me."

His jaw tightened, thinning his lips. He rounded the table, pulled the barstool from beneath the tall table, put it in the center of the floor and patted it. "Come, sit. I have to go get something." He walked to the office next door.

She took a controlled breath and blew it out, a yoga calming technique. "You can handle whatever it is," she whispered. "You are a strong, independent woman." She took another breath. "You've made it this far, and you're still standing." Well, she was sitting, but still—

"Close your eyes." His voice came from behind her.

"Danovan, if this is some kind of game, I'm going to thump you. You're really frightening me."

"Good, then we're even. Please, just humor me."

"Oh, all right." She closed her eyes.

In a few seconds, he said, "Okay, you can open them."

He was down on one knee in front of her, cradling a bottle of wine like a sommelier waiting for a diner's approval.

"What is this?"

"It's my signature wine."

It was a dark bottle, corked, with a deep blue foil label with gold script: Twice in a Blue Moon Merlot.

"Do you remember? You told me once that you were lucky, because love like you and Harry had only came along once in a blue moon."

She sat shocked to stillness. What was he saying? This was so opposite what she'd expected, her brain couldn't shift gears in time to catch up.

"I know I'm too brash, and I guess this bottle is proof." He turned it to face him and studied the label. "But I've also learned a lot about humility and the damage my arrogance has caused.

"These past months have taught me something else, too—that I can live without you." He set the bottle on the table. "They've also taught me that I don't want to."

When she would have interrupted, he held up a hand. "I'm not talking about business. You have your winery. I have mine." He stood, took her hands and lifted her to her feet, his eyes full of questions. "I love you, Indigo Blue. Would you be willing to take one more chance on me?"

When her lungs screamed for air, she inhaled.

How could she trust gold-foil words? Or the earnest look on a movie-star-handsome face?

Harder yet, how could she trust a gut instinct about as accurate as that fish, Dory, from the Pixar movie?

You can. Because you know it's right.

For once the voice didn't sound like a sarcastic teenager. It sounded…like her. An older, wiser version of her.

She remembered Jesse's advice to think of the worst that could happen. If you could live with that, you had your answer. If she gave her heart again to this man, and he lied, or tried to take over, or—

A flash of insight hit her like a searchlight in a night sky. None of that mattered anymore.

If the worst happened, she'd pick herself up and move on to whatever came next. And whatever came after that. Because she was her *own* Superman.

"I don't need you either, DiCarlo."

He looked as if he'd expected it. His face devoid of emotion, he nodded, looked away and dropped her hands.

"And thank God for that." She put her fingers under his chin and lifted it. "Because that makes it okay for me to want you. Better yet, it allows me to *have* you." She gave in to the tug that she could finally admit to feeling—the feeling she'd had since she saw him across the lawn the day of the grape stomping. She touched her lips to his. "Hello again."

He made a little whimper at the back of his throat, wrapped her in his arms, and seized her mouth. She felt every lonely night, every longing of the past months in that kiss. He lightened the pressure, then trailed kisses across her cheeks, her nose, over her eyelids. Tiny champagne kisses that went with the bubbles of happiness rising in her chest.

"Whoop!" When he lifted her into his arms and spun in a circle, she threw her head back and laughed.

He slowed their spin, the look in his eyes changing from a spark to a smolder. It was enough to catch her tinder; it burned on and fast. After a deep, searching kiss, she leaned her forehead on his and whispered, "Put me down. Let's go to the cabin."

He raised his scarred eyebrow. "Oh, lady, I know a place that's a lot closer than that."

He carried her to the manager's quarters, trailing kisses the whole way.

EPILOGUE

"THERE YOU ARE." Jesse stood on the porch of the cabin, hands on hips, in full lecture mode. "I thought I was gonna have to drive over there and haul you off the tractor. Holy poop, woman, you want to be late for your own wedding?"

Indigo trotted up the path, laughing. "No worries, Jess. If I'm late, the groom's late. He was with me." It was only fitting that they started this day together on a tractor. They'd been tilling over at what they called Danovan's winery, though it was now just a vineyard. When they'd decided that all wine making would take place at The Widow, they'd cannibalized the winery equipment, selling most of it—after she called dibs on the crusher.

"Don't get your frillies in a twist, Jess." She jogged up the stairs. "I'll hop in the shower, and then you can go to work on the makeup."

"Well, you'd better hurry. Masterpieces take time." Jesse followed her through the screen door. "Not that you need it. You're glowing, hon."

"I'm getting married today. Isn't that a requirement?"

"Good point. Your groom is pretty easy on the eyes, too. Your wedding photos could be in *Brides* magazine."

"No way. I'm done with public life. I want nothing more than what I can see from the front porch of this cabin." She hugged her friend. "Well, that and your milkshakes and a Yukon pizza now and again."

Jesse swatted her butt. "Will you get in the shower? You're gonna be late, I'm telling you."

Indigo practiced her vows in the shower. After that, time sped up, going by in a colorful whirl. And before she knew it, she was standing alone in the tasting room, facing the closed front door of the winery, dressed and made up, holding a nosegay of peach and white roses.

They'd decided against bridesmaids and groomsmen, and today, she was glad they had. It was only fitting that she'd do this alone.

She looked out past the porch, to where the little white bridge arched over the brook, leading to the white gazebo. The grapevines had taken hold in the lattice, and the vines dripped tiny delicate grape flowers from the roof. White folding chairs spread almost three hundred sixty degrees around it, filled with friends, customers and family. She could see her mother in the front row, and Danovan's family, who had arrived en masse two days ago.

She smoothed a hand down the peach chiffon dress she'd fallen in love with the second she'd seen it. The deep V-neck, ruffled cap sleeves and the hem at her knees in front, falling to her ankles in the back, made her feel like a princess from a fairy tale. The ballet slippers and white baby's breath that Jesse had twined in her hair had been just the right touch.

She pressed a hand to the butterflies in her stomach that had gotten a head start on the party. She might be nervous about the details of the day, but beneath that there was a solid bedrock of knowing.

This was right.

She shifted the bouquet to her other hand and reached for the door. But then she let her hand fall to her side. She shot a glance at the ceiling. "You know I'll always love you, Harry." Imaging his smile, she blew a kiss at the ceiling. "Wish me luck."

She opened the door and stepped onto the porch. The crowd fell silent. She walked to the bridge. Her eyes found Danovan, standing in the shade of the gazebo, hands clasped in front of him. He was as devastatingly handsome in his tux as he was in jeans. Or wearing nothing, for that matter.

Barney, dressed in a grapevine collar twined with peach roses, sat at his feet, panting a grin.

She crossed the bridge, walked onto the pristine white runner and took the final steps of a long path that would lead her to her new husband. She let the love that shone in his eyes pull her until she stood beside him at last.

Sooner than she thought possible, she stood, hands in his, looking into his eyes, and speaking her vows. "Just as the vines change with the seasons, so have I. You've helped me discover that there are more kinds of love in the world than just one. And I'm so incredibly lucky to have found one that was made just for me. I love you, Danovan DiCarlo, and promise to nurture, care for and cherish you, always."

He smiled down at her, eyes suspiciously bright. "And I love you, Indigo Blue. I promise to love you and give you space to grow, to flourish, always." His fingers tightened on hers. "More than anything, I promise not to take for granted a love that only comes twice in a blue moon."

* * * * *